TEXAS JOHN SLAUGHTER
THE EDGE OF HELL

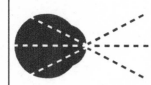

Texas John Slaughter
The Edge of Hell

William W. Johnstone
with J.A. Johnstone

WHEELER PUBLISHING
A part of Gale, a Cengage Company

GALE
A Cengage Company

Farmington Hills, Mich • San Francisco • New York • Waterville, Maine
Meriden, Conn • Mason, Ohio • Chicago

ALL RIGHTS RESERVED
Following the death of William W. Johnstone, the Johnstone family is working with a carefully selected writer to organize and complete Mr. Johnstone's outlines and many unfinished manuscripts to create additional novels in all of his series like The Last Gunfighter, Mountain Man, and Eagles, among others. This novel was inspired by Mr. Johnstone's superb storytelling.
Wheeler Publishing Large Print Western.
The text of this Large Print edition is unabridged.
Other aspects of the book may vary from the original edition.
Set in 16 pt. Plantin.

LIBRARY OF CONGRESS CIP DATA ON FILE.
CATALOGUING IN PUBLICATION FOR THIS BOOK
IS AVAILABLE FROM THE LIBRARY OF CONGRESS

ISBN-13: 978-1-4328-6513-9 (softcover alk. paper)

Published in 2019 by arrangement with Pinnacle Books, an imprint of Kensington Publishing Corp.

Printed in Mexico
1 2 3 4 5 6 7 23 22 21 20 19

AUTHORS' NOTE

This novel is loosely based on the life and times of legendary Old West lawman, rancher, and gambler John Horton "Texas John" Slaughter. The plot is entirely fictional and is not intended to represent actual historical events. The actions, thoughts, and dialogue of the historical characters featured in this story are fictional as well and not meant to reflect their actual personalities and behavior, although the authors have attempted to maintain a reasonable degree of accuracy.

In other words, none of what you're about to read really happened . . . but it could have.

CHAPTER 1

Exuberant shouts filled the air as a blaze-faced black stallion with four white stockings bucked and sunfished like mad in a desperate attempt to unseat the rider perched perilously on his back.

People crowded around the corral to watch the spectacle inside the fence. Most were men, but the group included several women as well.

The sweating rider had lost his hat, revealing that he was a young, fair-haired cowboy. He clung desperately to the horse's back as the animal pitched back and forth, leaped up and down, and switched ends with blinding speed.

It was just a matter of time, John Slaughter thought, before his brother-in-law Stonewall wound up on his butt in the dust.

The man standing beside Slaughter nudged him with an elbow, grinned, and said, "Your young man is quite good. But

Santiago's *El Halcón* will emerge triumphant in the end. You will see."

Slaughter — Texas John, some called him, since he hailed from the Lone Star State — figured his guest was right, but he was stubborn enough to say, "Oh, I don't know. I wouldn't count Stonewall out —"

Before Slaughter could continue, Stonewall lost his grip and sailed off the horse's back. He let out a yell as he flew through the air, a shout that was cut short as he crashed down on his back.

Another young man had started to scramble up the corral fence as soon as Stonewall left the saddle. When he reached the top, he vaulted over and landed lithely inside the enclosure. He was in his middle twenties, a little older than Stonewall, with olive skin and sleek hair as dark as a raven's wing. He ran toward the still-bucking horse and called, *"El Halcón!"*

The horse responded instantly to the name, which was Spanish for "The Hawk." He stood still except for a slight quivering in his muscles that was visible under the shiny black hide. His nostrils flared in anger.

Santiago Rubriz walked up to the horse and caught the reins. He swung easily into the saddle and began walking the horse around the inside of the corral. The transformation was astounding. *El Halcón* now appeared gentle enough for a child to ride.

"A one-*hombre* horse, eh?" Don Eduardo Rubriz, Santiago's father, said to Slaughter.

"Not much doubt about that," Slaughter agreed.

On his other side, his wife Viola looked anxiously between the fence boards and asked, "Is Stonewall all right?"

Stonewall Jackson Howell, who was Viola Slaughter's younger brother, still lay on his back, unmoving. Slaughter felt a moment of apprehension. Stonewall had landed pretty hard. He might have broken something. Maybe even his head.

But then Stonewall groaned, rolled onto his side and then on over to his belly, and pushed himself to hands and knees. He paused there for a few seconds and shook his head as if trying to clear it of cobwebs.

Then he staggered to his feet, looked around, spotted the grinning Santiago on *El Halcón*'s back, and said, "Son of a gun!"

That brought a laugh from the spectators, most of whom were either American cowboys or Mexican *vaqueros* who worked here on the Slaughter Ranch in southeastern Arizona's San Bernardino Valley. The crew was divided about half and half in nationality and nearly all of them were fluent in both languages. That wasn't surprising, because the Mexican border was a mere two hundred yards south of this corral.

Santiago rode over to Stonewall and said, "You did very well, *amigo.* You stayed on him longer than I expected."

"That ain't a horse, it's a devil," Stonewall muttered. "Why don't you call him *El Diablo?*"

Santiago patted *El Halcón* and said, "Because when he runs at full speed, he seems to soar over the earth like a hawk riding the currents of the wind."

That statement made Stonewall's blue eyes narrow speculatively.

"Fast, is he? Well, I bet we got a horse or two around here that can match him — or beat him."

Santiago arched a black eyebrow.

"Are you proposing a race, my friend . . . and a wager?"

Stonewall had waltzed right into that trap, thought Slaughter. He considered warning his brother-in-law, then decided against it. Stonewall was a grown man, a top hand here on the ranch, and one of Sheriff John Slaughter's deputies when they were back in Tombstone. Let him make his own mistakes.

Stonewall picked up the hat he had lost

10

when the horse started to buck, slapped it against his leg to knock some of the dust off it, and said, "You're dang right I'm talkin' about a race. As for a wager, we'll have to figure out the stakes."

"Very well," Santiago said. "We'll discuss it at the *fiesta* tonight, eh?"

"Sure," Stonewall agreed.

Viola turned away from the corral and said, "While my brother figures out some other way to make a fool of himself, why don't we all go back to the house? The sun's getting rather warm, and we can sit on the patio in the shade."

That sounded like a good idea to Slaughter. He linked arms with Viola and used his other hand to usher Don Eduardo and the don's American wife Belinda along the path that led beside a grove of cottonwood trees back to the sprawling ranch house.

The four of them made striking pairs. Both men were handsome, dignified, and considerably older than their beautiful young wives. There were contrasts, however. Slaughter was compactly built, below average height but muscular and possessed of a vitality that belied his years and the salt-and-pepper beard on his chin. Don Eduardo was taller, leaner, with a hawk-like face that was clean-shaven except for a thin mustache.

The two women were both lovely, but Belinda Rubriz was blond and blue-eyed while Viola Slaughter had dark hair and flashing dark eyes.

Their coloring wasn't the only difference. Belinda was from Boston, the daughter of a banker who had done business with the wealthy Don Eduardo, and had the pampered air of a young woman who had never done a day's work in her life.

Viola, on the other hand, was a cowgirl born and bred. She had been riding almost before she could walk, and she could handle a rifle better than a lot of men. Cool-nerved in the extreme, not much in life ever threw her for a loop — a quality that had come in very handy during times of trouble in the past.

John Slaughter loved her to the very depths of his soul and always would.

Like Viola, Belinda was a second wife. Don Eduardo's first wife, Santiago's mother, had been dead for many years. Slaughter had learned that during his correspondence with the Mexican rancher. Their letters had been concerned for the most part with the business arrangement they were making, but a few personal details had slipped in on both sides.

As Slaughter looked through the trees now, he saw grazing in the distance the concrete proof of their arrangement in the small herd of cattle Don Eduardo had brought up here from his *hacienda* ninety miles below the border.

Those cattle were some of the finest specimens Slaughter had ever seen, and he was paying a suitably pretty penny for them. He was eager to introduce the stock into his own herd and improve the bloodline.

Don Eduardo and his entourage, including his wife and son, had arrived with the cattle earlier today. Tonight, he and Slaughter would conclude their deal when Slaughter handed over the payment.

Then it would be time to celebrate. Slaughter had lived on the border long enough to adopt many of the Mexican customs, among them the idea that the chance for a party should never be wasted.

A white picket fence ran around the large compound that included the main ranch house, two bunkhouses, one with a kitchen attached where the meals for the crew were prepared, a chicken coop, and an ice house. An elevated water tank such as the ones found at water stops along the railroad stood to one side. Nearby, sparkling blue in

13

the afternoon sunlight, was a water reservoir contained within a retaining wall built of rocks.

Here in southern Arizona, where summers were often hotter than the hinges of hell and moisture was a precious commodity, having plenty of water on hand was important. Luckily, the San Bernardino Valley got more rain than some areas and there were also artesian wells located on the ranch that helped keep the reservoir and the water tank filled.

In fact, the Slaughter Ranch was an oasis of sorts, and John Slaughter was justly proud of what he had built here. When his term as sheriff of Cochise County was up, he intended to hand the badge over to someone else and spend the rest of his days on this spread.

Viola led her husband and their guests to a flagstone patio at the side of the house. Tall cottonwoods cast cooling shade over the area. A servant came out a side door, and Viola told her to bring a pitcher of lemonade and some glasses.

The two couples sat, and Belinda Rubriz said, "You have a lovely home, Mrs. Slaughter."

"Thank you," Viola said, gracious as always, adding with a smile, "You should call me Viola, though. We don't believe in a lot of formality around here."

"So, Señor Slaughter," Don Eduardo said, "is your brother-in-law correct? Do you have horses here on your ranch faster than *El Halcón*?"

"Well, I don't know," Slaughter said, letting a little of a Texas drawl creep into his voice. "I reckon Stonewall's right about how we can find out."

"And would *you* be interested in a small wager?"

Slaughter felt Viola's eyes on him. She knew that gambling was one of his weaknesses. Sometimes she tried to rein in that particular tendency.

Now, though, when he glanced at her, he saw her head move a fraction of an inch in an encouraging nod. She didn't believe in being reckless, but the honor of the Slaughter Ranch was at stake.

"Oh, I imagine we can work out something suitable," he said.

He and Don Eduardo both smiled in anticipation.

The servant came back with the cool, tart lemonade, which never tasted better than on a hot afternoon like this. When Slaughter's glass was full, he lifted it and said, "To good friends and good times."

"A most excellent toast," Don Eduardo said. "To good friends and good times."

The afternoon couldn't get much more pleasant, Slaughter mused as he swallowed some of the lemonade.

And that made a shiver go through him that had nothing to do with the temperature.

He was old enough to know that if a man ever let himself believe things couldn't get any better, that was when all hell was liable to break loose.

CHAPTER 2

In the foothills of the Chiricahua Mountains northwest of the Slaughter Ranch, a man lowered the spyglass through which he had been peering. His dark eyes gleamed in anticipation under the blue bandanna tied around his forehead to hold back the crudely cropped, shoulder-length black hair.

He was dressed in a blousy blue shirt, breechcloth, and high-topped boot moccasins. A strip of cloth dyed bright red was tied around his lean waist as a sash. He carried a knife tucked into that sash. A Winchester leaned against the rock by which he stood.

The man lifted his arm, pointed toward the southeast, and said in his native Apache, "There lies the ranch of the one called Slaughter. We will go there tonight and spill much blood."

The fifteen warriors to whom he spoke erupted in yips and shouts of excitement.

17

Several of them lifted their rifles above their heads and pumped the weapons up and down.

A few yards away, a white man stood watching with his hat tipped forward so that the brim shaded his face. Normally a white man who found himself in the company of sixteen bronco Apaches would be getting ready to fight or die. Probably both.

He'd be praying, too, either way, but this *hombre*'s lips didn't move except to curve into a sardonic smile.

"You're really gettin' 'em worked up, Bodaway," he said in English to the leader of the war party. The Apache had lived on a reservation and had even worked for a time as a scout for the cavalry, so he had no trouble speaking or understanding the white man's tongue.

"You know I am called *El Infierno*," the war chief said with a glare. "The Fires of Hell."

"Sure, sure," the white man said. "I'd forgotten how you *hombres* sometimes take Mex names."

Ned Becker hadn't forgotten at all. Calling *El Infierno* by the name he'd been given when he was born was Becker's way of reminding the Apache that they had known each other since they were boys.

Indians had long memories, sure enough, but sometimes if their blood got hot enough, they conveniently "forgot" that they had promised not to kill a fella. Especially a bloodthirsty bunch like these renegade Mescaleros.

Becker went on, "I know the ranch is too far away for you to see it from here, even with that telescope, but my scouts report that Don Eduardo is there with his herd of crossbreeds. They'll be celebratin' tonight, you can take my word for that."

"This man Slaughter is said to be a good fighter. He will have guards."

"Sure he will," Becker agreed. "But they'll be thinkin' about how they're missin' the barbecue and the wine and the dancin', and they won't be as alert as they ought to be. Your men should be able to slip past them."

Bodaway gave the white man a cold look.

"My warriors are like spirits in the night," he said. "No one will see them until they are ready to be seen."

Becker nodded and said, "Fine. You hold up your end of the deal and I'll hold up mine."

They understood each other. Indians liked to bargain. Becker knew that. That and his old friendship with the war chief had made him bold enough to ride into Bodaway's camp hidden in these rugged, isolated mountains when most men wouldn't have dared do such a thing.

Ned Becker wasn't most men, though, as those who had been unlucky enough to cross him had found out.

He was almost as dark as the Apaches, but black beard stubble covered his lantern jaw. His eyes under the pulled-down hat brim blazed with hatred. He kept those fires banked most of the time because he knew it was dangerous for a man to let his emotions get out of control.

But every now and then the flames inside him leaped up and threatened to consume him from the inside out if he didn't cut loose. When he did, somebody usually died.

Becker figured if anybody ought to be known as The Fires of Hell, it was him. He wasn't going to argue about it with Bodaway, though. The war chief was too useful to risk making him mad.

"Remember, hit 'em hard and fast," Becker went on. "That'll draw Slaughter's crew and Don Eduardo's men away from the herd. My men and I will take care of everything else."

Bodaway's lip curled slightly in disdain. To an Apache's way of thinking, stealing more cattle than you could eat was a waste of time and effort. For that matter, they would rather steal horses, since a warrior could ride a horse — and they preferred the taste of horse meat to beef.

"You will deliver the rifles?" he said to Becker.

"In two weeks or less," the outlaw promised. "Just as we agreed. Fifty brand-new Winchesters and a thousand rounds of ammunition for each."

Bodaway nodded in solemn satisfaction. Offering him money wouldn't have accomplished a damned thing, Becker knew. The Apaches didn't have any use for it.

But the lure of rifles had been more than the war chief could resist. Only a few of Bodaway's men were armed with Winchesters. Most of the others carried single-shot Springfields taken from dead cavalrymen. A couple even had muzzle-loading flintlocks that had been handed down for generations after being stolen from fur trappers farther north.

Most of the Apaches were on reservations now, but isolated bands of renegades still hid out in the mountains. It was Bodaway's dream to mold those groups into a band large enough to do some real damage to the cavalry and to the white settlements in the territory. With modern rifles to use as a lure, he might well succeed in bringing together all the bronco Apaches.

In the night, he probably thought about doing all the bloody things Cochise and Geronimo had never been able to accomplish. Becker knew what that was like.

He had a dream of his own.

His old friend Bodaway didn't know anything about that, and there was no reason to tell him. As long as Bodaway and his men did what Becker needed them to do, that was the only thing that mattered. If they did . . .

If they did, then Becker's long-sought vengeance would be right there in front of him where he could reach out and grasp it at last.

Evening settled down on the San Bernardino Valley, bringing some cooling breezes. Viola Slaughter loved this time of day. It gave her great peace and happiness to step out into the dusk and gaze up at the spectacular wash of red and gold and blue and purple in the sky as the sunset faded. Often she stood there drinking in the beauty of nature and listening to the faint sounds of the ranch's activities winding down for the day.

Today wasn't like that, however. The

sunset was as gorgeous as ever, but the air was filled with the sound of preparations for the evening's festivities.

Servant girls chattered as they brought plates and silverware from the house and set them on the tables under the cottonwoods. Cowboys and *vaqueros* called to each other and laughed from the great spit where a beef was roasting over a crackling fire. Fiddlers and guitar players tuned their instruments for the dancing later. Children from the families of the ranch hands ran around playing and shouting. Among them were some Indian youngsters. The peaceful Indian families in the area knew they were always welcome when the Slaughters had a party. Everyone was welcome, in fact. That was just the way it was on the Slaughter Ranch.

Viola's husband came up behind her, slipped his arms around her waist, and nuzzled her thick dark hair.

"I say, you've done a fine job with this *fiesta,* as usual," John Slaughter told her.

Viola leaned back in the comfortable embrace of his arms and laughed.

"I haven't done much of anything, John, and you know it. The people who work for us deserve all the credit."

"Without your planning and supervision,

there wouldn't even be a party," Slaughter said. "And *you* know *that.*"

She turned to face him and asked, "What do you think of Don Eduardo?"

"A fine fellow. Very straightforward." Slaughter shrugged. "A bit arrogant, perhaps, but that's common with these grandees. It's the Spaniard in 'em, I suppose. Europeans have a weakness for the aristocracy."

"What about his wife?"

"Doña Belinda? She's all right, I suppose. We don't really have anything in common with her, what with her being from back east and all."

"Maybe that's why I'm not sure I like her," Viola said quietly.

"What?" Slaughter looked and sounded surprised. "I thought you liked everyone."

"Not everybody," Viola said, a little tartly now. "She's pleasant enough, I suppose, but I'm not sure I trust her."

"Well, luckily you don't have to," Slaughter pointed out. "Her husband seems trustworthy enough, and he's the one I'm doing business with." Slaughter stepped back, slipped his watch out of his vest pocket, and opened it to check the time. "In fact, I ought to get back inside. I'm supposed to meet Don Eduardo in my study and deliver

24

the payment for those cows to him. Then we can get the *fandango* started."

"All right, go ahead," Viola said as she patted her husband's arm. "I'll see you when you're finished."

Slaughter nodded, put his watch away, and turned to stride back into the house with his usual vigor. He was not a man to do things in a lackadaisical manner, whether it was pursuing lawbreakers as sheriff, working with the hands here on the ranch, or making love to his beautiful young wife.

Viola checked with the servants to make sure the preparations were going as they were supposed to, then walked out to talk to the *vaqueros* and see that the meat would be ready. Assured that it would be, Viola started back toward the house.

Her route took her near the elevated water tank. She was surprised to see movement in the shadows underneath it. The area where the *fiesta* would be held was brightly lit by colorful lanterns hanging in the trees, but their glow didn't really reach this far. Twilight had deepened until the gloom was nearly impenetrable in places.

Viola had keen eyes, though, and she knew it was unlikely that any of the servants or the ranch hands would be around the water tank right now. She gave in to curiosity and walked in that direction, moving with her usual quiet grace.

As she came closer she heard the soft murmur of voices, but she didn't recognize them and couldn't make out any of the words. She started to call out and ask who was there, but she stopped before she said anything.

Her natural caution had asserted itself. If whoever was lurking under the water tank had some sort of mischief in mind, it might not be wise to let them know she was there.

Instead she stuck to the shadows herself and slipped closer, and then stopped as she began to be able to understand what the two people were saying.

They spoke in Spanish, the man with a fluency that indicated it was his native tongue. The woman's words were more halting as she tried to think of how to express what she wanted to say.

It was perfectly clear to Viola that they were lovers, and passionate ones at that. After a moment they both fell silent, and she assumed that was because they were kissing.

She had recognized the voices and understood the words as well. One of them belonged to Santiago Rubriz.

The woman was his stepmother, Doña Belinda.

Viola knew there had to be a reason she didn't like or trust the blonde from Boston, she thought as she stood there in the darkness, her face warm with embarrassment from the secret she had unwittingly uncovered.

CHAPTER 3

Before Don Eduardo came in, Slaughter had already worked the combination lock on the massive safe bolted to the floor in his study. All he had to do now was twist the handle and swing the heavy door open. He reached inside and pulled out a pair of leather saddlebags, grunting a little at their weight.

The saddlebags clinked meaningfully as Slaughter deposited them on the desk.

"Payment in gold, as we agreed, Don Eduardo," he said to his visitor. "Double eagles. Feel free to count them if you'd like."

Rubriz waved a hand dismissively. "I trust you, Señor Slaughter," he said. "I pride myself on being an excellent judge of character, and I have no doubt whatsoever that you are an honest man."

"I appreciate that," Slaughter said with a faint smile. "Unfortunately, not everyone I've dealt with in the past has felt that way."

"Then they were mistaken." Don Eduardo's shoulders rose and fell in an eloquent shrug. "Such things happen."

"Be that as it may, if you'd like to count the money, it won't offend me."

"And I say again, it will not be necessary. Besides —" Don Eduardo's eyes twinkled with good humor, but a glitter of steel lurked there as well, Slaughter noted. "If you were to try to cheat me, as the old saying goes, I know where you live, señor."

That brought a laugh from Slaughter, a laugh in which his visitor joined. Don Eduardo picked up the saddlebags, hefted them approvingly, and went on, "We may consider our arrangement concluded. Now that it is, if I might request a favor of you . . ."

"Of course," Slaughter said.

"If you would not mind keeping this locked up in your safe until we depart tomorrow, I would be in your debt."

"Certainly, if you'd prefer it that way," Slaughter said. He reached out and took the saddlebags from the don.

"It's not that I don't trust my people, or yours," Rubriz said as Slaughter locked the double eagles in the safe again. "But I wish to enjoy the evening's festivities without the slightest hint of worry in my mind."

"Can't blame you for that. It should be quite a shindig."

"I hope my wife enjoys it. Belinda has had a bit of trouble adjusting to our Western ways since coming to live at my *hacienda*. She finds us somewhat . . . uncivilized."

"Sorry to hear that," Slaughter muttered.

Don Eduardo waved an elegantly manicured hand. "I'm sure it is only a matter of time until she becomes accustomed to life on the ranch," he said. "But for now, I'm glad she has the friendship of such a fine lady as Señora Slaughter. That will make it easier for her to adjust."

Slaughter just nodded. He couldn't very well say anything about what Viola had told him earlier. Anyway, he was certain that despite how his wife might feel about Doña Belinda, Viola would treat her with the utmost courtesy and kindness. To do otherwise would be to go against everything she believed about being a good hostess.

Slaughter came out from behind the desk and suggested, "Why don't we go and see how the preparations are coming along? I reckon it ought to be time pretty soon to get this *fandango* started."

"An excellent idea," Rubriz agreed. Together, the two men left the study.

Viola didn't want to move for fear of making a noise and giving away her presence. It was bad enough that she had stumbled upon this illicit rendezvous. She didn't want Doña Belinda and Santiago to know that she was aware of their affair.

After a few more moments that seemed longer to Viola than they really were as she waited in the shadows, Belinda and Santiago moved apart. Belinda murmured an endearment in Spanish and then added in a mixture of Spanish and English, "Later, *mi amor.* When your father is asleep, I will come to you."

"*Sí,*" Santiago breathed. "I will count the seconds until then."

In the darkness, Viola rolled her eyes. All too often, young men in love sounded as if they were reading lines from a second-rate melodrama.

Santiago faded away quietly, disappearing into the warm, early evening gloom as he headed toward the house.

Viola expected Belinda to follow him — after a suitable interval, of course — but instead the woman stayed where she was in the shadows under the water tank. Viola began to get restless.

She jumped a little as Belinda said in a quiet but clear voice, "You can come out now. I know you're there."

Viola didn't budge. She hoped the other woman would decide that she had been mistaken.

Instead, Belinda said, "There's no need to pretend, Mrs. Slaughter."

That took Viola even more by surprise. She stepped forward and said, "How —"

"How did I know it was you?"

Viola was close enough now that even in the poor light, she could see the faint gleam of Belinda's teeth as the blonde smiled.

"I smelled your perfume," Belinda went on. "I remembered the scent from earlier."

"I wasn't wearing it then," Viola said.

"Maybe not, but enough of it lingered about you that I noticed. I'm observant about things like that."

"I'm observant, too," Viola said. Her tone was a little sharp now. "Sometimes I notice things that I wish I hadn't."

"How much . . . did you see?" Belinda asked with only the faintest of catches in her voice.

"Enough. You and your stepson —"

"Please," the other woman broke in. "You don't have to tell me. I was here, after all."

The note of wry humor in Belinda's voice irritated Viola even more. She was not a stiff-necked prude. In fact, according to her mother, she had always been a bit too earthy for her own good.

But she also had a code she lived by and a firm sense of what was right and what was not. There was no excuse for a woman to be carrying on with her own stepson.

"What you do is your own business, Doña Belinda," Viola said coldly. "But I hope you understand that I won't tolerate any improper behavior under my own roof."

Belinda sighed. "You don't understand," she said.

"That's what people always say when they know they're doing something wrong."

"Have you never gotten carried away by your emotions and done something you shouldn't have?"

"I married a man considerably older than myself when I was still a teenager," Viola pointed out. "My family didn't think that was a good idea."

"But you did it anyway, didn't you?"

"I was in love. I still am."

"Then you can sympathize." A worried note entered Belinda's voice. "Surely you won't say anything —"

"To your husband? You don't think Don

Eduardo deserves to know the truth?"

"I don't think he deserves to be hurt for no good reason!"

The vehemence of Belinda's response surprised Viola. She said, "You sound almost like you love him."

"I do love him. I just —" Belinda broke off with an exasperated sigh. "Arguing isn't going to do any good. All I can do is ask you not to tell my husband and to throw myself on your mercy, Mrs. Slaughter."

A moment of awkward silence passed. Finally, Viola said, "A lot of work went into this party, and I don't want it ruined. Since you and your husband are leaving tomorrow, I don't see any need to say anything to him about this matter."

"Thank you," Belinda said. The words sounded heartfelt and sincere.

"But surely you can . . . conduct yourself with propriety . . . for one night," Viola added.

"Don't worry. We won't do anything to bring shame on your house."

Viola felt a flash of anger. It almost sounded as if Belinda were mocking her. But she had already promised not to tell Don Eduardo what she had seen and heard, and she wasn't going to go back on her word.

"I'll see you again in a few minutes," she said. "We'll act as if nothing happened."

"All right. Thank you again."

Viola didn't say anything. She turned and walked away. She would be glad when this night was over, she thought.

And she would be even happier when their guests from below the border were gone.

Stonewall spotted Santiago Rubriz on his way back to the house and hailed him.

In the light from the lanterns in the trees, Santiago looked a little flushed and breathless. Stonewall wasn't sure what he might have been doing to cause that, but it didn't really matter. Stonewall had something else on his mind.

"Have you been thinkin' any more about that race?" he asked.

A grin stretched across Santiago's face.

"I have been thinking about nothing else, *amigo*," he said. "Have you settled on a horse that you think will put *El Halcón* to the test?"

"Yeah. We got a roan we call Pacer that's mighty fast. I'd like to match him against *El Halcón*."

"And will you be in the saddle, my friend?"

"You're dang right I will," Stonewall

35

declared. "Fact of the matter is, I rode Pacer in the race at the last Fourth of July picnic in Tombstone."

"And did you win?"

"Well . . . no," Stonewall admitted. "But we came in second, and there were ten horses in that race. The horse that won nipped us by a nose, right at the finish line."

"Then I'm glad you and Pacer will have a chance to redeem yourselves." Santiago shook his head. "It's too bad you're destined to lose again."

"We'll just see about that." Stonewall frowned and went on, "But when? Your pa's headed back to his *rancho* in the morning, right?"

"That's true. My stepmother, however, is not what you would call an early riser. We probably won't leave until midmorning. Perhaps we can hold our race at dawn?"

"That's a good idea," Stonewall enthused. "Fellas fight duels at dawn, don't they? We'll have it out, only with horses, not pistols."

Santiago clapped a hand on his shoulder and laughed. "Yes, that's much more civilized," he agreed. "And no one dies."

"I better not drink too much tonight," Stonewall said. "I'll need a clear head in the mornin' if we're gonna be racin'. How long are we talkin' about? A mile?"

"That's fine with me."

Santiago's easy agreement made Stonewall wonder if he should have chosen a different length for the race. But it was too late now. The deal was done . . . except for the stakes.

"What are we bettin'?" he asked.

"I thought that was understood," Santiago said. "The stakes are our mounts, *amigo*. Whoever wins walks away with the other man's horse."

CHAPTER 4

Slaughter and Don Eduardo had just emerged from the house when the don's wife reached the other side of the patio. She hurried to meet them and laid a hand on her husband's arm.

"Oh, Eduardo, everything is so beautiful," Belinda said. "Señor and Señora Slaughter have gone to great lengths to celebrate our visit."

"As well we should, ma'am," Slaughter said. "It's not every day we have a lady such as yourself on the ranch, all the way from Boston."

She shook her head and laughed lightly. "I'm not from Boston anymore," she said. "I'm from Mexico now."

"This is what I have longed to hear," Rubriz said. "You accept my home as your home."

"Well, of course it is," Belinda told him. "We're married, aren't we?"

"We most certainly are."

With that, Don Eduardo leaned down and kissed her with a passionate intensity that was clearly visible.

When her husband stepped back, Belinda went on, "At any rate, Señor Slaughter, you have a wonderful lady here on the ranch in your wife, no matter where she's from. I never met a more gracious and caring person."

"Well, that's certainly true," Slaughter agreed. "Meeting Viola was a great stroke of luck for me. Convincing her to become my wife was an even greater one." Slaughter looked around. "Have you seen her recently?"

"Not in the last few minutes. I'm sure she's around somewhere, making sure that everything is done properly for the party."

"No doubt about that. I believe I'll go and find her. I'm sure things will be getting under way soon. If you two would like to freshen up, I can have one of the servants take you back to your quarters."

"That would be excellent, Señor Slaughter," Don Eduardo said.

"Please, call me John."

"Texas John, is it not?" Rubriz asked with a smile.

"That's true. Arizona is my home now,

but I'm still a proud son of the Lone Star State. Always will be."

Slaughter beckoned to one of the servants and told the girl to escort Don Eduardo and his wife to their quarters. She lowered her gaze and murmured, "*Sí,* Don Juan."

When they were gone, Slaughter looked around, pleased at the preparations he saw. He was even more pleased when he spotted his wife coming toward him a moment later. Viola looked slightly flushed but as lovely as ever. She had probably been scurrying around making sure everything was done right, thought Slaughter.

"There you are, my dear," Slaughter said. He took both her hands in his. "I trust all the preparations are to your satisfaction?"

"What? Oh, yes, the party. It's fine."

She was definitely distracted by something. Slaughter frowned slightly and asked, "What's wrong?"

Viola gave a little laugh and said, "I never could hide much from you, could I, John? It's nothing for you to worry about, I promise."

"You're sure?" Slaughter pressed her.

"Absolutely certain. In fact, I'm going to put it out of my mind myself." She squeezed his hands and smiled at him. "We're not go-

40

ing to worry about anything this evening except having a good time."

There was enough food for an army, as the old saying went, and by the time people began filling their plates, it seemed as if an army had descended on the Slaughter Ranch. Word of the celebration had gone out to all of John and Viola Slaughter's friends on neighboring ranches and in the town of Douglas, eighteen miles to the west. Everyone was invited, and most of them had shown up for the festivities.

Slaughter and Viola sat at the main table with Don Eduardo, Doña Belinda, and Santiago. Their plates were piled high with barbecue, beans, potatoes, greens, and corn-bread. Attentive servants saw to it that wineglasses never ran dry.

Eventually Slaughter had to push himself away from the table. He patted his belly and said, "I believe I could live for a month on what I've eaten tonight."

"It was an exceedingly fine meal," Don Eduardo agreed. "My compliments to Señora Slaughter."

"Oh, I didn't have much to do with it," Viola said. "The cooks deserve all the credit."

Belinda said, "You'll have to visit us at

41

our ranch. We'd love to return the favor, wouldn't we, Eduardo?"

"*Sí,* of course," Rubriz said. "The two of you will be most welcome at any time."

"We'll take you up on that," Slaughter promised.

He noticed that Viola didn't chime in and agree with him. Not only that, he also thought he saw a hint of coolness in her eyes. That told him it was unlikely they would be accepting Belinda's invitation anytime soon, and her attitude puzzled him slightly. Normally Viola was a very sociable person and loved visiting friends.

Then he recalled what she had said earlier and figured that she didn't consider Belinda Rubriz to be a friend. Slaughter was still puzzled over the reason for that, but he didn't suppose it was any of his business.

Not long after the meal was over, the musicians who had stationed themselves on the other side of the road, near the cottonwoods that bordered a large stretch of open ground, fired up their fiddles. The Mexican guitarists joined in, and within moments the jaunty strains of a lively tune filled the air. It was a siren song that drew the guests away from the tables and their empty plates. They streamed across the road and began dancing.

Belinda put her hand on her husband's arm and said, "Come and dance with me, Eduardo."

"You know my leg is a bit too stiff for that, my dear," Rubriz told her. "Santiago, lend a hand here. Dance with your stepmother."

"Of course," Santiago said as he got to his feet. Slaughter thought he showed a noticeable lack of enthusiasm for the task. Stiffly, Santiago held his hand out and Belinda took it as she rose from the table. He led her across the road to the area where the dancing was going on.

Slaughter heard a faint sniff from where Viola sat beside him. He looked over at her and asked quietly, "Are you all right?"

"I'm fine," she said. "Shall we dance, John?"

"We shouldn't leave Don Eduardo alone —"

"Please," Rubriz interrupted. "Do not let me hold you back, *por favor.* By all means, Juan, dance with your lovely wife. The two of you should enjoy this beautiful evening."

"Well . . . all right, then," Slaughter said. He stood and extended his hand to Viola. "If you would do me the honor, Mrs. Slaughter?"

"I'd be happy to, Mr. Slaughter," she said as she smiled at him and took his hand.

43

■ ■ ■ ■

Viola knew it was all an act, the way Belinda and Santiago were carrying on toward each other. Their coolness, their demeanor of not actually liking each other all that much, all of it was intended to fool Don Eduardo. To keep the image of his wife and his son locked in a passionate embrace from ever even entering his mind.

And it seemed to be working, otherwise he never would have been so casual about telling the two of them to dance together.

"You're thinking about something again," Slaughter said as he held her close to him and they turned in time to the music. "And it's not me or the tune the fellows are playing."

"I'm sorry, John. It's true I'm a bit distracted tonight."

"It's Belinda, isn't it? You said earlier that you didn't like her."

For a moment Viola considered telling him what she had discovered. After all, she had promised Belinda only that she wouldn't say anything about the affair to Don Eduardo. She hadn't mentioned anything about whether or not she would tell her own husband.

But that would violate the spirit of the promise, if not the letter, she decided. John wasn't very good at hiding his feelings, either. If he knew the truth, he might not be able to act the same toward their guests.

Viola didn't want a scene, didn't want anything to ruin the evening for everyone else.

So she said, "I'll tell you all about it later, John, I promise. But not until the time is right."

When their visitors were gone, she added silently to herself.

Slaughter sighed and nodded.

"Very well," he told her. "If there's one thing I've learned over the years we've been together, it's that I'd be wasting my time and energy arguing with you." He pulled her even closer and nuzzled her ear. "It's much more pleasant agreeing with you."

"Later you'll see how much more pleasant it can be," she whispered.

"I'll hold you to that, my dear," Slaughter said.

Stonewall slipped away from the party and went along the tree-lined path to the barn and corrals. It was difficult for him to leave when there was dancing going on, especially when there were so many pretty señoritas eager to go for a spin around the "dance floor" with him.

But he couldn't stop thinking about the race with Santiago Rubriz in the morning. He wanted to go check on Pacer and see how the roan was doing.

Stonewall wouldn't have admitted it to anybody, but he had his doubts about being able to beat *El Halcón*. Santiago's horse was something special. Stonewall knew that, but his own stubborn pride had prodded him into issuing the challenge. Once he'd done that, it was too late to take it back.

But Pacer was a heck of a horse, too. They had a chance, Stonewall told himself. That was all he had ever asked out of life.

As he walked through the darkness, Stonewall reflected on how he'd be making evening rounds right about now if he'd been back in Tombstone, where he served as one of his brother-in-law's deputies. Slaughter had left Tombstone in the capable hands of his chief deputy Burt Alvord while he made this trip to the ranch to meet Don Eduardo and accept delivery of the cattle he'd bought.

Stonewall had told Slaughter he would stay in town if that's what the sheriff wanted, but it had been a half-hearted offer. He knew there would be a big party to celebrate

Don Eduardo's visit, and Stonewall hated to miss out on a party.

Slaughter knew that, too, and had told his brother-in-law to come along. Stonewall hadn't wasted any time in agreeing.

A lantern burned in the barn, its warm yellow glow spilling out through the open double doors. A couple of ranch hands sat on three-legged stools in the broad center aisle between the stalls, using a crate for a table as they played cards. They looked up and nodded greetings to Stonewall.

"Surprised to see you here, youngster," one of them said. He was a wizened wrangler named Pete who had been around the Slaughter Ranch for years. "Figured you'd be at the *fandango,* dancin' with all the pretty girls and tryin' to convince 'em to slip off into the trees with you."

"Maybe they all told him no," the other cowboy suggested with a grin.

Stonewall said, "As a matter of fact, there are at least a dozen gals up yonder I could be sparkin' right now if I wanted to. But I got a race in the morning to uphold the honor of the ranch, and that's more important. I came down to check on Pacer."

"He's fine," Pete said. "You insin-yoo-atin' that I don't know how to take care of a hoss? I been handlin' horses more'n twice

47

as long as you been alive, boy."

"I know that. I just wanted to take a look at him for myself."

Pete waved a gnarled hand at the stalls and said, "Go ahead and he'p yourself. Ain't nobody gonna stop you."

Stonewall walked over to the stall where Pacer stood. Even in the dim light from the lantern, the horse's hide seemed to glow with a reddish fire. He tossed his head and whickered a greeting to Stonewall, who reached over the gate to scratch between Pacer's ears.

"You're gonna run your heart out in the mornin', aren't you, big fella?" Stonewall murmured.

Pacer didn't answer, of course.

Stonewall stood there a few moments longer, talking quietly to the horse in encouraging tones that he knew were aimed as much at himself as they were at Pacer. The roan appeared to be in fine shape. He had left the party for nothing, Stonewall thought.

"Who the hell —" Pete suddenly said.

Stonewall heard the note of alarm in the wrangler's voice and turned his head to look just as Pete came up off the stool and took a step toward the barn's entrance.

Then there was a quick fluttering sound

followed by a thud, and Pete swayed back a step and half-turned as he clutched at the shaft of an arrow buried in his chest. He made a plaintive gurgling noise as bright crimson blood trickled from a corner of his mouth.

The other cowhand yelled and jumped to his feet just in time to catch an arrow in the throat. The arrowhead went all the way through his neck and emerged out the back of it, accompanied by a flood of gore. He collapsed on the hard-packed dirt like a puppet with its strings cut.

Pete fell to his knees but stayed upright for a second while he continued fumbling at the arrow in his chest. Then he fell over onto his side and didn't move again.

Stonewall stood in front of Pacer's stall, momentarily frozen in shock and horror. He had been talking to both of those men only minutes earlier, and now they were dead, struck down by a threat that came out of the darkness.

Three men stepped from the shadows into the lantern light, filling the barn's entrance. Stonewall stared at them, at the bow one of them held and the rifles in the hands of the others, recognizing the fierce faces of Apache warriors who had come to the Slaughter Ranch to kill.

And unless he did something mighty quick, he was next.

CHAPTER 5

Hector Alvarez tried not to resent the fact that he was stuck out here guarding this herd of cattle instead of being at the main house half a mile away enjoying the *fiesta* Señor and Señora Slaughter had thrown for their guests.

Somebody had to watch the cattle and keep them from straying. The animals were in a strange place, after all, having been driven up here from the Rubriz ranch south of the border. They might take it into their heads to try to go back there. Cows were funny creatures. You never could tell for sure what they might decide to do.

So three of Señor Slaughter's hands and three of the *vaqueros* Don Eduardo had brought with him had been chosen to ride night herd. As one of the youngest of Slaughter's men, and one who had been working on the ranch for less time than most of the others, it made sense that Hector had been picked as a night herder.

But that didn't mean he had to like it.

Hector could see the lights in the distance, shining brightly and merrily on those lucky enough to be enjoying the good food, the music, and the dancing. From time to time when the night breezes were right, he could hear the sprightly strains of the fiddles. He even thought he heard laughter now and then, but that might have been his imagination.

The slow, gentle thud of hooves came toward him. The nighthawks crossed paths occasionally as they endlessly circled the herd, and Hector knew that was probably what he heard.

Even so, he reined in and waited, and as he did he placed his right hand on the butt of the old Colt Navy .36 he carried in a crude holster at his waist.

A voice softly hailed him in Spanish, asking who he was. Hector gave his name, then added, "I ride for Don Juan Slaughter."

The rider came closer and said, "And I ride for Don Eduardo Rubriz, so you can take your hand off that gun, young one."

"How did you —" Hector began.

"How did I know you were ready to draw on me?" The man laughed. "Because I heard your voice and knew you weren't very old and figured you were probably nervous. And my eyes are good — like those of the cat. In fact, they call me *El Gato.*"

"They do?" Hector asked, impressed by the name.

"No, you young fool!" The man laughed again and went on, "My name is Hermosa. No one has ever called me *El Gato.* So don't start, all right?"

A match flared to life. Hermosa had turned in the saddle, leaned over, and cupped his hand around the match to shield the flame before he snapped it alight with his thumbnail. It was a sensible precaution to take around cattle.

Hermosa held the match to a thin brown cigarette he had rolled. Then he snuffed out the flame between thumb and index finger.

That one moment of light was enough to reveal a lean, leathery face with a wide mouth framed by drooping mustaches. Hermosa was old, or at least he seemed that way to Hector, who had yet to see twenty summers.

Hermosa didn't take the quirly out of his mouth but rather asked around it, "Have you run into any trouble out here tonight?"

"None," Hector answered. "Everything is peaceful."

"Good. That's what we want."

Hector gave in to impulse and asked the older man, "Don't you wish you were back at the house so you could go to the party?"

"Bah. A bunch of noise and commotion."

"And food and wine and dancing and pretty girls —"

"All things that are important to a young man. I prefer a good horse, comfortable boots, and a warm place to sleep."

"A man who feels like that is barely alive," Hector said without thinking. As soon as the words were out of his mouth, he realized that he might have insulted Hermosa — and the hard planes of the *vaquero*'s face had a cruel slant to them, Hector recalled.

Hermosa didn't seem to have taken offense, though. He puffed on his smoke and said, "Barely alive is still better than dead."

"I suppose." Hector thought it might be a good idea to change the subject. "What is it like to work for Don Eduardo?"

"Good. He is a hard man, but he treats his people fairly. Life on his ranch is the only thing I have ever known. And my father worked for his father, back in the days when Don Vincente founded the *rancho* with his partner. Before we started our own. Many years ago, boy. Long before you were born."

"You've spent your whole life in the same place?" Hector could barely wrap his mind around that idea.

"It's not so bad," Hermosa said as he snuffed out the butt of the quirly and snapped it away. He added dryly, "You get used to it."

"I'd like to go places," Hector said. "Faraway places. I'd like to see big cities and gaze out over the sea. But tonight I would settle for going to that *fiesta.*"

Hermosa growled, "You're young. There will be other *fiestas.*" With that he lifted his reins and nudged his horse into motion. "We had better get back to our jobs," he said.

Hector heaved a sigh, stared longingly at the lights glittering at the ranch house, and said, "I suppose —"

He stopped short as he heard several sharp reports. The sounds were muted somewhat by distance, but they were unmistakable.

Gunshots.

Hermosa lifted himself in his stirrups, muttered an exclamation, and said, "Don Eduardo." He dug the rowels of his fancy spurs into his mount's flanks and sent the horse leaping forward as he called over his shoulder, "Stay here with the herd, boy!"

"But —" Hector began as worry for John Slaughter and the lovely Señora Slaughter filled him.

"Stay here!" Hermosa ordered again, and then he was gone, galloping away into the darkness.

Hector hesitated. He didn't have to follow the commands given to him by Don Eduardo's man, but on the other hand, Señor Slaughter had ordered him to watch the herd.

Torn between concern for his employer and his desire to do as Slaughter had told him, Hector agonized for a moment before deciding that he would stay here with the cattle. He was convinced it was the right thing to do.

Besides, Hector had no doubt that whatever the trouble was, John Slaughter could handle it.

Stonewall wasn't armed. He hadn't figured it would be necessary to bring a gun to a *fandango.*

But he knew there was a shotgun inside the tack room. Pete kept it there to chase off the wolves that occasionally came down from the mountains.

Those Apaches were more dangerous than any wolves, Stonewall knew.

He made a desperate leap for the tack room door, which stood open about a foot.

As he moved, one of the raiders fired. The man's rifle was an old single-shot weapon. Stonewall heard the bullet hum past his ear like a bee, rather than the high-pitched whine of rounds fired by more modern rifles.

An arrow flew past him as well and lodged in the jamb as his shoulder struck the door and knocked it open the rest of the way. He half-stumbled, half-fell into the tack room and spotted the shotgun hanging on pegs beside the door. As he reached for it, one of the Apaches bounded toward him with a strident yell.

Now that a gun had gone off, there was no longer any need for stealth. Stonewall had a sinking feeling that these three renegades weren't the only ones on the ranch tonight.

The Apache charging him couldn't see the shotgun hanging on the wall just inside the door. He had jerked a knife from the colorful sash around his waist and raised it high as his face contorted with hatred. Clearly, he planned to kill Stonewall in hand-to-hand combat.

Stonewall had no interest in going *mano a mano* with the warrior. He jerked the scattergun from the pegs, swiveled toward his attacker as he used his thumb to ear back both hammers, and touched off the right-hand barrel.

The load of buckshot traveled only a couple of feet, so it was still bunched up as it slammed into the Apache's chest, shredding his blousy shirt and blowing a fist-size hole clean through him. The charge's impact was great enough to lift the warrior off his feet and throw him backward.

The intruder crashed down on his back with his shirt on fire from the tongue of flame that had licked out from the shotgun's muzzle. He would never get any deader.

Another rifle blasted and a slug chewed splinters from the doorjamb near where the arrow had lodged. Stonewall swung the shotgun up and fired the second barrel at the two men in the barn's entrance. They dived back into the darkness. Stonewall couldn't tell if he had hit either of them.

He retreated into the tack room and kicked the door shut. A box of shotgun shells sat on a shelf. He reached into it and grabbed a handful. It took him only a couple of seconds to break open the gun, dump the spent shells, and slide fresh ones into the barrels. As he closed the shotgun, he heard more gunfire, confirming his hunch that the ranch was under a general attack.

He needed to be out there with his friends and relatives, defending their home.

But if he stepped out of the tack room, he might run right into a rifle bullet or an arrow.

What happened next took the decision out of his hands. He smelled smoke wafting under the door.

The sons of bitches had set the barn on fire.

Slaughter had brought Viola back to the table after the dance ended. Belinda and Santiago had returned as well. Belinda sat close to her husband, while Santiago slouched several chairs away, toying with a glass of wine.

After seeing that Viola was seated, Slaughter walked over to the young man and asked, "Did you and my brother-in-law settle the details of that race you were talking about this afternoon?"

Santiago's interest perked up. He smiled and said, "It is all arranged, Señor Slaughter. We will race at dawn, Stonewall's Pacer against my *El Halcón*."

Slaughter picked up one of the chairs, reversed it, and straddled it.

"That ought to be something to see. I can

tell by looking at him that horse of yours is fast."

"*Sí,* very fast," Santiago nodded.

"But Pacer's got some speed, too. I'll enjoy watching them." Slaughter looked around. "Where is Stonewall?"

Santiago shook his head and said, "I have not seen him."

"I thought he'd be out there dancing," Viola said.

"Perhaps he is nervous about the race," Don Eduardo suggested. "Señor Slaughter . . . Juan . . . I was wondering . . . perhaps you would care to make a small wager on the outcome?"

"I might be persuaded to do that," Slaughter replied. "What sort of stakes were you thinking of?"

He was destined not to know Rubriz's answer, because at that moment a terrified scream ripped through the festivities and made the musicians abruptly fall silent. Slaughter bolted to his feet, looked around, and saw one of the young women who worked for them running toward the house, panic-stricken.

A shot rang out. Slaughter automatically identified the whipcrack report as that of a rifle.

The servant threw out her arms as her

mouth opened in a wide "O" of shock. She stumbled and pitched forward on her face. Slaughter saw the bright red stain on the back of her white shirt and knew she had been shot.

Screams and shots and high-pitched whoops suddenly filled the air, along with more gunshots.

Instinctively, Viola leaped to her feet and cried, "John!"

Before she could say anything else, Slaughter tackled her and bore both of them to the ground. The tables and chairs would provide a little protection as long as she stayed low.

"Stay down!" he told her as he looked around. A few feet away, Don Eduardo had pulled Belinda to the ground, too. He knelt beside her with a derringer in his hand. Slaughter hadn't known that the don was armed, but it didn't surprise him.

As a matter of fact, Slaughter had a gun himself, a short-barreled, single action .38 Smith & Wesson he carried in a holster under his left arm, hidden by his jacket. As he stood up he drew the revolver and looked around for somebody to shoot.

That didn't take long. Chaos filled the area that had been used for dancing, as the couples there scattered in the face of an attack by what appeared to be at least a dozen renegade Apache warriors. Some of the men were trying to fight back, but they were unarmed and a few had already fallen. Slaughter spotted one of the Apaches raising a knife high above his head. The renegade was about to plunge the blade into the chest of a man at his feet.

Even though the range was long for a handgun, Slaughter drew a bead and fired. He aimed at the Apache's chest, but the bullet went high. Just as well, though, since it entered the renegade's left cheek just below the eye and bored on into the brain, dropping the man like a stone before he could strike that killing blow with his knife.

"Santiago!" Don Eduardo bellowed.

Slaughter jerked around to see that the younger Rubriz was running toward the fight. Slaughter admired Santiago's courage, but the youngster's actions were rather foolhardy since he was unarmed.

Santiago had something in mind, though. He grabbed up an overturned chair, brought it crashing down on the ground so that it shattered, and charged on into battle, using a broken chair leg in each hand as clubs.

Slaughter saw that he couldn't risk any more shots — there was too great a chance of hitting one of the innocents — so he reached down and took hold of Viola's arm with his free hand. As he lifted her to her feet, he told her, "Take Belinda and get inside the house. You'll be safe there." He pressed the .38 into her hand. "Anybody tries to stop you, gun 'em down."

Viola acknowledged the order with a curt nod. Slaughter knew from the grim expression on his wife's face that she would do what he told her. Any Apache who got in her way would have a fight on his hands.

Viola ran to Belinda's side and told her, "Come with me."

The blonde didn't respond at first. Clearly she was too terrified to move. Her husband had to take hold of her, lift her to her feet, and shove her toward Viola.

"Go with Señora Slaughter," he told her. "I love you, Belinda. Never forget that."

"Eduardo —" She clutched at his coat.

"Go!"

Belinda obeyed, stumbling along beside Viola as the other woman held her arm to steady her. Rubriz turned toward Slaughter, opened his mouth to say something, and then jerked up the derringer and fired instead.

Slaughter heard the bullet go past him and thud into something behind him. He turned to see one of the Apaches collapsing with a hole in the center of his forehead where Don Eduardo's slug had struck him.

The warrior had been armed with a Henry rifle. Slaughter snatched it from the dead man's hands and brought it to his shoulder as he said "Much obliged" to Don Eduardo.

"You have fought these bronco Apaches before?" Rubriz asked.

The rifle in Slaughter's hands cracked. One of the Indians across the road spun off his feet as the bullet ripped through him.

"Many times," Slaughter said in response to the don's question. "But they haven't dared attack the ranch in quite a while."

"We should turn this table on its side and use it for cover," Don Eduardo suggested.

"Good idea," Slaughter said. He lowered the Henry and held it in one hand while he used the other to help Don Eduardo tip the table onto its side. Platters of leftover food, plates, silverware, wineglasses, all went flying.

The mess could be cleaned up later — if they survived.

Slaughter knelt behind the table and fired several more shots from the Henry. The sight of two Apaches collapsing rewarded his efforts.

Don Eduardo crouched beside him and said, "Where is Santiago? I don't see —"

"There," Slaughter said as he spotted the younger Rubriz. Santiago was using the broken chair legs to fight off an Apache who was attacking him with a knife. He blocked the thrusts and tried to strike back, but the warrior was too quick, too experienced in such combat. The Apache's foot shot out, hooked behind one of Santiago's knees, and jerked him off his feet.

"Santiago, no!" Don Eduardo cried as he saw his son fall. The don straightened up in alarm and then fell back.

At the same time, Slaughter fired and blew away a chunk of the Apache's skull before the warrior could plunge his knife into the fallen Santiago.

"I got him," Slaughter said. "Santiago's all right."

Don Eduardo didn't respond. Slaughter turned to see the don lying there with a hand pressed to his side as blood welled between his fingers.

CHAPTER 6

Through the tack room door, Stonewall heard the terrified shrieks of the horses and knew the smoke had spooked them, too. He couldn't let them burn, and if he stayed in here the flames would consume him as well.

Even if the Apaches were waiting for him, he had to get out of here.

With the shotgun held ready, he kicked the door open and lunged through it into the barn's center aisle, which was clogged with black, billowing smoke. He ducked his head, but that didn't really do any good. The stuff still stung his eyes, nose, and throat, leaving him half-blind, coughing, and choking.

He fought his way through the smoke, figuring that if he couldn't see the Apaches, they couldn't see him, either. As he came to each stall, he threw the latch open and flung the gate back to let the horse inside stampede out. The panicky animals would have a chance to escape, anyway.

When the renegades saw the horses emerging from the barn, they would figure out that he was letting them loose and know he was still alive. So they would be expecting him to come out, too, any time now.

Stonewall had a surprise in mind for them, though.

He wasn't going to emerge from the barn by himself.

He saved Pacer's stall for last, and when he came to it he saw the roan lunging back and forth within the sturdy wooden walls.

"Pacer!" Stonewall said. "Pacer, settle down. Settle down, boy, it'll be all right."

The words were punctuated by hacking coughs, so he supposed they might not be as reassuring as they would have been otherwise. There was nothing he could do about that. Something in what he said must have gotten through to the horse, though, because Pacer stopped trying to batter his way out of the stall. He threw his head up and down and whinnied as if asking Stonewall to do something, anything, about the inferno spreading around them.

The walls were on fire, and when the flames reached the hay in the loft, that fuel would turn the barn into a gigantic torch. It couldn't be saved. Stonewall glanced in the direction where the two bodies lay but couldn't see them because of the thick smoke.

He would have liked to get Pete and the other cowboy out of here, but that wasn't going to be possible. He would be doing good to save himself. As he swung the stall gate open, he continued talking to Pacer in calm, steady tones. If the roan bolted, Stonewall wouldn't be able to stop him.

Pacer didn't run. Stonewall opened the gate wide and used it to help him throw a leg over Pacer's back. He leaned forward over the roan's neck, held the shotgun in one hand and Pacer's mane with the other, and banged his heels on the horse's flanks.

Pacer took off like a shot.

Instinct must have guided the horse through the smoke toward the barn entrance. Pacer burst out into the open. Stonewall's eyes were streaming tears from the smoke; he couldn't see a thing. He was doing good just to stay mounted, riding bareback like he was.

Fresh air flooded against his face. His vision began to clear a bit as he heard rifles cracking. Some of the Apaches were shooting at him, he realized, but Pacer was moving too fast for them to draw a bead on him.

Stonewall galloped along the road through

the cottonwoods that led back to the house. One of the attackers leaped into his path and fired a Winchester. The shot missed, but it spooked Pacer and made the roan shy violently. Stonewall almost fell off. Somehow he managed to hang on.

The Apache worked the rifle's lever for a second shot. Stonewall had no choice but to thrust the shotgun at him and fire it one-handed. The short-range blast blew the Apache's head off his shoulders, but the recoil ripped the weapon out of Stonewall's hand.

The thunderous blast also made Pacer rear up and paw at the air. This time Stonewall wasn't able to stay on. He slipped off the roan's back and crashed to the ground.

Slaughter knew that Don Eduardo must have been hit by one of the bullets flying around. He dropped to a knee beside the wounded man and asked him, "How bad are you hit?"

"I . . . I don't know," Rubriz gasped. "But don't worry . . . about me . . . Juan. Protect my wife . . . my son . . ."

"I'll do my best," Slaughter promised. "In the meantime . . ."

He set the Henry aside, whipped off his coat, and wadded it up. As he pressed it hard against the wound in Don Eduardo's side, he went on, "Hold this on there to slow down the bleeding."

"I will . . . be all right . . . *mi amigo,*" Rubriz said. "Now go. Deal with those . . . damned Apaches."

Slaughter nodded and picked up the rifle. He turned back to the fight.

Not as much shooting was going on now. The battle had turned into mostly hand-to-hand combat. The actual number of attackers had been relatively small, Slaughter realized. The Apaches were outnumbered, and their only advantages had been surprise and the fact that most of the partygoers weren't armed.

Eventually the odds had worked against them, however, and as some of the Apaches had fallen, the guests and Slaughter's cowboys had snatched up the weapons the dead warriors had dropped. That had helped turn the tide even more.

Slaughter stalked across the road, seeking out targets and bringing the Henry smoothly to his shoulder to fire every time he spotted one of the renegades still on his feet. There was plenty of light for shooting because the barn was on fire, flames shooting a hundred feet into the air as they consumed the structure.

The barn could be rebuilt, but Slaughter hoped the horses had gotten out all right. And some of his men might have been in there, too, he thought grimly. If they had been killed, he would make sure their deaths were avenged.

Not one of the renegades would leave the ranch alive.

He looked for Santiago Rubriz and felt a surge of relief when he spotted the young man. Slaughter was even more relieved when he recognized the smoke-grimed figure Santiago was helping along.

"Stonewall!" he called. "Over here."

Stonewall and Santiago hurried toward him. Stonewall said, "John! Thank the Lord you're all right. Where's Viola?"

"I sent her and Doña Belinda into the house."

"My — my stepmother!" Santiago said. "Was she hurt?"

Santiago had seemed rather cool toward Belinda earlier, but clearly he was concerned about her safety now. Slaughter told him, "She was fine the last time I saw her."

"Thank God!"

"But your father . . . I'm afraid he was hit, Santiago."

The young man's eyes widened. He said, "Is he . . . was he —"

"I don't know how bad it is," Slaughter said. He turned and pointed. "Over there, behind the table where we were sitting earlier."

Santiago took off in that direction at a run.

The shooting had stopped completely now, but the area between the ranch house and the barn wasn't silent. Angry shouts and the moans of the wounded filled the air. Bodies, white and Apache alike, littered the ground.

Stonewall looked around at the carnage and said, "John, the Indians around here have been peaceful lately. What the hell was this all about?"

"I don't know," Slaughter said, "but I intend to find out."

Hector Alvarez was in agony as he sat on his horse and listened to the gunshots and watched the flames leaping up. From this distance, the fire was just a garish orange blob and Hector couldn't tell what was burning, but he thought it might be the barn.

Whatever it was, that didn't really matter right now. What was important was that Señor and Señora Slaughter and all of Hector's friends and fellow cowboys were in danger, and he wasn't doing a single thing to help them.

But his orders had been to stay with the herd no matter what happened. He prided himself on being a faithful *vaquero* and doing what he was supposed to.

Hermosa and the other nighthawks had disregarded their orders, though. They had galloped back to the ranch to find out what was going on and help if they could. Hector had heard the swift hoofbeats of their horses in the darkness and knew he was alone out here with the herd.

He thought about one of the maids who worked in the main house, Yolanda Ramos. She was about a year younger than Hector and very beautiful. He had walked out with her several times when neither of them was working, and once he had even been bold enough to kiss her. Nothing he had ever tasted had been sweeter than Yolanda's lips.

Soon, when they had known each other longer, Hector planned to ask Yolanda to marry him. He had hopes that she would say yes, and if she did, then they would live in one of the small cabins where Señor Slaughter's married hands made their homes. Yolanda would continue to work for Señora Slaughter — at least until her belly was too big with their first baby for her to do so.

There would be other babies, many of them, and Hector would grow old surrounded by the love of children and grandchildren and great-grandchildren and most of all his beautiful Yolanda. It was a dream that he held close to his heart and cherished.

A dream that would be destroyed if anything happened to Yolanda.

As that horrible realization sunk into Hector's brain, he knew he couldn't wait any longer. Orders or no orders, he had to make sure she was safe from whatever terrible thing was happening there at the ranch.

He had just lifted his reins when he heard hoofbeats nearby. Were Hermosa and the other nighthawks coming back? The shooting was still going on, and the fire still blazed.

Hector hesitated as large shapes loomed up in front of him. Men on horseback, he told himself. He put his hand on the butt of the .36 and called softly, "Hermosa?"

Something thudded against his chest as if someone had just thrown a rock at him. Whatever it was, it didn't bounce off like a rock, though. He reached up to feel, and as his fingers touched the leather-wrapped handle of a knife, pain welled up inside him, a greater pain than he had ever known.

He realized the blade was buried deep in

his chest.

A numb weakness followed the pain. Hector tried to draw his gun, but his muscles refused to work properly. The Colt came out of its holster but then slipped from Hector's fingers. He swayed in the saddle and grabbed for the saddle horn instead. That steadied him for a second, but then he lost that grip as well and toppled off the horse.

A hot, salty flood filled his mouth. He knew it was blood, knew he was dying. He fumbled at the knife sticking out of his chest but couldn't dislodge it.

Fingers pushed his aside, gripped the knife, pulled it out. A shape loomed over him, a deeper patch of darkness in the night, and a man's voice said in English, "You should've gone back to the house with the others, kid. Might've stood a chance that way."

Hector's head fell to the side. Blood welled out of his open mouth. His lips moved, and he whispered, "Yolanda . . ." just before he died.

CHAPTER 7

Viola and Belinda had almost reached the house when one of the servants came shrieking after them with an Apache in pursuit. As Viola looked over her shoulder and saw what was happening, she remembered the poor girl who had been gunned down when the attack first began. She was determined not to let another of her people be killed.

She pushed the sobbing, stumbling Belinda toward the door and snapped, "Get inside."

Then she turned back, raised the Smith & Wesson, pulled back the hammer, and fired.

The Apache's head jerked back. His legs kept running for a couple more steps, then folded up underneath him. As the dead man tumbled to the ground, Viola stepped forward and caught hold of the hysterical servant.

The girl screamed and fought, not knowing or caring who had hold of her. Viola said, "Stop it!" then recognizing the girl she added, "Stop it, Yolanda! Stop fighting me!"

Her urgent words must have gotten through to the servant's terrified brain. She stopped struggling and gasped, "Señora Slaughter?"

Viola pushed her toward the front door that Belinda had left open behind her. "Get inside. Find Doña Belinda and take care of her." Giving Yolanda a job to do might help her keep calm.

"What . . . what are you going to do, señora?"

"I'll make sure none of those Apaches get in," Viola said in a flat, hard voice.

As soon as Yolanda had hurried into the house, Viola stationed herself in the doorway and watched the battle unfold. Her heart seemed to twist in her chest when she saw the flames through the trees and realized the barn was on fire. She was afraid for the men and horses who might have been caught in there, but it was just one more worry on top of her fear for the safety of her husband and her brother.

With the iron-willed, icy-nerved determination that had proven so valuable in times past, she kept those fears tamped down deep inside her. She couldn't afford to give in to them while the outcome of the attack was still in doubt.

Fortunately, that didn't last too much longer. The shooting died away. The lanterns still burned in the trees, casting the same light they had before terror and death replaced dancing and gaiety. Viola's eyes searched desperately for John and Stonewall.

When she spotted them and saw that they appeared to be all right, the relief that surged through her was so powerful it made her gasp. Her knees went weak for a second before she stiffened them.

"Señora . . . ?"

Yolanda's voice made Viola turn. The maid stood there, calmer than before but obviously still very agitated.

"What is it?" Viola asked.

"I found Doña Belinda like you said, señora, but she . . . she collapsed. I cannot get her to wake up, señora. I think she is dead!"

By the time Slaughter and Stonewall reached Don Eduardo, Santiago was already kneeling at his father's side. He had lifted Don Eduardo and leaned the wounded man against him.

Rubriz's eyes were open. He gazed up at his son and asked in a weak voice, "Santiago . . . you are unharmed?"

"I'm fine, Papa," Santiago assured him. "Don't try to talk. Just rest."

Thin lines of blood had trickled from the corners of Don Eduardo's mouth. Slaughter hunkered on the other side of him and said, "Let me take a look, Santiago."

Rubriz still had Slaughter's coat pressed against the wound. Slaughter lifted it away. There was no strength left in Don Eduardo's fingers. Slaughter pulled the don's shirt out of his trousers and lifted it along with the short charro jacket Rubriz wore. When the bloody garments were out of the way, an ugly red-rimmed hole in his side oozed crimson.

Slaughter reached around and felt for an exit wound. When he didn't find one, he said, "The bullet's still in there. No way of telling how much damage it's done. We need to get him inside, stop that bleeding, and let him rest."

"The bullet must come out," Santiago said.

"Try to dig it out now and you'll finish him off," Slaughter said. "He needs to get stronger first. Tomorrow, maybe."

"He could have blood poisoning by then," the younger man argued.

Slaughter knew Santiago was right. This

was a fine line they had to walk. Too much delay in getting the bullet out would prove fatal, but subjecting Don Eduardo to a lot of cutting and probing in the shape he was in now would kill him, too.

"We'll do everything we can for him, Santiago, I give you my word. I'll send a man to Douglas tonight for the doctor. They should be back by morning."

"Will my father still be alive by then?" Santiago asked bitterly.

"S-Santiago . . ." Don Eduardo rasped. "*Mi amigo* Juan . . . is right. What I need now . . . is to know that my wife . . . is unharmed."

"I sent her into the house with Viola," Slaughter told him. "We'll take you in there so you can see her. You need to be resting in a bed anyway."

Of course, moving the wounded man might be dangerous, too, Slaughter thought, but they couldn't leave him out here in the open all night.

Before he and Stonewall and Santiago could pick up the don, rapid hoofbeats pounded nearby. Slaughter thought the likelihood of another attack tonight was very slim, but he picked up the Henry rifle he had set aside and straightened to his feet anyway.

80

Several men rode up in a hurry. Slaughter recognized the rider in the lead as one of Don Eduardo's men, an older, saturnine *hombre* who had the look of a *bandido* about him even though Slaughter had no reason to think he was anything more than an honest *vaquero.*

The leader of the newcomers swung down from his saddle and said, "Don Eduardo —"

"I am all right, Hermosa," the don said. His voice sounded a little stronger now, but Slaughter had a feeling he just didn't want to seem any weaker than he had to in front of his men. "What about . . . the cattle?"

"They were fine when we left," Hermosa replied. "We had to make sure you were safe."

A shock went through Slaughter as he realized these were the men Rubriz had picked to watch over the herd while the party was going on. Not only that, but he spotted two of his own hands among them and recognized them as men who were supposed to be acting as nighthawks.

"Wait a minute," Slaughter said sharply. "Who's out there keeping an eye on the herd?"

"One of your young cowboys, señor," Hermosa said. "I told him to stay behind while we rode in."

"Son of a —" Slaughter bit back the rest of the curse. He turned to his men who had come in with the *vaqueros* and said, "Get down from those horses. Help carry Don Eduardo into the house. Mrs. Slaughter will know what to do. Stonewall, you up to coming with me?"

"Sure, John," Stonewall said. His voice was raspy from the smoke he'd inhaled in the barn. "What's wrong?"

"That's what I intend to find out."

The two confused cowboys dismounted and turned their horses over to Slaughter and Stonewall. Both saddles had scabbarded Winchesters strapped to them, so Slaughter left the Henry rifle behind. He set a fast pace toward the bed ground half a mile away, where the herd he'd bought from Don Eduardo was settling in.

As they rode, Stonewall said above the hoofbeats, "I think I've got it figured out now. That raid by the Apaches was just a distraction."

"That's what I'm afraid of," Slaughter said. "Raise hell, draw in all the men, then hit the herd."

"Apaches usually don't go in for rustling on a scale like that," Stonewall pointed out.

"No, but somebody could have gotten

them to do it. Paid them off with rifles, maybe, or something else they'd want."

As Slaughter put this theory into words, he knew it made sense. He might be wrong — he hoped he was wrong — but he wasn't going to be surprised if he and Stonewall found that the cattle were gone.

They rode hard at first, then Slaughter slowed and told his brother-in-law, "Better get that rifle out. There's no telling what we're going to run into."

With Winchesters in hand, they advanced at a more cautious pace. Slaughter felt his hopes disappearing as he scanned the countryside in the light from the moon and stars and failed to find the dark, irregular mass that should have greeted him.

"They're gone," Stonewall said, his voice hollow. "All those cattle you just bought from Don Eduardo — gone!"

"Yes," Slaughter agreed grimly. "That appears to be the case."

He spotted something else, though. A single, much smaller shape huddled darkly on the ground. He pointed it out to Stonewall.

The young cowboy cursed. All the members of the crew were his friends. It was impossible not to like Stonewall, and he felt the same way about almost everybody he met.

"Take a closer look," Slaughter told him. "I'll watch for any trouble, but I don't think we're going to find any." His voice held a note of bitterness, too, as he added, "Whoever was out here a little while ago, they're all gone now."

Stonewall dismounted and walked over to the shape on the ground. He knelt and rolled the body onto its back. With a catch in his voice, he called, "It's . . . Hector Alvarez."

Slaughter sighed. Young Alvarez hadn't been working on the ranch for very long, but in the time he'd been here, he had demonstrated that he was a devoted, capable hand.

He was courting one of the maids who worked in the house, too, Slaughter recalled Viola telling him.

Now any future together they might have had was over, ripped away by ruthless men.

Somebody would pay for hurting his people, thought Slaughter.

"Can you tell what happened to him?" he asked.

"Let me strike a match," Stonewall said.

He snapped a lucifer to life and held it so that its feeble, flickering glow washed over the unfortunate Hector Alvarez. Even from horseback, Slaughter could see the large bloodstain on the young man's shirt.

"Doesn't look like he was shot," Stonewall said. "More likely he was stabbed. He must've let whoever it was get pretty close to him, to get stuck like that."

"Not necessarily," Slaughter said. "The killer could have been good at throwing a knife."

"Yeah, I guess." The match had burned down almost to Stonewall's fingers. He shook out the flame and dropped it.

"Strike another one," Slaughter told him. "Let's have a look at the hoofprints around here."

As Stonewall did so, he said, "Apaches aren't really horse Indians, like the ones back on the plains."

"No, they're not," Slaughter agreed. An Apache was just about as likely to eat a horse as he was to ride it. These renegades preferred to travel on foot. Some of their hideouts in the mountains were impassable even by horse.

"Only hoofprints I see are shod ones," Stonewall reported. "White men's horses. Looks like your idea of rustlers working with the Apaches was the right one, John."

"It's not a coincidence that this happened

tonight," Slaughter said. "Not when Don Eduardo just delivered this herd today. Somebody knew these cattle would be here and came after them specifically."

"You reckon one of the don's men is workin' with the rustlers?"

Slaughter frowned in thought for a moment, then said, "Maybe, maybe not. They could have been keeping an eye on his ranch, waiting for the right moment to make a move against him. Some old enemy of Don Eduardo's, maybe."

"Or an enemy of yours," Stonewall suggested.

Slaughter shook his head. "Not likely. I have plenty of enemies, but I don't see how any of them would have known the don was bringing that herd up here. Not in time to set that up with the Apaches, anyway." Slaughter scraped a thumbnail along his jawline. "No, this is somebody who wants to get back at Don Eduardo for something. Unfortunately, since earlier this evening when that money changed hands, those are my cows that they stole."

"And that means . . . ?"

"That means I'm going to get them back," Slaughter said.

CHAPTER 8

Viola was practically holding her breath as she hurried after Yolanda. She would have sworn that Belinda Rubriz hadn't been wounded. What could have happened to her?

Maybe Belinda had been hit by a stray bullet on their way into the house and hadn't even realized it herself. Viola had heard of people being shot without knowing it.

The maid led Viola into the parlor, where Belinda was slumped on the floor in an untidy heap. Viola dropped to her knees beside the blonde and placed a hand on Belinda's chest, searching for a heartbeat.

To her great relief, after a few seconds she found it.

Belinda was alive, just unconscious.

"She's not dead," Viola told Yolanda, who crossed herself and offered up a quick prayer of thanksgiving. Viola went on, "Help me check her for injuries."

They looked the visitor over and found no sign of blood on her clothes. Viola checked her head, searching through the thick blond hair, thinking that maybe Belinda had been creased by a bullet. That turned out not to be the case, either.

Viola lifted one of Belinda's eyelids and saw that the blonde's eyes had rolled back in their sockets.

"It looks to me like she just fainted from fear and strain," Viola said.

"Do people really do that, señora?"

"High-toned ladies from Boston do, I guess," Viola said. "Help me lift her onto the sofa."

She took Belinda's shoulders while Yolanda grasped her ankles. Together they lifted her and placed her on one of the sofas in the parlor. Viola loosened Belinda's clothing.

"We'll give her some air and wait for her to wake up," she said. "That's about all we can do right now."

Heavy footsteps sounded from the house's main entrance. Yolanda whirled in that direction, put a hand to her mouth, and gasped, "Señora!"

Viola had slipped the .38 Smith & Wesson her husband had given her into a pocket of her dress. She reached in and grasped the gun now. She lifted it and had her thumb on the hammer as the shapes of several men appeared in the entrance to the parlor.

She relaxed slightly as she recognized Santiago Rubriz and Don Eduardo. Santiago was on one side of the don, holding him up, while one of Don Eduardo's *vaqueros* supported him on the other side.

The don's clothes had a lot of blood on them. His head sagged forward limply. He appeared to be unconscious.

Viola put the revolver away again as she hurried to meet the men.

"Señora Slaughter —" Santiago began.

"Put him over there," Viola interrupted as she pointed to the room's second sofa. "Was he shot?"

"*Sí.* Your husband said the bullet was still in him."

"I'll have a look at him," Viola said with an efficient nod. "I've patched up gunshot wounds before. There's a good doctor in Douglas, too, and a rider can be there in a few hours."

"*Sí, señora,* Señor Slaughter said he would send a man for the doctor."

As Santiago and the *vaquero,* an older, hawk-faced man, carefully placed Don Eduardo on the sofa, Viola asked, "Where is my husband?"

"He and your brother rode off in a hurry, señora," Santiago said. He stepped back from the sofa and added, "They did not say where they were going, but they seemed quite upset about something, especially Señor Slaughter."

John had plenty of reason to be upset, thought Viola. His home had been attacked, his friends and family endangered.

Texas John Slaughter wasn't going to take that outrage lying down.

Santiago seemed to notice his stepmother for the first time. His eyes widened at the sight of Belinda lying on the sofa, and he exclaimed, "*Dios mio!* Belinda! She is —"

He had started toward her, but Viola caught hold of his arm and stopped him.

"Your stepmother is fine," she said. "She just fainted."

Unless Belinda had told him earlier in the evening, Santiago didn't know that Viola was aware of their affair. Don Eduardo's men wouldn't know about it, either, and Viola was sure Belinda would want it to stay that way. Several of the don's *vaqueros* had crowded into the parlor, and they might become suspicious if they saw Santiago carrying on too much about his stepmother.

With a visible effort — visible to Viola,

anyway — Santiago controlled his rampant emotions and asked, "You are sure she's all right?"

"I told you, she fainted. As soon as she wakes up, she'll be fine. Now, I need to tend to your father."

Santiago swallowed and nodded. He said, "Anything you need, we will help."

"I want to clean the area around the wound first. Yolanda, get some clean rags and a basin of hot water. I'll need some whiskey or something like that, too."

The piratical-looking *vaquero* asked, "Will tequila do?"

"I don't see why not," Viola said.

The man reached into a pocket inside the brown leather vest he wore and brought out a silver flask.

"Then we have that," he declared with a grim smile.

Viola took the flask from him and said, "I'm sure there are wounded people outside who need help, too. Go out there and see about making them comfortable. Those who are hurt the worst need to be brought in here."

The sharp tone of command in her voice might have rankled some men, especially one who didn't work for her and technically didn't have to do what she told him.

91

But the *vaquero* just smiled faintly again, touched the brim of his gray felt sombrero with a tobacco-stained finger, and murmured, *"Sí, señora,"* before he left the room.

There was no doubt who was in charge here at the moment.

Viola spent the next quarter-hour working on Don Eduardo, first using rags soaked in hot water to clean the blood from the area around the wound. She was gentle and tried not to hurt the don any more than she had to.

His eyes were closed. He had passed out, and he didn't come to as Viola tended to his injury. When the bullet hole was clean and open, she uncapped the *vaquero*'s flask of tequila and poured some of the fiery liquor into the wound, filling it until it overflowed in reddened streaks.

The tequila's fierce bite was enough to make Don Eduardo groan, even though he didn't regain consciousness.

Viola didn't know her husband had returned until Slaughter touched her shoulder and asked, "How is he?"

She turned quickly toward him and instead of answering his question asked one of her own. "Are you all right, John?"

"Fine," Slaughter replied with a curt nod. Viola saw anger and pain in his eyes, though.

Not physical pain, she thought, but grief at what had happened here tonight. The people who worked for the Slaughters were like family, and some of them had been lost.

Slaughter nodded toward the sofa and asked again, "What about the don?"

"He's lost a lot of blood," Viola said. "But he seems to be breathing all right, and the last time I checked his heartbeat it was a little ragged but still strong. I don't think the bullet did a tremendous amount of damage inside, or else he wouldn't be hanging on like he is. He ought to be all right if we can get the slug out of him."

"That's what I thought," Slaughter said. "Do you want to go after it, or should we wait for Dr. Fredericks to get here from Douglas?"

"I'd rather let the doctor do it, if we can wait that long. You're going to send a rider?"

"Already did it, as soon as Stonewall and I got back. Orrie's on his way into town now, on the fastest horse we could find."

"Pacer," Stonewall added. He had come into the parlor behind his brother-in-law.

Slaughter glanced over at Santiago, who hovered near the sofa where his stepmother lay.

"Is that all right with you?" he asked. "We'll wait for the doctor to operate on your father in the morning?"

Santiago took a deep breath and nodded. "If you think that is best, señor."

Slaughter frowned as he looked at the unconscious blonde and asked, "What happened to her?"

"Fainted," Viola answered dryly. "She'll come around."

"Oh."

From the doorway, the old *vaquero* said, "Señora, there are more people who need your help. Shall I have them brought in, as you commanded?"

"Of course," Viola said. "Yolanda, fetch blankets. We'll make pallets on the floor. Stonewall, help me move some of this furniture back to make room."

As the maid hurried out, Slaughter touched Viola's arm and asked quietly, "That's Yolanda? The one young Alvarez was courting?"

"That's right," Viola said. She caught her breath. "John, you said 'was' courting?"

With a bleak expression on his bearded face, Slaughter nodded.

"He was riding nighthawk. The others left him with the herd when the trouble started. Then he was jumped by wide-loopers who went after the cattle." Slaughter paused for a second. "They killed him."

94

Viola pressed a hand to her mouth and breathed, "No. That poor boy . . ."

"I'll tell the girl when she comes back —"

"No," Viola said. "I'll tell her, John. But later." A determined look came over her face. "Right now, we have wounded to take care of. There'll be time enough later to talk about what happened — and what we're going to do about it."

When the final tally was made, six people had been killed by the Apaches in the attack at the ranch: Pete the wrangler and the other cowboy, Jesse Harper, in the barn; the first victim at the *fandango* itself, a servant girl named Elena; two more of the ranch's cowboys, Al Fraley and Ben Baxter; and one of Slaughter's neighbors, a rancher named Carl Stevens. Hector Alvarez was the seventh victim, killed by the men who had stolen the herd.

In addition to the fatalities, nine men and three women were wounded, some of them seriously. That included Don Eduardo Rubriz.

Fifteen Apaches lay dead, here and there around the ranch. Slaughter believed that the renegades must have fought to the last man.

Viola and some of the other women stayed

busy all night, nursing the wounded. Yolanda had cried when Viola broke the news of Hector Alvarez's death to her, but after a while she dried her eyes and went on helping, grim-faced.

Doña Belinda woke up after a while, but she was no help. She was still half-hysterical, especially after she saw her husband lying there so pale with makeshift bandages wrapped around his midsection. She fell to her knees beside him and would have grabbed him, but Viola held her back.

"You don't want to jostle him around any more than he already has been," Viola said. "We don't know exactly where that bullet is, but we know the don is hanging on the way things are. We don't want to cause it to shift and maybe hurt him worse."

"But . . . but he looks so bad," Belinda wailed. "Like he's already dead."

"But he's not, and we want to keep him that way." Viola looked around, spotted Santiago sitting across the room in a straight-back chair, his head hanging down and his hands clasped between his knees. He must have felt her eyes on him because he lifted his head and looked at her. Discreetly, she motioned with her head toward Belinda.

Santiago was good enough to have an affair with his stepmother, Viola thought. The least he could do was take care of her now and keep her out of everyone else's way.

Santiago sighed, stood up, and came over to the sofa where his father lay. He put his hand on Belinda's shoulder and said, "They are doing everything they can for him. We must let him rest."

It took a couple of minutes, but Santiago was able to persuade her to stand up and stop trying to climb onto the sofa with his father. He put an arm around her shoulders and started to turn her away.

Don Eduardo stopped them by whispering, "S-Santiago . . ."

Viola leaned over him, a bit surprised that the don had regained consciousness. She had halfway expected him to be out until the bullet could be removed.

"Don Eduardo, you must rest —" she began.

"My son . . . Santiago . . ."

"I'm here, Father," Santiago said.

Belinda tried to pull loose from his grip. She sobbed, "Eduardo."

Rubriz ignored her. His eyes didn't open, but he said, "Santiago . . . I think I heard talk . . . the cattle we brought . . ."

"Stolen," Santiago said grimly. "Señor Slaughter believes the Apaches were working with rustlers, that their attack was a distraction."

"*El Señor Dios* protect us . . . if those savages begin working with . . . *bandidos.* You must help . . . must help . . ."

"Must help what, Father?"

Rubriz lifted a trembling hand. Santiago let go of Belinda and stepped closer to clasp his father's hand in both of his.

"You must go after them," Don Eduardo rasped. "You must bring those cattle back . . . Our family's honor demands it."

Slaughter had been standing back, listening to the conversation. He stepped forward now and said, "I already paid you for those cows, Don Eduardo. Losing them is my problem. And I assure you, I intend to get them back."

"Take Santiago . . . with you," Don Eduardo pleaded. "Those thieves . . . they stole from me, too. They put my son and my wife . . . in danger. They must be . . . punished."

"Eduardo, that's crazy," Belinda said. "If you send Santiago after them, then you're putting him in danger, too."

"It's different," Santiago said. "I understand what he means." He squeezed his father's hand. "And I'll do it. I'll uphold our family's honor."

A trace of a smile crossed Don Eduardo's lips. Barely audible, he said, "That is good . . . I knew I could count on you . . . my son . . ."

The last word came out of him with a sigh. Belinda lifted both hands to her mouth and stared in horror as she said, "Eduardo!"

"He's still breathing," Viola told her. "He's just asleep again. Talking even that much wore him out. You should probably get some rest, too."

"I . . . I want to help. If there's anything I can do —"

"There's not," Viola said.

One of the last things she wanted right now was to have Belinda underfoot, weeping and wailing.

Santiago turned to Slaughter and said, "You heard what my father said, señor. When are you going after those rustlers?"

"At first light," Slaughter said.

"Then I will be going with you. I can bring most of our *vaqueros* with me, too. A few should be left behind, though, to protect my father since we don't know how long he will be here."

"I agree," Slaughter said. "And I appreciate the offer, Santiago."

"It's not an offer. It is my duty."

"All right. We'll ride together." Slaughter

looked over at Stonewall. "Too bad you fellas won't get to have your race in the morning."

"I reckon this is more important," Stonewall said.

"*Sí,*" Santiago agreed. "And there will still be a race. Justice — against the men responsible for this tragedy."

CHAPTER 9

Ned Becker waited in the mouth of the canyon. A quirly drooped from his lips. From time to time his fingers brushed the leather-wrapped handle of the knife sheathed at his waist.

The knife he had used to kill that young *vaquero* with one deadly accurate throw.

A couple of hundred yards behind him, the cattle moved restlessly, making noises familiar to any man who had spent much time as a cowhand. They were tired and they were angry because they had been driven so hard to get here before dawn.

Now they could rest for a while, though, before some of Becker's men moved them on deeper into the mountains. It was still more than an hour until sunrise, and Becker didn't figure John Slaughter would start after him until first light.

It would probably take that long just to clean up the mess from that little visit by

Bodaway and his Apaches, Becker thought as a wry smile curved his lips.

A footstep behind him made Becker look back over his shoulder. In the shadowy canyon, he couldn't see the man who approached him, but he recognized the voice as that of his *segundo,* Herb Woodbury.

"You sure you should be out here alone waitin' for those redskins, boss?" Woodbury asked. "They could decide to double-cross you. Maybe cut your throat just for the spite of it. You can't never tell what them blood-thirsty savages'll do."

"Bodaway would never betray me," Becker said. "We've been friends for too long."

Woodbury came closer now, close enough that Becker could see him in the starlight. He was a tall, gaunt man with a sandy mustache that straggled across his upper lip.

"It ain't none o' my business, but I can't help but wonder how in blazes you wound up pards with a damn Apache."

"You're right," Becker snapped. "It's none of your business."

Woodbury started to fade back, muttering, "Sorry, boss —"

"But that's all right," Becker went on, his tone softening a bit. "Bodaway and I both grew up around army posts and reservations. His father, you see, was a scout who worked for the army and helped them hunt down his fellow Apaches."

Woodbury grunted. "Lord. That must not've set too well with the redskins who wanted to keep puttin' up a fight."

"No, it didn't," Becker agreed. "To many of the Apaches on the reservation, Bodaway's father was hated and reviled. It was inevitable those feelings reflected over on him, too. He grew up being despised."

"Reckon that's what makes him hate white folks so much now," Woodbury said.

"More than likely. He feels like he's got a lot to make up for. He'll never come in peacefully. He's had his fill of reservations."

"What were you doin' there?" Woodbury asked. "Your pa must've been one of the soldiers, I reckon."

"No," Becker said.

"Sutler, then? Civilian scout?"

Becker considered telling Woodbury to go back with the others and leave him alone. The man's questions were stirring up old memories that were better left alone.

Becker knew from experience that as long as he kept his past buried deep inside him, he could control it instead of the other way around. He could use the bitter hatred as fuel to drive him on.

On the other hand, no man could keep everything bottled up inside him forever. It might feel good to let some of it out for a change.

"My father was dead by then," Becker told his *segundo*. "It was my mother who worked around the forts and the camps. She cooked, did laundry, sold herself to the troopers."

He said the words casually, but there was nothing casual about the way something inside him twisted as he spoke.

"So you see," he went on, "it was natural for Bodaway and me to become friends. My mother was a whore, and his father was being paid to betray his people. We were alike in so many ways."

For a long moment Woodbury didn't say anything. Then the outlaw said in a clearly uncomfortable voice, "Boss, I never meant to pry —"

"Don't worry about it, Herb." Becker's voice hardened again. "But know one thing: I won't be gossiped about. What I just told you, that stays between the two of us, understand?"

Becker heard the other man swallow. Woodbury said, "Sure, boss. I won't say anything to anybody."

Becker knew that he meant it, too. Woodbury was too afraid of him not to honor the request. Woodbury had seen him kill — savagely, suddenly, without warning.

No, Woodbury wouldn't say anything, Becker thought with a smile.

Then he stiffened as he heard an owl hoot somewhere outside the canyon.

Only it wasn't an owl, Becker knew. He recognized the sound from childhood. He turned, slipped a match from his vest pocket, and struck it with his thumbnail. He moved the flame back and forth in front of him three times, then snuffed it out and dropped the match at his feet.

Less than a minute later, a lithe figure trotted out of the darkness.

Alone.

Becker tensed even more. He had expected Bodaway to lose some men in the attack, but it appeared that the Apache war chief had arrived at this rendezvous by himself.

"Bodaway," Becker said quietly. *"El Infierno."*

Bodaway came to a stop in front of him and grunted.

"What happened?" Becker asked. "Your warriors —"

"All dead," Bodaway said, his voice flat and devoid of emotion. "We took the white men by surprise, but they fought well.

Especially a few. The little one with the beard slew many of my men."

"Slaughter," Becker said with a note of hatred. Until now he hadn't had anything personally against John Slaughter. His grudge was against someone else. But the rancher and lawman had made himself an enemy tonight.

Becker knew that was a little irrational. Of course Slaughter would fight back when his ranch was attacked. But Becker hated him for it anyway, the same way he hated anyone who dared to oppose his plans.

Setting that aside for the moment, Becker asked, "What about Don Eduardo? Your men knew he was not to be harmed."

"You ask too much, Becker," the Apache snapped. "No man's safety is guaranteed in the middle of a fight."

Becker suddenly felt as if he were standing at the edge of a high cliff, with everything falling away into nothingness at his feet. If Rubriz had been killed, that would ruin everything. He couldn't die without knowing the reason. He just couldn't.

"What happened?" Becker forced himself to ask. "Was he killed?"

"I do not know, and that is the truth, Becker. You told me what he looks like, and I saw such a man fall." Bodaway shrugged.

"That is all I know."

Becker struggled to maintain his composure. This didn't really change anything, he told himself. He would still go through with his plan. Even if Rubriz was dead, that wouldn't finish things.

There was still more killing to do.

"All right. I'm sorry about your men, Bodaway. I'll honor our bargain, though. I'll get the rifles for you —"

"With no warriors, I have no need of rifles now," the war chief cut in. "Later, when I have raised another band. Then you will give us rifles."

"Of course," Becker agreed.

"But now . . ."

"Whatever you want, Bodaway, if it's within my power."

"I want to kill that little man, the one you called Slaughter. I want to strip his skin off inch by inch and burn him over a fire for a long time before I allow him to die."

Becker smiled and nodded and said, "I think that can be arranged."

The eastern sky was gray with the approach of dawn when Slaughter held a council of war in his study.

Stonewall was there, and so was the ranch's foreman, Jess Fisher. Slaughter had invited Santiago Rubriz, too, and Santiago had brought along the older, rakish *vaquero,* who he introduced as Augustín Hermosa.

"Jess, I'm leaving you in charge here on the ranch," Slaughter told the foreman. "I want you to pick out ten good fighting men to come with me after those cows."

Fisher, who had also served as one of Slaughter's deputies in Tombstone from time to time, frowned and said bluntly, "I'd rather go with you after those damned rustlers myself, boss."

"I know that. But I'm not going to ride off and leave the ranch unprotected. I'm not expecting any more trouble . . . but I wasn't expecting the trouble last night, either."

With obvious reluctance, Fisher nodded and said, "All right. When are you riding out?"

"No later than an hour from now," Slaughter said. "Sooner if we can get everything together."

"I had the remuda brought in, like you ordered earlier. You'll want to take extra horses."

"One per man," Slaughter agreed with a nod. "This shouldn't turn into a long chase. We can move faster than those cattle can. But I spoke to the cook about supplies, too.

We'll take a couple of pack horses and carry enough provisions for several days."

Santiago spoke up, saying, "I can provide eight men, not counting myself. Our force will number almost two dozen. We should be more than a match for the thieves."

"We'll have to catch them first," Slaughter said. He looked at Hermosa. "You're Don Eduardo's foreman, aren't you?"

"Me?" Hermosa's shoulders rose and fell in a languid shrug. "I'm just a simple *vaquero,* señor."

Slaughter knew better than that. All he had to do was look at Hermosa to recognize that the *hombre* was a top-notch fighting man. He was glad they were going to be on the same side.

He turned his attention to Stonewall and said, "I suppose you're going to insist on coming along, too."

"Those Apaches tried to burn me up in the barn," Stonewall said. His voice was still a little hoarse from the smoke he'd inhaled. "And they were workin' for the varmints we're goin' after. So, yeah, you can dang well bet that I'm comin' along."

"Apaches don't really work for anybody," Slaughter pointed out. "But there's no doubt they had an arrangement with the men who stole that herd. It's unusual, no doubt about it, but the conclusion is inescapable. Those two things didn't happen the same night by coincidence."

It was agreed that the party going after the rustlers would assemble on the road in front of the ranch house. As soon as everyone was ready, they would start in pursuit.

Slaughter knew the trail ought to be easy to follow. The herd was a relatively small one, only about five hundred head, but that many cattle couldn't be moved without leaving plenty of signs.

"I want to see how my father is before we leave," Santiago said. "But we will be ready to ride, Señor Slaughter, have no doubt of that."

"I don't have any doubts," Slaughter told him. "The rest of us will be saying our good-byes, too."

The meeting broke up. Slaughter went to the parlor, where Don Eduardo was still resting on the sofa. He looked around but didn't see Viola. One of the servants tending to the wounded men noticed what he was doing and told him, "Señora Slaughter is in the kitchen, señor."

"Gracias," Slaughter said. He went on out to the kitchen and found Viola supervising the packing of provisions for the men who were going after the rustlers.

She smiled at him and asked, "Will you be leaving soon?"

"Soon," Slaughter confirmed.

"I don't suppose it would do any good to tell you to be careful."

"I'm always careful," he protested. "I'm a cautious man."

"You can be," Viola admitted. "Maybe even most of the time you are. But then you get some crazy, reckless hunch, and nothing will do except that you follow through on it."

He grinned and said, "You mean like when I decided I was going to ask this wild young cowgirl to marry me?"

Viola laughed and then moved closer so she could rest her forehead against his shoulder.

"Honestly, John," she said quietly, "don't get yourself killed over some cows. You can always buy more cattle."

"That's true . . . but I can't buy the lives of the people who were killed last night. Murdered while they should have been enjoying themselves at that *fandango* you threw."

"And that's the real reason you're going after the rustlers, isn't it?"

Slaughter inclined his head in acknowledgment of her point.

"Just come back to me safely," she said. "That's all I've ever asked."

"And I always have. I always will."

Promises like that were easy to make, he thought.

Sometimes not so easy to keep. But he would do his best.

"You'll look after Stonewall?"

"Of course. But that brother of yours can look after himself, you know. I wouldn't say it to his face for fear of giving him a swelled head, but he's a fine young man."

"Yes, he is." Viola put her hands on Slaughter's arms and leaned in to kiss him. She didn't have to come up on her toes very far to do that, since he wasn't much taller than she was. "All right, let me get back to work. The sooner you chase down those rustlers, the sooner you can bring our cattle back and things can settle down here."

Slaughter nodded and went back out to the parlor. He found Santiago there, sitting on a chair he had drawn up next to the sofa where Don Eduardo lay.

"He seems to be resting fairly comfortably," Santiago said as he looked up at Slaughter. "Will the doctor be here soon?"

"Should be. I expect him and the rider I sent to Douglas by dawn, or at least not long after that. But that's only if Orrie was able to locate Dr. Fredericks right away. The doc could have been out somewhere on a call. In that case, Orrie would have to wait for him to get back to town."

"I have prayed for my father. That's all I can do." Santiago's face hardened. "Except for going after the men responsible for what happened to him."

"Where's your stepmother?" Slaughter asked.

"She's gone to her room to rest. She didn't want to leave my father's side, but I convinced her."

"I reckon there's really not much she could do. Viola will let her know if they need her help."

"Your wife is a fine woman, Señor Slaughter."

Slaughter chuckled and said, "You're not telling me anything I don't already know, son."

He could count on Viola to take care of things here at the ranch. Otherwise, he never would have been able to chase off after those rustlers like he was about to.

He wasn't acting in his capacity as a lawman in this case, but justice was going to be done anyway.

The sooner the better.

Chapter 10

Viola stepped out the front door of the ranch house and used her hand to shade her eyes from the glare of the sun rising to her left. Almost two dozen men were gathered on the other side of the picket fence that enclosed the house. They had mounted up and were ready to ride. Her husband, wearing a black Stetson, blue work shirt, and denim trousers, would take the lead.

The range clothes were considerably different from the suit that the nattily dressed John Slaughter usually wore, even here on the ranch, but they were much more appropriate for chasing down rustlers.

Santiago Rubriz, in tight trousers, charro jacket, and steeple-crowned sombrero, was much more dapper. His face was pale and drawn, though, which prevented him from looking dashing.

He was mounted on *El Halcón*. The blaze-faced black stepped around nervously. With her ranch woman's experienced eye, Viola wasn't sure the horse was the best animal for the job of chasing down rustlers. *El Halcón* was fast, no doubt about that, but he might not have the staying power this task would require.

But that was none of her business, Viola told herself. Her concern at the moment was keeping the ranch safe while John was gone, as well as taking care of the people who had been wounded in the Apache attack.

Dr. Neal Fredericks still hadn't arrived from Douglas. It was pretty obvious by now that something had happened to delay him.

If the doctor didn't show up soon, Viola knew she would have to try to remove the bullet from Don Eduardo. Every hour the chunk of lead stayed inside him lessened his chances for survival.

She had already said her good-byes to her husband. They had caught a moment alone in the house and shared an embrace and passionate kiss. The difference in their ages that had caused some people to look askance at their marriage had never meant a thing to them. They loved each other wholeheartedly, always had, always would.

From the back of his horse, John lifted a hand to her in farewell. She returned the wave, trying to ignore the pang of worry that went through her. She already missed him, and he wasn't even gone yet. She couldn't even begin to comprehend what it would be like if something happened to him and he never returned.

"Let's move out," Slaughter called. Santiago repeated the order in Spanish for the Rubriz *vaqueros,* even though Slaughter's command of the language was as fluent as a native's. In the absence of Don Eduardo, though, his men looked to Santiago for leadership.

Viola hoped the young man could provide it. If he didn't, that might wind up putting John Slaughter in danger.

Maybe this whole affair would help Santiago grow up a little.

That thought was in Viola's mind when someone tried to hurry past her. She looked over, saw Doña Belinda, and caught hold of the blonde's arm to prevent her from rushing out to the road.

"Let go of me," Belinda said. "He's leaving. I didn't get a chance to say good-bye to him."

"If you're talking about your stepson, you can still wave to him," Viola said. "If I could trust you to give him a motherly kiss, you could go out there. But since I can't . . ."

Belinda glared at her and demanded, "Who are you to judge me? I've heard about you. You married a grown man — a widower — when you weren't much more than a child."

Viola struggled with the impulse to slap this woman from back East. She said, "I was old enough to know what I wanted, and it's worked out. We have the happiest, strongest marriage I know. And I've always been faithful to him."

"You can get off your high horse," Belinda said coldly. "You don't know anything about me and my marriage."

"I know more than I wish I did."

"I love my husband," Belinda went on as if Viola hadn't said anything. "I wanted to help take care of him. You wouldn't let me."

Maybe she had a point about that, Viola thought. Maybe the dislike she felt for Belinda had prompted her to keep the woman at arm's length, even from her own wounded husband.

Right now, though, Viola didn't care. Her husband and brother were riding away, quite possibly to risk their lives. The group of riders had covered about a hundred yards, moving at a fast lope as they headed for the place where they would pick up the trail of the stolen herd. Dust rose in the air

117

from their horses' hooves, blurring their dwindling figures.

"You might as well go on back in the house," she told Belinda. "They're gone . . . and all we can do is pray that they'll be safe while we wait for them to come back."

Slaughter led the way to the spot where the herd had been bedded down the day before. The group had to pass the place he and Stonewall had found the body of Hector Alvarez. Slaughter didn't pause, but he pointed it out to the others and said, "At least one of the fellas we're going after is good with a knife, so be ready for that."

"I don't intend to let any of 'em get close enough to me to use a knife," Stonewall said.

The *vaquero* called Hermosa plucked a Bowie knife from a sheath at his waist and said, "I can handle a blade fairly well myself, Señor Slaughter. Perhaps I will meet up with this *hombre* who killed young Alvarez."

That would probably be a good fight to see, thought Slaughter.

Finding the trail the cattle had left when they were driven away was no problem. The tracks led almost due north. If they continued in that direction, eventually they would reach the Chiricahua Mountains on the other side of Cave Creek. If they curved west, they would get to the mountains sooner, and if they went east they would find themselves in the wasteland of southern New Mexico Territory.

Whatever direction the rustlers took, Slaughter intended to stay on their trail. He set a brisk pace, but not fast enough to wear out the horses. They had extra mounts, but he wanted to keep all the horses in as good a shape as possible.

You never knew when you might need to make a hard run for some reason.

"I wish the doctor had gotten there before we left," Santiago said. "My mind would rest easier if I knew my father was going to be all right."

"He's in good hands," Slaughter told the young man. "My wife has tended to many wounded men before. If the doctor doesn't show up soon, she'll do what needs to be done."

"I suppose you're right. And my father is a very strong man, very tough. He has been shot before, you know."

"No, I didn't know that," Slaughter said. "I'm not surprised, though. He mentioned in one of his letters that he started his ranch almost thirty years ago. Northern Mexico's still pretty rugged today, but it was really wild back in those days. Not much around except Apaches, Yaquis, and *bandidos.*"

"That is true," Santiago said, "but it was none of those who shot him. It was his own partner. An American named Thaddeus Becker."

As the sun rose, Ned Becker told the eight men who would be taking the cattle deeper into the mountains, through twisting canyons to the high, isolated pasture where they would be kept, to get ready to move out.

Eight men would have their hands full driving the herd, but it could be done. That left eighteen gunhands to accompany Becker on the next part of this job.

Or maybe he had nineteen men, he thought as he approached the spot where Bodaway hunkered on his heels next to the ashes of a campfire, soaking up what little warmth still came from it in this chilly dawn.

"What are you going to do now, Bodaway?" Becker asked his old friend.

The glance the Apache lifted to him was almost as cold as the desert air around them.

"I will start looking for more warriors to fight the white men," Bodaway said, as if the answer to Becker's question should have been completely obvious.

"That can wait a while. Why don't you come with me? I know we were supposed to split up after this rendezvous, but there's no reason to do that now."

"You mean since all my men are dead."

"I'm sorry about that, I truly am," Becker said in response to the flat comment. He knew what Bodaway had to be thinking, and he wanted to head that off if he could. "In a way it's my fault they're dead. I understand why you'd feel that way. You were there at Slaughter's ranch because of me. I knew you'd probably lose a few men, but . . ." Becker sighed and shook his head. "Damned if I ever thought you'd lose all of them. I really didn't, Bodaway."

The Apache regarded him through dark, slitted eyes for a long moment before saying, "All the way here, I thought I would kill you as soon as I saw you. As you said, I blamed you for their deaths. I wanted to avenge them by killing you. But that would not bring them back . . . and you did not take their lives. Slaughter and his people did. The Mexican don and his people did."

"That's right," Becker said, trying not to sound too eager to exploit what Bodaway had just said. "And you can take your vengeance on them if you come with me."

Bodaway straightened to his feet. He asked, "Will they not come after the cattle?"

"Slaughter will. I've heard enough about him to know that. I figured Rubriz would come with him, but you said he was wounded."

"Or killed."

"Or killed," Becker agreed with a shrug. "But I'm not going to accept that until I know for sure. I'd planned to make him come to me begging on his knees, but if he's still at the ranch that'll work out even better."

Bodaway frowned slightly and said, "I never really understood what you mean to do."

That was because he had never really explained it to anybody else, not even Woodbury or any of his other men, Becker thought. The details of the plan had remained fluid in his mind, capable of being changed to take circumstances into account, and as things were turning out, that was good.

Bodaway was perhaps the only person cunning enough to follow his reasoning, though, so he said, "Your raid on the ranch was a distraction to allow us to steal Don Eduardo's herd."

Bodaway nodded.

"But the rustling was a distraction, too, to lure nearly everybody away from the ranch. I figured Don Eduardo would come along with Slaughter and try to get the herd back. That way I could take some of my men and circle around and go back to the ranch. There wouldn't be enough of Slaughter's crew there to stop us from taking over."

"But you thought the Mexican would not be there."

"Yeah, but his wife would be. With her as a hostage, Rubriz will do anything I tell him to, even give himself up to me so I can torture him."

Bodaway nodded gravely and said, "This is much hate in you, to go to so much trouble instead of just killing the man."

"Just killing him's not enough. I want Don Eduardo Rubriz to suffer as much as possible, in as many ways as possible, before he dies."

"Why?" Bodaway asked.

"Because the son of a bitch murdered my father."

CHAPTER 11

Viola stood next to the sofa where Don Eduardo lay and looked down at his slack, pale face. If not for the fact that she could see his chest rising and falling, she might have thought that death had already claimed him.

An hour had passed since John and the others left in pursuit of the rustlers. The doctor still hadn't arrived from Douglas. Viola glanced at the big grandfather clock in one corner of the parlor to check the time.

She would give it another half-hour, she decided, and then she would have to try to extract the bullet from Don Eduardo's body herself.

A soft step sounded behind her. Viola turned and saw Belinda standing there.

"How is he?" the blonde asked.

"The same as before. He's sleeping."

"Unconscious, you mean," Belinda said in

an accusing tone.

"I'm not sure I'd call it that. His body is doing everything it can to preserve the strength it has left."

"How long are you going to wait for the doctor?"

"I was just thinking about that," Viola admitted. "Another thirty minutes or so. That much time shouldn't make any —"

Before she could finish, a small Mexican boy, the son of one of the married *vaqueros,* ran into the room and said excitedly, "Señora, señora, someone comes."

"Who is it, Paco?" Viola asked.

"A man in a buggy, señora. That's all I know."

It was enough, Viola thought. She knew that Dr. Neal Fredericks drove a buggy when he called on his patients. She put a hand on the boy's head for a second, said, "*Gracias,* Paco," and hurried to the door.

Belinda was right behind her.

Viola looked west along the road leading to Douglas and saw the buggy drawn by a tall, sturdy horse. A thin plume of dust rose into the sky behind it.

Another man rode alongside the vehicle. That would be Orrie, the cowboy John Slaughter had sent to town to fetch the physician. As they came closer, Viola recognized the horse Orrie was riding as Pacer, and seeing the roan confirmed her hunch.

"Is that him?" Belinda asked anxiously. She shaded her eyes with her hand, even though the sun was behind them. "Is that the doctor?"

"It is," Viola said.

"Thank God."

Viola looked at the other woman and said, "You sound like you mean that."

"You'll never understand how things are between my husband and me," Belinda snapped. "Don't even waste your time trying."

"Fine," Viola said. Maybe she was being too judgmental, although she didn't think so. But either way, it didn't really matter right now. Saving Don Eduardo's life was the important thing.

Dr. Fredericks brought the buggy to a halt in front of the picket fence. Viola already had the gate open, ready for him. He climbed out of the buggy, a tall, heavyset man with a squarish head and close-cropped gray beard. He wore a gray suit and a flat-crowned black hat and carried a black medical bag.

"Good morning, Mrs. Slaughter," Fredericks greeted Viola as he came into the yard. "I hear you had quite a commotion out here last night."

"You could call it that," Viola said.

"I knew about your party and thought I might attend, but I was called away. It was Mildred Bankston's time. Triplets, can you believe that? It was quite an ordeal for everyone involved. Anyway, I didn't get back until long after midnight. That's why your man had to wait for me."

Belinda said, "Can't you stop talking and go inside?"

Fredericks looked at her and raised his bushy eyebrows in surprise. Viola said, "This is Doña Belinda Rubriz, doctor. Her husband is in the worst shape of those who were injured in the attack."

"Then by all means let's go have a look at him," Fredericks said. He gave Belinda a curt nod and added, "I'm sorry to be making your acquaintance under such trying circumstances, ma'am."

Belinda didn't say anything else. She followed Viola and the doctor into the house.

Viola took Fredericks straight to Don Eduardo. He pulled a chair over next to the sofa and set his bag on it, then untied the bandages and pulled them back to reveal the bullet hole in the wounded man's side.

Belinda gasped a little at the sight of it, but Viola thought the hole actually looked pretty good, considering. The flesh around it wasn't too red, and she didn't see any streaks running away from the wound, which would have been a sign that it was festering and spreading.

Dr. Fredericks seemed to agree with her. He said, "It appears you did a fine job here, Mrs. Slaughter. I believe your man said the bullet is still in the victim's body?"

"That's right. We didn't find any other wounds, so it has to be."

Fredericks nodded.

"The next thing to do is get it out. I'll give the don just a bit of laudanum to make sure he remains unconscious through the procedure."

"See?" Belinda whispered to Viola. "I told you he was unconscious, not just asleep."

Fredericks heard her anyway and chuckled.

"What you call it doesn't matter, Señora Rubriz. What's important is that your husband doesn't wake up and start moving around while I'm going after that bullet."

"Should we try to move him?" Viola asked. "We can put him on the dining room table so you can operate there."

Fredericks shook his head and said, "No, I'd prefer that he stay right where he is until we get that bullet out of him." He took off his hat and coat and started rolling up his shirt sleeves. "I'll be needing some hot water and clean rags."

Viola turned and nodded to one of the servants standing nearby. The woman hurried off to fetch what the doctor wanted.

"Now, before I start this procedure let me take a quick look at the other wounded, so I'll have an idea of what else I'll need to do this morning," Frederick said.

Ten minutes later, after checking his other patients, Fredericks perched on a chair next to the sofa where he could reach Don Eduardo and got ready to extract the bullet. He had a long, slender probe and a pair of forceps in his hands. Before he got to work he looked over his shoulder and said to Belinda, "You might want to step out of the room, madam."

"I'm not going anywhere," she declared. "I'm going to stay right here until my husband is out of danger."

"All right, but I warn you, there's liable to be more bleeding."

"I don't care. I'll be all right."

"Suit yourself."

Fredericks inserted the probe into the wound and began using it to search for the bullet. As he had warned Belinda, blood welled out of the bullet hole around the probe.

Viola heard a faint moan and glanced over at the blonde. She saw how pale Belinda was, how wide her eyes were, and how hard she was breathing as she watched the operation. Viola moved a little closer to her.

It was a good thing she did, because Belinda moaned again and her knees buckled. Viola was there to catch her under the arms and keep her from falling.

Without looking up from what he was doing, Fredericks said, "Fainted, eh? That didn't take long."

"About as long as I figured it would," Viola said. "Doña Belinda seems to have a tendency toward passing out."

She motioned with her head, and a couple of servants hurried to take hold of Belinda and carry her over to an armchair. They lowered her into it gently.

A few minutes later, Fredericks held up a misshapen lump of lead that he gripped with the forceps.

"There it is," he said to Viola as he showed the bullet to her. "I believe, considering its location, that it didn't damage any major organs or fracture any ribs. The don was lucky. He lost enough blood to make him pass out, but as long as the wound is kept clean, with plenty of rest he ought to be fine."

"I'm glad to hear that, doctor."

Fredericks used one of the rags to wipe blood off his hands as he stood up.

"Now I'll get started on the other cases." He smiled and added, "When you and your husband throw a party, Mrs. Slaughter, it's always quite an event. I'll be sure to attend the next one — just in case my services are needed again!"

"Where the hell are they going with those cows?" Stonewall asked as the trail of the stolen herd continued to lead north toward the Chiricahuas. "Do they plan to drive 'em all the way up to Galeyville or around the mountains to Fort Bowie?"

Slaughter rode at the head of the group of pursuers with Stonewall on his right and Santiago Rubriz on his left. Santiago hadn't explained his earlier comment about his father being shot by an American partner, and Slaughter hadn't pressed him for details. He didn't figure it was any of his business. If Santiago wanted to talk about it, he could.

Instead Santiago asked now, "Could they sell the herd to the army at this fort? Soldiers always need beef."

131

"It would be a shame to use those cattle for beef," Slaughter said. "I bought them to improve the bloodline of my herd, so I want them around for a while."

"They still have my father's brand on them, not yours, Señor Slaughter," Santiago pointed out.

And since Mexican brands most closely resembled a skillet full of writhing snakes, those markings wouldn't mean anything to an army quartermaster, Slaughter mused. All the rustlers had to do was convince the quartermaster at Fort Bowie that the stock was legally theirs, and they might collect for it.

For that matter, Slaughter knew that the army sometimes turned a blind eye to the possibility that animals with Mexican brands might be what they called over in Texas "wet cattle," meaning they had been driven across the Rio Grande — usually in the dead of night.

As Santiago had said, soldiers needed beef, and the men charged with providing it often weren't too particular about where it came from.

Those thoughts ran through Slaughter's mind, and then he said, "That may be what they try to do, but it seems like a lot of trouble for what they'd make out of the deal. This is a small herd. The payoff won't be big enough once it's split up among them to make it worthwhile — especially since they had to run the risk of involving those Apaches, too." He frowned. "I have a hunch that there's something else going on here, but I'll be damned if I can figure out what it is."

"We'll just catch up to the varmints and ask 'em," Stonewall said.

Slaughter chuckled and said, "Yes, that might be the best plan."

They kept moving, stopping now and then to switch horses and let the animals rest a bit. The sun had risen high enough now to generate a considerable amount of heat.

It was during one of those pauses, while Slaughter had his hat off and was using his sleeve to wipe sweat off his forehead, that he noticed something. Several miles away to the east, a thin haze of dust rose in the air as if a large group of riders was on the move over there, heading south.

It couldn't be the rustlers doubling back, he told himself. The dust was moving too fast for that. They couldn't push those cattle at such a pace and hope to control them.

A cavalry patrol, he thought. That was a more likely answer. Possibly word of the Apache attack had reached Fort Bowie, and the commander there had sent a troop to check it out and chase any renegades who were left.

If that was the case, they were too late for that, Slaughter thought. By now all those Apaches would be buried in shallow graves.

He put the matter out of his mind for now and told the men to mount up. They were moving out again.

Whoever those riders in the distance were, they had nothing to do with the deadly errand on which John Slaughter found himself occupied today.

CHAPTER 12

Ned Becker knew that Bodaway was still curious about the origins of his vendetta against Don Eduardo Rubriz, but the Apache didn't ask any questions. Bodaway wouldn't; that wasn't the sort of man he was. He would wait for Becker to offer details, and if that never happened, Bodaway would just put the whole matter out of his mind.

As with his conversation about his mother with Herb Woodbury the night before, though, the idea of letting out some of the demons that gnawed on his brain and guts appealed to Becker. During a halt to rest the horses around midmorning, Becker went over to his old friend and said, "I'll tell you about it if you want."

"It is nothing to me whether you do or not," Bodaway answered without looking at him. He had been given a horse to ride, and he was checking the animal's saddle.

"My father was Rubriz's partner," Becker said. "He'd done some fighting in Mexico. He went down there on a filibuster and stayed to work for one faction or another. Those Mexes are hell on wheels when it comes to overthrowing their government. Doesn't matter who's in charge, there's always a revolution brewing."

Bodaway grunted. He was starting to look interested in spite of himself.

"He and Rubriz became friends somehow," Becker went on. "When the side Rubriz supported came to power, he wound up with a big land grant in northern Sonora. He asked my father to help him start a ranch there. Before they left Mexico City, though, they each got married. Their wives were high-born ladies with mostly Castilian blood."

Becker started trying to roll a cigarette as he talked, but when he mentioned his mother his fingers began to shake. She had gone from the pampered surroundings of a wealthy family in Mexico City to selling herself in an Arizona Territory cavalry camp. Was it any wonder he hated the man responsible for that downfall?

He crumpled the half-rolled quirly and threw it aside.

"They worked together side by side to

establish that ranch," Becker continued. "They fought Indians and bandits and drought and sickness. And they made something out of the place. I was born there."

"You are fortunate the warriors of my people never visited your ranch," Bodaway said. "You probably would not have survived infancy."

Becker responded with a grim chuckle.

"I reckon maybe you and me were meant to be partners, Bodaway. That's why the Apaches never tried to kill my folks."

Bodaway just grunted.

Becker said, "Things went along all right for a while. No telling how long they would have stayed that way if Rubriz hadn't started sniffing around my mother. It wasn't bad enough he wanted to cheat on his wife. He had to go after his own partner's wife."

"This is none of my affair," Bodaway said.

The story had started to spill out of Becker, though, and he didn't want to stop it. He said, "When my pa found out what was going on, he wanted to take me and my mother and leave the ranch. But he couldn't bring himself to just walk away from everything he'd done. He had put as much time and hard work into the place as Rubriz had. He told Rubriz he had to buy out his half. If he didn't, then my father was going to send word to my mother's family back in Mexico City about what was going on, and to the family of Rubriz's wife, too."

Several more of Becker's men had drifted up and started listening to the tale. Becker was in the habit of keeping everything bottled up, so their presence almost made him stop.

But then he decided that they had a right to know. They wouldn't just be getting a payoff for this job. They were helping him right a wrong. For once in their mostly misbegotten lives, they were doing a good thing.

Sure, some innocent folks had wound up dead already because of Becker's plan, and more would surely die before it was over, but that couldn't be helped.

Vengeance trumped everything else.

"Rubriz was afraid of both families back in Mexico City. In those days they had more money and power than he did. So when my father threatened him, he should have backed off. I guess he just wanted my mother too much, though. He pretended to mend fences with my pa, then lured him out on the range one day and —"

Becker had to stop and swallow hard before he could go on.

"Rubriz shot my father in the back," he

138

grated after a moment. "Pa managed to turn around and get off a shot of his own. He wounded Rubriz and got away from him. But he was hurt bad and barely made it back to the ranch before he died. He lived long enough to tell my mother what had happened, though. She was afraid Rubriz would try to hurt me, too, so that I couldn't grow up and settle the score. She took me and ran, to save my life. She figured Rubriz would expect her to head for Mexico City and her family, so she went the other way to fool him. We wound up in Arizona Territory. She planned to circle around and get back home, but we didn't have any money or food and Ma . . . Well, Ma had to do things so we could survive. After that, she was too ashamed to go home, so we got by any way we could." Becker shrugged and concluded, "You know the rest, Bodaway. Wasn't long after that you and I met."

One of the other men spoke up, asking, "Is that story true, Ned?"

"Would I have told it if it wasn't?" Becker snapped.

Bodaway said, "You have good reason for wanting this man Rubriz to suffer. But it will not bring back your father, or change any of the bad things your mother endured."

"I figured you'd understand about a blood

debt if anybody would," Becker said.

"I understand," the Apache said. "And I stand ready to help you get what you want. But what you want may not be what you think it is."

"It'll do. As long as Don Eduardo Rubriz dies screaming in agony, knowing that everything he holds dear is dead, it'll do."

Several of the other patients at the ranch had serious injuries, though not as life-threatening as Don Eduardo's had been, so by the time Dr. Neal Fredericks had finished tending to everyone, the hour was approaching midday.

"I hope you'll stay and have lunch with us before you start back to Douglas," Viola told him.

Fredericks nodded as he rolled down his shirt sleeves and fastened them. He was standing beside the pump behind the house where he had just spent several minutes scrubbing blood off his hands.

"I'd be glad to, Mrs. Slaughter," he said. "I appreciate the invitation. It's been rather a long morning." Fredericks canted his head to one side and added, "Longer for you, though, I expect. Just how long has it been since you had any sleep?"

"Oh, I don't really know. Thirty hours or

more, I suspect."

"At least, I'd say. I'm going to prescribe a nice long nap for you after we've eaten."

"Someone needs to keep an eye on Don Eduardo and the other wounded," Viola protested.

"And someone can. Someone else. The don's wife, for example. Surely she's capable of taking care of him."

Viola couldn't stop herself from letting out a ladylike snort.

"I wouldn't be so sure of that," she said.

"It would take a blind man not to see that the two of you don't care for each other," Fredericks commented as they started toward the back door. "Why the hostility?"

"Some people just don't get along, I guess," Viola said. She was still reluctant to expose Belinda's secret, even though she had only sworn not to tell Don Eduardo.

Anytime a secret was shared, it was well on its way to not being a secret anymore, she thought.

"I suppose it shouldn't come as a surprise," the doctor mused. "The two of you come from very different backgrounds, after all. Other than being married to older men, I wouldn't think you'd have much in common." He added, "And I'm not saying anything bad about you being married to

141

an older man, by the way. I know you and John well enough to know how well-matched you are."

"Thank you, doctor. Not everyone has always felt that way."

As they went inside, Yolanda came to meet them. The maid's features still looked a bit drawn with grief over the death of Hector Alvarez, but she had been busy all day and Viola knew that must have helped her cope with the loss.

"Señora, Don Eduardo is awake," Yolanda reported. "He is asking for Doña Belinda."

"Where is she?" Viola wanted to know.

"In her room, maybe?" Yolanda shook her head. *"Quien sabe?"*

"I'll go see. But first I want to look in on Don Eduardo."

They went into the parlor, which was still serving as a makeshift hospital. Don Eduardo was not only awake, he was also trying to sit up on the sofa. One of the other maids leaned over him and told him in Spanish that he should rest.

"The young lady is right, sir," Fredericks said as he strode up. "You risk further injury by carrying on like this."

"Who are you?" Don Eduardo demanded as he glared up at the physician.

"Dr. Neal Fredericks. I'm the one who

removed that bullet from you."

"Then I owe you my gratitude, doctor, but not my obedience. Where is my wife? Where is my son?"

Don Eduardo was a little wild-eyed, Viola thought. He was flushed, too, and breathing hard.

"Doña Belinda is around here somewhere," Viola told him. "I'll find her and let her know you're awake, but you really should lay back and rest."

"What about Santiago?"

Viola was a little surprised that he didn't remember telling Santiago to go with John. He must have been a little out of his head at the time.

"He went with my husband after those men who stole the herd of cattle you brought up here," she explained.

"The cattle . . . ?" The confused expression faded from Don Eduardo's face. He sank back against the pillows and went on, "Ah, I remember now. The Apaches were just to keep everyone busy while the real evildoing went on."

Viola would have said that killing innocent people was more evil than rustling cattle, but she knew what the don meant.

Rubriz went on, "You say Santiago went after the thieves as well?"

143

"You insisted that he should."

Don Eduardo closed his eyes and murmured, "Good. The honor of our family demands it. May *El Señor Dios* watch over the boy."

Now that the don was calmer again, Fredericks reached down and rested a hand briefly on his forehead.

"He seems to have developed a bit of a fever," the doctor told Viola as he straightened. "Well, that was always a possibility and one of the things we needed to watch out for."

"What should we do now?" she asked.

"All we can do is keep him as cool and comfortable as possible and let his body fight it. He needs to stay calm, too, so why don't you go find his wife?"

Viola nodded. As she left the parlor, she heard Fredericks telling one of the servants to fetch a basin of cool water and some clean cloths, so she could bathe Don Eduardo's face.

The first place Viola checked was the room that had been intended for the don and doña's use if things had gone as planned. She knocked on the door twice and was about to give up when she heard a faint response from within.

"What is it?"

Viola opened the door. She saw that the curtains had been pulled tightly closed, but enough of the midday light came in through cracks around them that she had no trouble spotting Belinda on the big four-poster bed. Belinda was fully dressed and lying on top of the comforter.

"Your husband is awake and asking for you," Viola said. "Also, he's running a little fever."

Belinda sat up sharply and said, "What? I knew I shouldn't have trusted that back-water quack —"

"Dr. Fredericks is a very competent doctor," Viola said. "I have no doubt that he could practice in Boston if he wanted to and do just fine. Instead of worrying about that, why don't you come and see if you can help?"

Belinda swung her legs off the bed and stood up. As she straightened her clothes she glared at Viola and said, "You've no right to talk to me that way. I'm a guest here, remember?"

"Trust me, I remember." Viola didn't add that it was her own stubborn hospitality that kept her from slapping some sense into the blonde. "The doctor said Don Eduardo needs to remain calm. You don't need to go in there acting angry and upset."

"All right. I understand." Belinda's chin jutted defiantly. "I'm getting tired of you judging me, though."

"Then how about in the future I just steer clear of you as much as possible?"

"I think that's a very good idea."

The two women left the room. As a tense silence hung between them, Viola led the way back to the parlor.

Belinda went straight to the sofa where her husband lay. One of the servants sat in a chair beside Don Eduardo and wiped his face with a cool, damp cloth. Smiling, Belinda said, "Why don't you let me do that, dear?"

The maid turned the job over to her, and as Belinda stroked the cloth over Don Eduardo's face, he looked at her and said, "My darling, are you all right?"

"Of course I'm all right, Eduardo," she told him, "and you will be, too, very soon now. Just lie there and rest and let us take good care of you."

Rubriz sighed. His eyes slowly closed as the taut lines of his face relaxed.

Standing back a ways, Fredericks said quietly to Viola, "See, she's doing him some good already."

Viola had her arms crossed over her chest as she struggled to keep an expression of dislike off her face. She said, "I suppose so."

"Let's leave the two of them alone."

Viola nodded and turned away. She needed to go see about getting a midday meal ready, she remembered.

Before she could do that, Jess Fisher appeared in the doorway, holding his hat in one hand. Viola knew instantly from the ranch foreman's worried expression that something was wrong.

She went over to him and asked, "What is it, Jess?"

"There's a good-size bunch of riders coming in," Fisher said.

Viola's spirits rose for a second when she heard that. She said, "John and the others are back already?"

"No, ma'am," Fisher said, his face turning even more grim. "Best I can tell, these fellas are strangers — and they don't look like the friendly sort."

Viola's breath seemed to catch in her throat. More trouble was exactly what they didn't need right now.

But trouble never waited until it was convenient. She said, "Get as many of the men together as you can. If these visitors are looking for a fight, that's exactly what we'll give them."

CHAPTER 13

Slaughter and the other men ate in the saddle, making a skimpy midday meal out of tortillas and bacon brought from the ranch. They were in the foothills of the Chiricahua Mountains now. The trail of the stolen herd had led to a canyon that wound through the hills and gradually climbed higher.

There was something odd about the sign they had found at the mouth of the canyon. The droppings indicated that the cattle had stopped there for a while, probably to let them rest after the hard nighttime run that had brought them to this point.

Slaughter could understand that, but what didn't make sense was that the tracks indicated the herd had been driven back and forth a few times, right there in the same area. He had pointed that out to Stonewall and asked, "What do you make of that?"

The young man just frowned, shook his head, and said, "I don't know, John."

The *vaquero* called Hermosa leaned forward in his saddle and said, "They were trying to hide something, Señor Slaughter." He waved at the vast muddle of hoofprints. "What man could make any sense out of that?"

Hermosa was right, Slaughter realized. The tracks made it impossible to be sure how many men were with the herd.

As soon as that thought leaped into his head, Slaughter's keen brain carried it further. He muttered, "Some of them could have turned back."

"Why would they do that?" Stonewall asked.

Slaughter didn't have an answer for that question, but he couldn't help thinking about the dust he had spotted a few hours earlier. It worried him now more than it had then.

But there was nothing he could do. The tracks of the herd led deeper into the mountains. There was no denying that. Everything else was sheer speculation. He couldn't know for sure that the rustlers had split up, or if they had, where the second bunch was headed.

As Viola had pointed out, though, he was

well-known for following his hunches. That applied equally in all areas of his life — lawman, rancher, gambler.

He gave in to one of those hunches now, saying, "Stonewall, I want you to go back to the ranch."

"What?" The young man looked shocked. "But I'm chasin' after those rustlers with you, John."

"We have a good-size force. We can afford to lose one man." Slaughter looked at Hermosa. "Or two."

"What do you have in mind, Señor Slaughter?" the *vaquero* drawled.

"I want the two of you to get back to the ranch as quick as you can and make sure there's no trouble there."

"What trouble would there be?" Stonewall asked. "We wiped out those Apaches."

"There's something deeper going on here," Slaughter pointed out. "We know that, we just don't know what it is. But I'd feel better about things if I knew there were a couple of good men headed back to the ranch."

Stonewall didn't like the idea of going back at all, not when the rustlers and the stolen herd were still ahead of them. Hermosa, though, just murmured, "With all due respect, Señor Slaughter, I ride for Don

Eduardo, not you."

"And I represent my father," Santiago said. "I don't know if Señor Slaughter is right, Hermosa, but if he wants you and Stonewall to return to the ranch, I think that is what you should do."

Hermosa's shoulders rose and fell in an eloquent shrug.

"Of course, señor."

Still grumbling, Stonewall had gone with Hermosa. Slaughter hated to lose a couple of good fighting men, but his gut told him Viola might need help.

The rest of the group had pressed on, and now as the heat grew even more oppressive in the early afternoon, Slaughter could tell from the tracks that the cattle had slowed. The hoofprints were fresher. He and his men had cut considerably into the rustlers' lead.

"You know this country much better than I do, Señor Slaughter," Santiago said as he rode alongside. "Where do you think they are taking the herd?"

"Well, they're not headed for Galeyville or Fort Bowie," Slaughter said. "If they were bound for either of those places, they wouldn't have come into the mountains like this. Although I suppose they could still reach the fort if they know of some pass through the Chiricahuas. But it would have been faster if they had gone around." Slaughter scratched his bearded jaw. "It's almost like they're just trying to lead us up here. That's another reason I'm worried that some of them might have doubled back to the ranch."

"How many men are there now?"

"No more than a dozen, I reckon. But the house is sturdy. We've had to fort up in it before. My wife comes from pioneer stock, too. If there's trouble, she won't panic. Anybody comes riding in on the prod, she'll give 'em a hot reception."

"I wish I knew that my father was safe. And . . . my stepmother."

Slaughter heard the hesitation in the young man's voice and said, "It's none of my business, but you don't like Doña Belinda very much, do you?"

"My father loves her. I would not want her to come to any harm."

"I reckon maybe she got a little more than she bargained for when she moved out here. This part of the country isn't nearly as civilized as Boston."

Santiago shook his head and said, "I don't know anything about that. I have never been to Boston. My father has, but not me."

"Well, maybe you'll visit Doña Belinda's

family someday."

"Perhaps," Santiago said, but he still sounded doubtful.

A few more minutes went by as they followed the herd's tracks through a broad, steep-sided canyon. As Slaughter looked ahead, he saw that the canyon took a turn around a fairly sharp bend several hundred yards in front of them.

A place like that would be a pretty good spot for an ambush, he thought. Considering the trickiness the rustlers had already demonstrated, he wouldn't put such a thing past them at all. Because of that, he reined in and motioned for the others to do likewise.

"I think we'd better do a little scouting," he said. "I'll go have a look around that bend."

"I'll come with you," Santiago volunteered without hesitation.

"Better not," Slaughter said. "If anything were to happen to me, somebody will need to take charge."

Santiago looked surprised by that statement. He said, "You would entrust such a task to me?"

"You're Don Eduardo's son. His men will follow you. So will mine, if I tell them they're supposed to." Slaughter crossed his hands on his saddle horn and turned a level gaze on the young man. "Are you up to the job, Santiago?"

"I — I will do my best to be, Señor Slaughter."

Slaughter shook his head and said, "Trying's not good enough. You either do it or you don't."

Santiago's backbone stiffened. He gave Slaughter a curt, solemn nod and said, "I will not let you down, señor."

"That's more like it." Slaughter lifted his reins and got ready to heel his horse into motion again.

Before he could do that, he heard a rumbling sound, like an approaching thunderstorm. The sky was clear, however, except for a few puffy white clouds against the crisp, startling blue.

The other men heard it, too, and a worried mutter went through their ranks. Slaughter was about to tell them to settle down when a cow bolted around that bend in the canyon up ahead. Another animal followed it, then another and another . . .

As the rumbling grew louder and a cloud of dust welled into the air, a solid line of spooked beef rounded that bend and thundered toward Slaughter and his companions. The herd they'd been chasing all day was now coming to them . . .

In the form of a stampede!

Viola hurried to get John's spyglass and then went back outside. Jess Fisher had told her that the strangers were coming from the northeast, so she climbed the ladder attached to the framework holding up the elevated water tank until she could see over the house.

This certainly wasn't a very ladylike thing to do, Viola thought as she wrapped an arm around the ladder to steady herself. She had never worried all that much about comporting herself properly, though. At heart she was still a wild cowgirl.

She spotted the group of riders in the distance, then lifted the spyglass to her eye and squinted through the lens. It took a second to locate them through the glass, but then the face of the leader sprang into sharp relief.

It was a beard-stubbled, hard-planed face. More details were hard to make out because the man had the brim of his hat tugged down fairly low. That threw a shadow over his features. Even so, it struck Viola as a cruel face.

She caught her breath as she swung the spyglass to one side and saw the man riding to the leader's right and just behind him. His face was cruel, too, and it was easy to see because he wore no hat, only a bandanna tied around his head to keep his thick mane of black hair back. The man was an Apache. He didn't seem to be a prisoner. He looked more like an ally of the men approaching the ranch.

Viola used the spyglass to take a look at the other men. They all had the stamp of the owlhoot on them. Tough, brutal, ruthless men who would stop at nothing to get what they wanted. There were at least a dozen of them.

That meant the members of the crew John had left here at the ranch were outnumbered, but not by that much, Viola thought. And they had the advantage of being able to fight a defensive action, behind the thick walls of the house.

She closed the spyglass and climbed down as quickly as she could. As she went back to the house, she met Dr. Neal Fredericks at the front door. The doctor had his coat draped over one arm and carried his medical bag in his other hand.

"Doctor, you should get in your buggy and leave right now," she told him. She estimated that the riders wouldn't be here for another four or five minutes. That would give Fredericks time to get clear before any trouble started.

He frowned and said, "What's wrong, Mrs. Slaughter? You seem upset about something."

"There are riders coming in," she said. "I think they may be some of the rustlers who stole that herd of cattle last night."

"They've come back for more?"

"I don't know," Viola said. "I hope I'm wrong about them. But in case I'm not, you should leave while you still can, doctor, before there's any trouble."

"You mean shooting," Fredericks said heavily.

"It could come to that."

"Then I'm not going anywhere," he declared. "My services may be required here."

"It may not be safe —"

"I didn't swear an oath to help people only when it was safe or convenient. You may have more wounded, so this is where I need to be." Fredericks grunted. "If it comes down to that, I know how to use a gun, too, not just how to patch up bullet wounds. It would go against my code to inflict them, unless it was absolutely necessary to prevent further harm."

Viola saw that it wasn't going to do any good to argue with him, and she didn't have

157

time for that, anyway.

"All right, doctor, but go back inside and stay away from the windows. And thank you. I have to admit, I do feel a little better knowing you're here."

Fredericks disappeared inside the house as Jess Fisher emerged from the bunkhouse with eight more members of the crew. Each man carried a rifle, and most of them had holstered revolvers strapped around their waists as well.

"These are all the fellas I could round up, Miz Slaughter," Fisher reported as they trotted up to the fence. "You want us all inside, or should we spread out?"

"Who's the best marksman among you?" Viola asked.

One of the men stepped forward and said in a Texas drawl, "That'd be me, ma'am. Joe Sparkman."

None of the other men disagreed with Sparkman's assessment of his skills.

"All right, Joe," Viola said. "I want you to climb up on top of that water tank. You have plenty of cartridges for that Winchester with you?"

"Yes, ma'am, a whole box of .44-40s."

"All right. I won't lie to you, it's a very dangerous position. You'll be more exposed than anyone else. But you'll have a better field of fire than any of the rest of us, too."

"Yes, ma'am." A grin creased Sparkman's leathery face. "I wouldn't rather be nowhere else."

He hurried off toward the water tank while Viola led the rest of the men into the house.

"There are too many windows and not enough of us," she said as she took a Winchester down from a rack of rifles in the front room. "We can't cover all of them. So you'll have to spread out and do the best you can. We'll try to cover all the approaches to the house. Luckily their numbers aren't overwhelming. They can't really hit us from more than one direction at once."

Yolanda stepped into the arched doorway between the front room and the parlor. She said, "Señora, do you need more people to fight? Some of the servants know how to shoot."

"That's a good idea," Viola said. She didn't really expect any of the maids to hit anything, but they had plenty of rifles and ammunition. The women could make a lot of racket, anyway, and maybe the attackers would believe the ranch house's defenses were stronger than they really were.

She was getting ahead of herself, Viola thought. She didn't know for sure those men intended to attack the place, no matter what they looked like. Even the fact that they had an Apache warrior with them didn't have to mean they were hostile. Some Apaches worked as scouts for the army, didn't they? Maybe this was one of them.

She was like a little girl whistling on her way past a graveyard, hoping the tune would ward off evil spirits, she told herself. Reason and logic meant little in a situation such as this. Viola trusted her instincts a lot more, and they insisted that those men were trouble.

She told Yolanda, "Bring any of the women who want to fight in here and let them get rifles. Then help the men cover the windows. The rest of you should help the wounded get as far out of the line of fire as possible."

The rifle Viola held didn't have a round in the chamber. She worked the Winchester's lever to rectify that and then strode toward the front door.

From the window where he had taken up position, Jess Fisher said in an alarmed tone, "Ma'am, what're you doin'?"

"This is my house," Viola said as she held the rifle at a slant in front of her, across her chest. "I'm going to go greet our guests."

Chapter 14

"We gonna ride in shootin', boss?" Herb Woodbury asked as they approached the ranch.

"No need for that," Becker said. "I'm sure they've spotted us by now. They know we're coming. We'll keep this as civilized as we possibly can."

From beside him, Bodaway said, "The woman knows."

Becker glanced over at the Apache and asked, "What do you mean?"

"The woman climbed the ladder on the water tank and looked at us through a telescope. I saw her."

Becker laughed.

"You've got better eyes than I do, *amigo*. I missed that. But I was right, they know we're here, and if the gal you saw had a spyglass, she probably got a pretty good look at us. So she has a pretty good idea that we're not friendly."

Woodbury muttered, "With this bunch o' cutthroats, I reckon not."

"Still, I'm going to try talking to her first. You never know what people will agree to until you ask them."

Bodaway just grunted, but the sound was packed with skepticism.

They came in past a row of cottonwood trees and a building made of adobe bricks that had two sides and a covered dogtrot in the middle, in the style of Texas cabins. It appeared to be empty at the moment.

Becker reined in and signaled a halt. He said, "The rest of you stay here. I'm going on up alone."

"I don't know how smart that is, Ned," Woodbury said. "They could be holed up in there with a bunch of rifles."

"I'm sure they are. That's exactly why I want the rest of you to stay here instead of riding right up into their gunsights."

"Yeah, but what about you?"

"The Slaughters are law-abiding people. Hell, he's the sheriff of Cochise County! Mrs. Slaughter's not going to gun down a man who just wants to parley."

Woodbury grimaced and said, "I hope you're right. If you ain't, you'll be just askin' to get ventilated by ridin' up there like that."

"I'll take the chance," Becker said. He

hitched his horse into motion again.

Despite his confident tone, he felt his nerves crawling as he rode toward the ranch house. He didn't think anybody in there would start shooting without talking to him first and finding out what he wanted, but like everything else in life, there were no guarantees of that.

He had just reined to a stop in front of the gate in the picket fence when the front door opened and a woman stepped out of the house carrying a rifle.

Becker's first impulse was to reach for his gun, but he stopped himself from doing that since the woman wasn't pointing the Winchester at him. She held it ready in front of her.

She was damned good-looking, too, with a trim figure and dark hair that at the moment was pulled back in a loose knot behind her head. Her chin lifted in a show of stubborn defiance. Becker could tell that she was cautious but not scared of him, not really.

That was a mistake on her part. She needed to be scared of him — scared enough that she would cooperate and let him have what he had come here to take.

The woman lifted her voice and said, "Normally when someone rides up to my gate, I tell them to get down from their horse and come inside. I think it would be better if you stay right where you are, though."

"You're Mrs. Slaughter?" Becker asked.

"I am. Who are you?"

Becker didn't answer the question. Instead he said, "I'm looking for Don Eduardo Rubriz, and his wife and son if they're here."

"I didn't ask who you were looking for," the woman snapped. "I asked who you are."

He didn't see how it would do any harm to tell her. He was going to have to reveal his identity anyway, in order to get the full measure of revenge on Rubriz. The don had to know it was Thaddeus Becker's son who was responsible for the hell on earth that was about to descend on him.

"My name is Becker, Ned Becker," he said. "If you tell Don Eduardo that I'm here, he'll know the name."

For the first time, he saw a trace of indecisiveness on the woman's face. She was prepared for war, but she wanted to hope that maybe he had come in peace.

That wasn't the case, of course, but Becker was willing to let her think that for the time being.

"Stay where you are," Mrs. Slaughter said again. She turned her head slightly to speak

164

over her shoulder without taking her eyes off of Becker. "Yolanda, go tell Don Eduardo that a man named Ned Becker is here."

A thin smile curved Becker's lips. The woman's words confirmed that Rubriz was here and still alive. Becker was sure the doña would be, too. She wouldn't have gone with Slaughter and the others after the stolen cattle. Santiago might be a different story, but Becker would deal with that when the time came.

"What do you want with Don Eduardo?" Mrs. Slaughter asked.

"I reckon that's between the don and me," Becker drawled. "You can rest assured, though, Mrs. Slaughter, that I don't mean any harm to you or your people."

"You don't mean any harm," she repeated. "But will you inflict it anyway if we get in your way?"

Becker's jaw tightened. He admired this woman for her beauty and bravery, but she was starting to annoy him.

Again he didn't answer the question she had asked him, choosing instead to ask one of his own.

"I heard the don was injured. How bad is he hurt?"

He knew that was a mistake as soon as

the words were out of his mouth. The woman's eyes sparked with anger. She said, "You wouldn't know that unless you were here last night, or someone who was here told you about it. That Apache who's riding with you and your men, maybe?"

Anger of his own welled up inside him. He was wasting time here. He leaned forward in the saddle and said, "I don't have anything against you, ma'am, but I'll have what I came here to get, one way or another. If innocent folks get hurt, that's on your head, not mine. Now bring Don Eduardo and his wife out here. You do that and we'll go on our way and leave you in peace."

That was a lie, of course. Becker didn't intend to leave any witnesses behind. When he was done here, when he rode away from this place, he planned to leave it burning. The flames would wipe out any trace that he had ever been here.

Mrs. Slaughter suddenly leveled the Winchester at him. She wasn't a large woman, but she held the heavy rifle rock-steady as she pointed it at him.

Becker stiffened and sat up straighter in the saddle, but he kept his hand away from his gun. He had no doubt that she would drill him if he gave her the slightest excuse to pull the trigger.

"Take it easy, ma'am —" he began.

"You've made a bad mistake, Mr. Becker," she said. "You think you hold the winning hand here, but you overplayed it. I don't know what your plan is and I don't care. All I know is that if you don't throw your gun away, climb down from that horse, and come in here, I'm going to kill you."

The herd of stampeding cattle filled the canyon almost from one side to the other.

Almost.

Some boulders littered the ground along the base of the canyon wall to the left, though. They were chunks and slabs of sandstone that had fallen from the wall in times past. Slaughter knew instantly that they represented the best chance for him and his men to escape the deadly onslaught of hooves and horns thundering toward them.

"Come on!" he shouted to the others as he yanked his horse around and kicked the animal into a gallop toward the rocks.

They might have been able to turn and outrun the stampede by heading back the way they had come. But they had been following this canyon for a couple of miles and Slaughter knew there was a good chance the runaway herd would overtake them before they could find a way out. If that happened, they were all doomed.

As usual when faced with danger, he had made the decision instantly, with no hesitation. A lot of men had died on the frontier from dithering around, and John Slaughter wasn't going to be one of them. If fate had finally caught up to him, it wouldn't be from lack of action on his part.

He glanced over his shoulder and saw that Santiago and the other men were close behind him. They understood what they had to do. They rode hard, leaning forward in their saddles and slashing their mounts with the reins.

Slaughter slowed as he neared the rocks. He pulled his horse aside and waved the others on. Like any good leader, his first concern was for the men who followed him. They raced past and crowded into the cluster of boulders.

The leading edge of the stampede was less than twenty yards away. The billowing dust cloud from it was already starting to reach Slaughter and the other men.

Slaughter swung down from the saddle and hauled his horse behind a sandstone slab. All the men were clear now. The stampede reached the rocks and flowed around them like a brown tide. The noise was deafening, a rumble that assaulted the ears. It sounded like the world was ending.

The dust choked the men, clogged their throats and noses, stung their eyes, made it difficult to see anything. Their horses were all spooked, and they had their hands full keeping the animals under control.

Faintly over the racket, Slaughter heard men yelling and shooting. That would be the rustlers, he thought, driving the cattle through the canyon and using them as living weapons.

Those varmints were in for a surprise, Slaughter told himself grimly. They were about to discover that their would-be victims hadn't been trampled into raw meat after all.

The terrible rumbling diminished slightly. That told Slaughter most of the stampede had passed them already. The rustlers would be along very shortly. He called to Santiago, who crouched behind a nearby rock, "Get ready! We'll hit 'em when they go past us!"

Santiago nodded and turned to give the order to the next man. Slaughter hoped the command would spread to all the others in his group.

He reached up and pulled his Winchester from its saddle sheath. The dust was thinner now. He began to be able to see out into the canyon.

Several riders loped out of the sandy clouds, still yipping and shooting. Slaughter brought the rifle to his shoulder and drew a bead on one of the rustlers. It would have been easy to blow the man out of the saddle, and he was tempted to do just that.

But he was a lawman, he reminded himself, even if he wasn't wearing his badge at the moment, and there was a right way and a wrong way to do things. He raised his voice and shouted, "You men are covered! Throw down your guns and elevate!"

Instead of obeying the order, the startled rustlers twisted in their saddles and started blazing away at the men hidden in the rocks. That was the wrong thing to do. Slaughter fired, and so did Santiago and the other men. A storm of lead tore through the rustlers and knocked them off their horses.

"Hold your fire!" Slaughter called. If any of the thieves were still alive, he wanted a prisoner he could question. He left his horse with reins dangling and strode out from behind the slab of rock where he had taken shelter from the stampede.

The rustlers' horses had bolted, following the runaway cows. That left three shapes sprawled on the ground.

Only three, Slaughter thought. An unknown number of the rustlers were unaccounted for.

Maybe one of the wounded men could tell him where the others were.

He was about fifteen feet away from the men when one of them suddenly twisted halfway up from the ground and thrust a revolver at him. Smoke and flame gouted from the weapon's muzzle. Slaughter heard the bullet whip past his ear and reacted automatically. He fired his Winchester and saw the man's head jerk backward.

The rustler's gun slipped from his fingers and thudded to the ground as he rolled onto his back. By the time Slaughter reached him, he was staring sightlessly at the lingering shreds of dust in the air. The bullet hole in the center of his forehead was like a third eye, but it was as blinded by death as the other two.

Pools of blood spread slowly around all three men, the sandy soil of the canyon floor soaking up the life-giving fluid almost as fast as it welled from the rustlers' bodies. Slaughter saw that the second man was dead, too, then was a little surprised when he heard a faint groan come from the third man.

Wary of another trick, Slaughter dropped to a knee beside the man, grasped his shoulder, and rolled him onto his back. The three crimson splotches of blood on the man's shirt — two on the chest, one on his belly down near his waist — were ample testimony that he no longer represented a threat. He was still alive, but barely, and that condition wouldn't last more than another minute or two at most.

The dying man was young, about Stonewall's age. Dark beard stubble covered his cheeks and jaws. His eyes were set in hollows that seemed to be made even deeper by the agony that gripped him now. Slaughter could tell by looking at him that he'd had a hard life.

That was no excuse for taking up rustling as a trade, though. Slaughter said, "You're dying, son. What's your name?"

The man's eyelids fluttered open. His mouth moved. It took a lot of obvious effort for him to force out, "St-Stoney . . . Carter."

"Listen to me, Stoney," Slaughter said. "We'll see to it that you're laid to rest properly, but you have to tell me what this is all about. Why did you steal those cattle? Were the Apaches working with you? Where's the rest of your bunch?"

Slaughter put more emphasis on the last question. That was the most important one.

172

He didn't think these three men had been handling that herd by themselves. There had to be more of them somewhere close by.

He hadn't forgotten that dust cloud he had seen, either, or the worry that some of the rustlers might have doubled back to the ranch for some reason.

Carter didn't reply. His eyes were still open but unfocused. Slaughter said, "Stoney! This is important. What's this all about? Did some of your men turn around and go back to my ranch?"

The youngster was slipping away in front of Slaughter's eyes. He didn't think Stoney Carter was ever going to say anything again.

But then the dying rustler whispered a word. Slaughter was leaning close over him, or else he wouldn't have heard it.

He heard and understood, though, and that one word was enough to make Slaughter stiffen and catch his breath. It was a name . . .

"Becker!"

Chapter 15

Stonewall and Hermosa had taken a couple of extra horses with them so they could switch back and forth and keep up a fast pace. Even though Stonewall hadn't wanted to turn back, now that he had he was beginning to get worried. He knew how smart his brother-in-law was, and he trusted John Slaughter's instincts, too.

If Slaughter thought something might be wrong back at the ranch, there was a good chance that it was.

Hermosa wasn't a very talkative companion. He rolled one quirly after another and smoked them as he rode. Stonewall was nervous, though, and when he got that way he talked even more than usual.

"You think whoever's behind this has got some grudge against Don Eduardo?" he asked the *vaquero* as their horses splashed across the shallow water of Cave Creek.

"Why not someone with a grudge against

Señor Slaughter?" Hermosa asked. "He is the sheriff, is he not? I never saw a lawman who did not have an abundance of enemies."

"Oh, I reckon John's got enemies, all right," Stonewall admitted. "Plenty of 'em, I'd say. And not just from him bein' sheriff, either. He had his share of trouble with folks while he was bringin' cattle over here from Texas and settin' up his ranch. Why, there was one *hombre* who accused him of rustlin'! Can you imagine that?"

"Was he guilty?" Hermosa asked dryly.

"What? You mean, was he a rustler? John Slaughter?" The disbelief was obvious in Stonewall's voice.

"Today's honest, upright man may not have always been that way," Hermosa said with a shrug. "And every story is different depending on who tells it."

"I reckon that's true," Stonewall said, only slightly mollified. "But you probably wouldn't like it if I started talkin' about Don Eduardo bein' some sort of outlaw."

Hermosa glanced sharply over at him and said, "Make no mistake about it, *amigo*, Don Eduardo has done things of which he is not proud. Things that many men would look down upon. But he has always stayed true to himself and the things he wished to achieve."

"You'd know, wouldn't you? You've been ridin' for him a long time."

"Many years. I was with him when he founded his ranch. He and his partner."

"Partner?" Stonewall repeated with a frown. "I didn't know anything about him havin' a partner."

"It was long ago. And it ended badly. But there were two of them, Don Eduardo and a *gringo* friend of his. And their wives." Hermosa shook his head. "If the women had not been there, things might have turned out very differently."

Hermosa fell silent. Stonewall allowed that to go on for a minute or so, then burst out, "Come on! You've got to tell me the rest of the story."

"It is none of your affair, *amigo.* Of the people who were most intimately involved, they are all dead and buried now . . . except for Don Eduardo. Let him keep his pain to himself."

Stonewall frowned and said grudgingly, "Well . . . all right. I guess you're right, it's not any of my business."

Hermosa nodded. He took the stub of a cigarette from his lips and snapped it away, then started building a new one. As he rolled the smoke, he said, "It was long ago,

176

but Don Eduardo still says prayers for the dead . . . all of them." He struck a match, held it to the tip of the quirly, and added from the corner of his mouth, "Even the man who tried to kill him."

From where Viola stood on the porch, just outside the front door, she heard the gasp from the parlor and the startled exclamation, "Becker!"

Clearly the hard-faced stranger was right: the name meant something to Don Eduardo.

There would be time enough later to find out what this was all about, Viola thought. For now, the moment had come to play her trump card.

Before Ned Becker could do anything else, she pointed the Winchester at him and ordered him to throw down his gun and surrender.

It didn't seem that likely that he'd do it, but you never could tell. Sometimes a man's personality changed when he found himself looking down the barrel of a gun.

Not this one, though, Viola saw despairingly. Becker regarded her coolly from under the pulled-down brim of his hat. He didn't make a move to disarm himself or get down from the horse.

Instead he gave her a smug, infuriating smile and said, "We both know you're not going to pull that trigger, Mrs. Slaughter."

He wouldn't be aware of it, but that was just about the worst thing he could have done. The arrogant mockery made her temper blaze up inside her. Her finger started to tighten on the trigger as she shifted her aim slightly to put a bullet through his right shoulder.

Before she could fire, something struck the rifle with stunning force and ripped it out of her hands. She cried out, as much from shock as from pain, and threw herself backward as she saw Becker clawing at the holstered revolver on his hip. Viola fell through the door and kicked it shut.

Jess Fisher was there to drop the bar into the brackets on either side of the door, sealing it from outside. As soon as he had done that, he turned to her and said, "Mrs. Slaughter, are you all right? Blast it, your husband'll kill me if you're hurt!"

Viola sat up and shook her throbbing hands.

"I'm fine, Jess," she said. "What happened?"

"Hard to tell from in here, but it looked like somebody shot that rifle out of your hands."

Viola thought that was what had happened, too. She held up her hands and looked for blood, but she didn't find any. The bullet had hit the Winchester but missed her.

"That was a hell of a shot!" she exclaimed in a mixture of anger and admiration.

She heard a swift rataplan of hoofbeats from outside. One of the ranch hands called from a window, "That fella's lightin' out, Miz Slaughter. You want me to let him go or try to knock him down?"

"Let him go," Viola said. There hadn't been any more shots. "Maybe they'll decide the house is too well-defended and leave."

She knew how unlikely that was. She had gotten a good enough look at Ned Becker to recognize the hatred burning in his gaze. Whatever grudge against Don Eduardo had brought him here, he wasn't going to just ride away and forget it.

Viola wanted to know more about that grudge, although she didn't see how the knowledge would change anything in this situation. She climbed to her feet and went to the parlor. Her fingers still stung a little, but they didn't hurt too badly.

Don Eduardo was sitting up on the sofa now with bandages wrapped tightly around his midsection. Belinda stood close enough that she could rest a hand on his shoulder.

Dr. Fredericks was nearby, too, with a worried look on his face. He spoke first, saying, "I heard one of the men ask you if you were all right, Mrs. Slaughter. What happened?"

"Someone shot the rifle out of my hands," Viola explained.

Fredericks let out a low whistle of surprise. He said, "I didn't think you ever ran across trick shooting like that except in Wild West Shows and dime novels."

"Those men have at least one excellent marksman among them," Viola agreed.

"But you're not hurt?"

She held her hands up and turned them so the doctor could see both front and back of each hand.

"You're lucky," Fredericks said. "You could have lost a finger."

"And it would have been my fault," Don Eduardo said.

"You didn't pull the trigger," Viola pointed out.

"No, but those men are here because of me. The one who spoke to you . . . he said his name is Ned Becker?"

"That's right. I take it the name is familiar to you?"

Don Eduardo sighed and nodded.

"It is one I have not heard in many years," he said. "A name that makes me ashamed to hear it now."

Belinda protested, "That's not fair. You don't have anything to be ashamed of, Eduardo."

Rubriz shook his head and said, "There are things about me you do not know, my dear. Things that happened long before the two of us met."

"If they happened before we met, then I don't care about them," Belinda said with a stubborn toss of her blond hair.

"You should," Don Eduardo said, "because they may mean the death of us all."

Becker slowed his horse and swung down from the saddle while the animal was still moving. His angry gaze swept over the men gathered behind the brick building that shielded them from the view of those in the ranch house.

"Who fired that shot?" he demanded.

"Talk to your Apache *amigo,*" Herb Woodbury said with a nod toward Bodaway, who stood there with a Winchester cradled in his arms. The war chief's face was as expressionless as ever.

Becker confronted his old friend and said, "I didn't give the order to start shooting."

181

"You would have rather I let the woman shoot you?" Bodaway asked coolly.

"She wasn't going to shoot me," Becker insisted. "She wouldn't have pulled the trigger."

"You're wrong. If I had not fired, you would be dead now, or at least wounded. I know when someone is about to kill."

"She's a woman, for God's sake!"

Bodaway actually smiled. His lips curved only a tiny fraction of an inch, but it was a smile.

"Have you not lived enough years to have learned how dangerous a woman can be?" he asked.

Becker blew out an exasperated breath and moved a hand in a curt, dismissive gesture.

"All right, what's important is that we know now Rubriz is in there," he said. "Mrs. Slaughter spoke to someone inside and had them tell the don my name. So he's here, and he's alive. I can still take my revenge on him. All we have to do is convince Mrs. Slaughter to turn him over to us."

Woodbury said, "I don't know if she'll do that, boss. She strikes me as a pretty stubborn woman."

"She'll do it if she wants to save her life and the lives of those other people in there,"

Becker insisted. "For now, spread out. Keep to cover, but search the place. I want to know if there are any other ranch hands around here, or if they're all forted up inside the house. That's what I'm betting on, but I'd like to be sure before I decide what we're going to do next."

Woodbury nodded and started pointing at the other men in turn, singling them out and telling them where to go.

"And keep your damn heads down," he added. "You waltz right into a bush-whackin', it won't be nobody's fault but your own."

Within minutes, only Becker and Bodaway were left at the adobe brick building. Becker went into the covered dogtrot and peered through the windows into the rooms on each side.

"I'll be damned," he said to the Apache. He pointed through the glass. "Look in there. Desks and chalkboards, by God. This is a schoolhouse. Slaughter must have somebody teaching all the little Mex brats that belong to his *vaqueros.*"

"It is said that sometimes the Apaches come here, too," Bodaway mused. "Not all of my people are enemies to John Slaughter. Some are his friends."

"I don't care about that. He can be friends

with all the Apaches he wants to, as long as he stays out of my way."

"I have heard as well that Slaughter is a good tracker," Bodaway said. "Once he starts on someone's trail, he never turns back until he catches his quarry."

"You're talking about those fellas I sent on ahead with the herd? I hope Slaughter stays after them. That's the whole idea, to keep him away from here until I've done what I came to do."

"They will be outnumbered. They will not have much chance to escape."

"You think I care about those cows?" Becker scoffed. "I came to settle a debt, that's all. Why do you think I've been holding up banks and trains for the past five years? I saved my share of the loot from those jobs so I could afford to pay Woodbury and those other fellas. So I could afford those rifles I promised to you — the rifles you're still going to get, by the way. I did all that because money doesn't mean a damn thing to me, Bodaway." Becker stared across the open space between the school and the ranch house. "All I want is right in there. The head of Don Eduardo Rubriz, the man who murdered my father."

CHAPTER 16

Slaughter had promised the dying Stoney Carter that he would be laid to rest properly after he crossed the divide. He kept his word, even though the delay chafed at him.

Slaughter had brought along a couple of folding prospector's shovels, thinking there might be a need for them, and several of the men had taken turns scraping out shallow graves for the young outlaw and the other two rustlers. Those graves had dirt mounded over them now.

Hat in hand, Slaughter spoke a brief prayer over the dead men. He, Santiago, and the cowboys who had dug the graves were the only ones here. Slaughter had sent the rest of the bunch to round up the herd.

With the burying done, Slaughter clapped his hat back on his head and turned to Santiago. He fixed the young man with a hard, level gaze and said, "The two of us have to talk."

Santiago frowned and asked, "What about, señor?"

Slaughter didn't answer directly. He figured some privacy would be best for this conversation, so he jerked his head for Santiago to follow him and said, "Come on."

They strode away, far enough to be out of easy earshot of the other men. Santiago still looked puzzled.

"What is this about, Señor Slaughter?" he asked again. "I thought we would either pursue the other rustlers or take the herd and head back to the ranch."

"We'll do one of those things, all right," Slaughter said, "but first I want to know the reason behind all this trouble."

Santiago appeared even more confused. He shook his head and said, "How would I know?"

"I didn't tell you the last thing that boy said before he died. It was a name. Becker."

Santiago stiffened. His face took on a grim cast.

"Earlier you said something about a man named Thaddeus Becker," Slaughter went on. "You mentioned that he was your father's partner, and that sometime in the past he shot Don Eduardo. But you didn't finish that story, and I think it's high time you did."

"Some things are private," Santiago said. "They should be kept within the family."

"I can respect that . . . but not when it brings trouble to my home and endangers people I love. When that happens I've got a right to know what's going on."

"It was all many years in the past," Santiago said with a stubborn shake of his head. "It cannot possibly have anything to do with what is happening now."

"Then how did Carter know the name Becker?"

"There could be many men with that name —"

"You don't believe that any more than I do," Slaughter said sharply. "Look, son, I don't want to pry in your family's personal business, but we've got to figure out what's going on here so we'll know what to do next."

For a moment, Santiago stared at him in stubborn defiance. But then the young man sighed.

"All right," he said. "I suppose you have a right to know. But I cannot tell you everything, Señor Slaughter, simply because I do not know it myself."

"Fair enough," Slaughter said with a nod.

"Just tell me what you do know."

"Many years ago, my father befriended an American named Thaddeus Becker. Becker was in Mexico because he had come there with a man named William Walker, an adventurer who tried to take over the country."

Slaughter nodded. He had heard of Walker, the notorious filibuster and would-be dictator.

"Becker and Walker had a falling out, but Becker remained in Mexico, selling his services as a military man to the highest bidder. Eventually he fell in with a rebel faction that included my father. When that faction came to power, my father and Becker took advantage of their newfound wealth and power to establish a ranch in northern Sonora."

"The same ranch your father has now," Slaughter said.

Santiago nodded.

"They brought their wives with them. High-born ladies from influential families in Mexico City. It was a hard, dangerous time. Bandits roamed the land, and Yaquis from the mountains raided the ranch on numerous occasions. But they were strong and met all the challenges until . . . until Thaddeus Becker's wife decided that she wanted my father."

"I can see where that would cause some trouble," Slaughter said.

Santiago nodded and went on, "My father turned aside her advances, of course, but in her anger at being refused, she told her husband that my father had attacked her. Becker was furious. He wanted to dissolve their partnership. My father and mother both did everything they could to save the friendship. Becker pretended to put all the hurt feelings aside, but really he was planning his revenge. One day, while they were out on the range, Becker shot my father with no warning. I don't know what he planned. Maybe he intended to say that a bandit ambushed my father. No one would have been able to prove otherwise. He must have believed that my father was dead, because he turned away, no doubt to return to the ranch. But my father regained consciousness and shot him."

"In the back?" Slaughter asked with a frown.

"You must understand," Santiago said, "my father believed he was dying. That was the only way he could strike back at the man who had slain him. After he fired, he passed out again. His *vaqueros* found him lying there later that day. They had gone to look for him after Becker returned to the ranch, mortally wounded. I don't know what he said to his wife before he died. A pack of lies, though, surely."

"But you don't know that's exactly how things happened," Slaughter pointed out. "The way you told the story, the two men were out there alone."

Santiago nodded and said, "That is true. But I believe my father."

Of course he'd take Don Eduardo's word for it, thought Slaughter. Just about any son would.

"My father was badly wounded," Santiago continued. "For many weeks, my mother nursed him back to health."

"What happened to Becker's wife?"

"No one knows. She disappeared from the ranch after her husband's death and took her son with her."

"You didn't mention a son," Slaughter said.

Santiago nodded again.

"His name was Ned. He was several years older than me. I remember him only vaguely."

"Ned Becker," Slaughter mused. "You don't know if he's still alive?"

"I have no idea," Santiago said. Slaughter was convinced the young man was telling the truth.

"If he was alive, that might explain some of this. Lord knows what his mother might have told him over the years. She could have blamed his father's death and anything else that happened on Don Eduardo. She could have filled his head with hate, to the point that by now he's wanting some revenge."

"You really think Ned Becker could come back from nowhere and do all this, Señor Slaughter?"

"Stoney Carter said Becker's name."

"Not Ned."

"Can you think of another Becker it might be?"

Santiago shook his head and admitted, "No, what you say makes sense, señor."

"And Ned Becker wasn't nowhere all this time," Slaughter said. "He was somewhere . . . somewhere nursing the resentment he feels toward Don Eduardo."

Now that Slaughter had put the theory into words, he was convinced that he was on the right trail. If the long-lost Ned Becker was behind the attack on the ranch and the rustling of the herd, then his ultimate goal had to be . . .

Revenge on Don Eduardo.

And Don Eduardo was back at the ranch.

Turning to his men, Slaughter ordered in

a curt, grim voice, "Saddle up. We're heading south."

"What about the rest of those rustlers, boss?" one of the cowboys asked. "They've got to still be up ahead in these mountains somewhere."

"I know," Slaughter said, "and I don't like letting them get away. But if I'm right, the man who put them up to it isn't with them anymore. The story's too long and complicated to go into it now." Slaughter reached for his horse's reins. "I want to be back at the ranch by nightfall —"

The sinister whine of a bullet slapping past his ear and the sharp crack of a rifle sounded at the same time, and a split-second later more shots blasted, their echoes filling the canyon.

"Help me up," Don Eduardo said as he struggled to stand. "Help me up, I say!"

"Eduardo, stop," Belinda said. Her hands fluttered uselessly in front of her. "Please, you can't get up. You have to rest —"

"Your wife is right, sir," Dr. Fredericks said as he stepped forward to rest a firm hand on Rubriz's shoulder. "You've lost a great deal of blood, and if you open that wound again, you'll lose more. I don't think you can afford to do that."

Don Eduardo sank back on the sofa cushions and glared around at them.

"I am to blame for what is happening here," he insisted. "I should be the one to put an end to it. I will go to this man Becker —"

"Don't be a blasted fool," Viola said.

Don Eduardo gave her a shocked, angry look. Clearly, he wasn't accustomed to anyone speaking to him like that, especially a woman.

Viola Slaughter wasn't like most of the women he had known, however. She returned his gaze without flinching and went on, "Even if you surrendered to him, do you really think he's going to let the rest of us live? With all due respect, Don Eduardo, I looked into the man's eyes, not you. He's a killer, pure and simple. Whatever he's got planned, when he's done with you he'll come after the rest of us and try to finish us off."

A frown creased the don's forehead. He asked, "Do you truly believe that, Señora Slaughter?"

"I have no doubt of it," Viola said.

Don Eduardo sighed.

"Then I have no choice but to accept your judgment. I have not seen Ned Becker since he was a boy, many years ago. But I can imagine he would grow into a man who hates me enough to do these things."

"But why?" Belinda asked. "That makes no sense, Eduardo. What could you possibly have done to make this man hate you so much?"

A stubborn expression came over Don Eduardo's face as he said, "I will not talk about it. Not here, not now."

"You don't think your wife deserves to know the truth?"

He looked up at her and said, "Perhaps if we survive this ordeal, my dear, then I will tell you what you want to know. But for now there are some things I will keep to myself, including Ned Becker's reasons for wanting to see me dead."

Viola said, "Whether you explain or not, Don Eduardo, we're left in the same position — defending this house."

"Give me a gun and help me to a chair beside a window. I can shoot."

"It may come to that," Viola said, "but not yet."

From the front room, Jess Fisher called, "Rider comin', Miz Slaughter!"

Viola hurried out of the parlor and joined Jess at the window. She crouched low, not wanting to give that sharpshooter a target, and watched as a man galloped along the lane that ran between the fence and open ground where the party had taken place the previous evening.

"Want me to see if I can knock him off that horse?" Fisher asked as he squinted over the barrel of his Winchester.

"No, hold your fire," Viola ordered. She raised her voice so the defenders in the other rooms could hear her. "Hold your fire until we see what he wants."

The rider didn't slow down as he raced past the fence. As he neared the gate he drew back his arm and threw something that sailed toward the house.

"It's a bomb!" Jess Fisher yelled in alarm. He snapped his rifle to his shoulder as the thrown object clattered on the porch.

"No!" Viola caught hold of the barrel and kept him from shooting until the rider had galloped on past and gone out of sight, probably to circle around and rejoin his companions. "It looked like a rock or something with a note tied around it."

"Are you sure about that, ma'am? I'd hate to have the place blow up."

"You and me both, Jess." Viola backed away from the window, not standing up until she was clear of it. "We need to find out what it was."

"Could be a trick to get us to open the

195

door," the foreman suggested.

"Maybe . . . but I don't think so. Give me your rifle."

Reluctantly, Fisher did so.

"Now take the bar off the door and open it," Viola went on. "Stand back when you do, though, so they won't have a good shot at you."

"What about you?"

Viola hefted the rifle and said, "I'll be ready if they try to charge the house."

Fisher still looked like he thought this was a bad idea, but he went to the door, took hold of the thick beam that served as a bar, and lifted it from its brackets. He grasped the knob, twisted it, and swung the door wide, standing behind the panel as it opened into the house.

Viola's heart hammered in her chest. In spite of what she'd told Fisher, she couldn't be certain this wasn't a trick of some sort. She had the Winchester pointed toward the door as it opened.

A chunk of rock a little bigger than a man's fist lay on the porch. A folded piece of paper had been wrapped around it and tied into place with a piece of string.

"I was right," Viola said. "It's a message."

She stepped toward the opening. Fisher said, "Careful, ma'am. I'll go and get it."

"No," Viola said. "No one is going out there."

She got down on her knees and inched forward. By thrusting the rifle out with one hand, she was able to hook the front sight against the rock and drag it toward the door without exposing herself. When it was close enough, she set the rifle aside, darted a hand out, grabbed the rock, and threw herself backward. Fisher shoved the door closed and dropped the bar across it again.

Viola climbed to her feet, untied the string, and removed the note from the rock. She handed the chunk of stone to Fisher, smiled, and said, "Here you go, Jess. Better hang on to it. You might need to throw it at one of the varmints."

"If one of 'em gets close enough, I'll dang sure do it, ma'am," the foreman promised as he weighed the rock in his hand. "This thing's heavy enough to bust somebody's skull open if you hit him just right with it."

Viola carried the note into the parlor without unfolding it. Everyone in there was waiting tensely. Belinda put what they were all feeling into words by asking, "Well? What was it?"

Viola held up the piece of paper and said, "They sent us a message." She unfolded the note and read the words printed there in a bold, easy to read hand. Her face grew more solemn as she said, "Becker is giving us until nightfall to turn you over to him, Don Eduardo."

The don sat forward again and said, "See, it is like I told you. I should surrender —"

"That's not all," Viola said. "It's not just you he wants. Becker says that we have to give him Doña Belinda, too — or he'll kill everybody on the place and burn it to the ground."

CHAPTER 17

Slaughter knew that he and his men were too exposed, standing out in the open this way next to the graves. He grabbed his horse's reins and said, "Head for the rocks!"

Those boulders had protected them from the stampede. They were the only real cover in the canyon. As Slaughter ran toward them, pulling his horse along with him, he searched for the source of the shots.

Bullets kicked up dirt around the men's feet as they hurried toward shelter. One of Slaughter's cowboys suddenly cried out in pain and stumbled.

Slaughter started to turn back to help him, but the man waved him on and said, "Keep goin', boss, they just nicked my leg!"

The cowboy took only one more step before he rocked back, making a strangling sound as crimson flooded from his throat. A bullet had ripped it open. He let go of his horse and flopped to the ground, writhing and jerking as he bled to death in a matter of a few heartbeats.

Rage filled Slaughter, but he kept moving. He couldn't do the man any good now except for avenging his death, and getting himself killed wouldn't accomplish that. In fact, it would just assure that the man had died for nothing.

Bullets ricocheted off the rocks as Slaughter, Santiago, and the remaining ranch hand, a man named Dixon, darted among them. Slaughter handed his reins to Dixon and motioned for Santiago to do likewise.

"Hang on to the horses, Chuck," Slaughter told the man as he pulled his Winchester from its sheath. "Stay back as close to the canyon wall as you can. Santiago, let's see if we can figure out where those bushwhackers are."

Slaughter's eyes swept the canyon as he crouched behind one of the boulders. The gunfire had stopped a moment earlier, but he figured the ambushers were just waiting for a good shot again.

The shots had come from farther up the canyon, the direction in which Slaughter and his companions had been pursuing the rustlers before the thieves stampeded the herd back at them. Slaughter was convinced the bushwhackers were the other men who had been driving the stolen cattle north. He had no way of knowing how many of them there were.

He could speculate about their motives, however, over and above wanting to avenge their comrades who'd been killed in the aftermath of the stampede. Slaughter had a hunch that Ned Becker had ordered the men to do everything in their power to delay the pursuers and keep them away from the ranch. That fit in with Slaughter's theory about what Becker was doing.

Becker didn't want to be disturbed while he went after his twisted revenge on Don Eduardo Rubriz.

"Did you see where the shots came from, Señor Slaughter?" Santiago asked.

"No, but when they start shooting again, I'm hoping I can spot their smoke."

"Be ready to watch, then," Santiago said, and with no more warning than that, he stood up and opened fire, spraying bullets wildly up the canyon.

Slaughter yelled, "Get down, you fool!" but Santiago was too far away for him to do anything else. He would have tackled the young man if he had been closer, but he couldn't reach Santiago without going out into the open.

A bullet spanged off the boulder in front

of Santiago, but the ricochet missed him somehow. Slaughter spotted a puff of smoke from the rimrock on the other side of the canyon about fifty yards north from their position and sent three shots toward it as fast as he could work the Winchester's lever.

At least one of them found the target, although in a case like this, Slaughter was under no illusions that he was a better marksman than the bushwhackers. It was luck or fate that guided his shots.

A man rose sharply to his feet and lurched into view, dropping his rifle as he did so. He pitched forward off the edge of the rim and turned over in midair as he plummeted to the canyon floor.

The thud as he struck the ground made an ugly sound.

Slaughter glanced over and saw that Santiago had dropped back down behind the boulder.

"That was a damn fool stunt you just pulled!" Slaughter told the young man.

"It worked, though," Santiato said. "And now we have one less enemy."

Slaughter couldn't deny that. And a moment later Santiago's tactic paid an unexpected dividend. Slaughter heard hoofbeats and realized at least two horses were heading north at a fast rate of speed.

From farther back in the rocks, Dixon called, "Sounds like they're lightin' a shuck outta here, boss."

Slaughter agreed, but he said, "Let's keep our heads down for a few minutes anyway, just in case it's a trick."

There were no more shots, and after five minutes, Slaughter risked standing up and moving out into the open. He didn't draw any fire as he walked over to the dead cowboy, a man named Callan.

Slaughter knelt beside the man just to make sure he was dead, although he didn't really have any doubt. No one could lose that much blood and survive. Callan's eyes were open, staring sightlessly at nothing.

Slaughter straightened and let out a grim sigh.

"We've got another grave to dig. We'd better get at it."

"You think the others are gone?" Santiago asked as he and Dixon emerged from the rocks.

"Seems like it."

Dixon said, "If you want to go take a look around, Mr. Slaughter, I'll take care of buryin' Callan."

Slaughter nodded. "All right, Chuck. That's a good idea. Come on, Santiago."

Slaughter and Santiago mounted and rode

up the canyon, rifles held ready for use. They went around the bend where the rustlers had held the herd until the pursuit caught up to them, and another hundred yards farther on, Slaughter and Santiago came to a narrow, twisting trail that led up to the rim on that side.

Slaughter nodded toward the trail and said, "Let's go take a look."

Cautiously, they rode to the top. When they reached the rim, they had no trouble locating the spot where the bushwhackers had waited. They found empty rifle cartridges littering the ground, as well as the stubs of several quirlies.

"Three horses," Slaughter said as he pointed out the tracks. "They took the extra one with them when they lit out, and it looks like they were in a hurry to put this part of the country behind them."

"The odds were no longer in their favor," Santiago said.

"Yes, that's the way it seems to me, too. From the looks of everything we've found, it appears that Becker sent six men on with the herd and took the rest of the bunch with him. I'd say the two who were left didn't care for the idea of being sacrificed on the altar of Ned Becker's revenge."

"What do we do now?"

"We'll catch up to the herd, leave a few men to drive it on back to the ranch, and the rest of us will go on ahead and get back as soon as we can." Slaughter glanced at the sky. "I started to say earlier that I wanted to get there by nightfall, but I doubt if we can do that. But we've wasted enough time. If our guesses are right, they could use our help back there, and the sooner the better."

Joe Sparkman lifted his arm and used the sleeve to wipe sweat off his forehead. He had been up here on top of the water tank for a couple of hours, with no shade from the sun, and the heat from the sun was intense.

It would be nice if he could lift the hatch in the top of the tank, lower himself into the cool water, and float around for a while. That would cool him off. But he couldn't keep an eye on what was happening from inside the tank.

As far as he could tell, the varmints who had laid siege to the ranch didn't know he was up here, and Sparkman wanted to keep it that way for as long as possible. Not for his own protection, although he sure as hell had no wish to die here today, but rather because he thought he could do the most good for Mrs. Slaughter and the others in the house if he took the outlaws by surprise when he finally announced his presence by drilling some of the bastards.

Joe had come close to shooting the fella who had ridden up to the front gate. It would have been easy to do while the gent was palavering with Mrs. Slaughter.

But that would have been cold-blooded murder. Sparkman was no saint, but he drew the line at such things.

So he'd waited, and for a second it looked like he'd made a bad mistake when he thought that Mrs. Slaughter had been shot. Texas John would go on a rampage if anything ever happened to that little gal.

Thankfully, he'd caught a glimpse of her a short time later when she opened the door to retrieve that note one of the outlaws had tossed up on the porch, so he knew she was all right. That was a big load off his mind.

Now he'd settled down to waiting again.

Hot, tedious waiting.

He was no strategist, just a cowboy from Zephyr, Texas, who'd discovered at an early age that he had a natural shooting eye. He had supplied countless squirrels and jackrabbits for his ma's stew pot when he was a kid.

But he was beginning to get a hunch that the outlaws were going to wait until dark to make their move. They could get around easier then without being seen. They might be planning to sneak up on the house.

Sparkman figured he'd better do something to spoil that plan while he still could.

The varmints were holed up behind the schoolhouse. Sparkman could look over the ranch house roof and see the Texas-style adobe brick building a couple of hundred yards away. Cottonwood trees grew behind and to one side of it, and the outlaws were using those for cover, too.

But from time to time he spotted some of them moving around. As Sparkman thought more about it, he decided that the *hombre* who had ridden up to the gate to talk to Mrs. Slaughter must be the leader.

Cut off a snake's head and the rest of it died, he thought. Any good ol' Texas boy knew that. Sparkman's eyes narrowed as he looked over the barrel of his rifle and waited to catch a glimpse of the boss owlhoot. His vision was exceptionally keen. Even at this distance he thought he could spot the man again.

And when he did, that would be the time to take his first shot. Kill that fella and the others might give it up as a bad job. Maybe not likely, but there was at least a chance of that happening.

Sparkman waited with the patience of a born hunter. He recalled the time he had waited almost an entire night, not moving a muscle, for a coyote that had been getting into his ma's chicken house and carrying off a hen every night. Finally the slinking critter had showed up, and Sparkman drilled him with a single shot from the hayloft in the barn. He'd hung that varmint's tail from the fence around the vegetable garden, proud of what he'd done.

If he could save the lives of everybody here on the ranch, it would be even better.

Caught up in those thoughts, he might not have heard anything behind him — even if there had been anything to hear.

But as it was, the form that pulled itself swiftly onto the top of the water tank moved in utter silence. The only thing that warned Sparkman he had company was a flickering shadow in the corner of his eye.

His heart leaping in alarm, he rolled onto his back as fast as he could. That saved his life, at least for the moment. The knife that the Apache had been about to drive into his back struck the tank's top instead and the point imbedded itself in the wood.

Sparkman tried to swing the Winchester's muzzle up and around so he could get a shot off, but the Indian knocked the barrel aside with a swipe of his other arm as he struggled to wrench the knife free.

Sparkman struck upward with the rifle's stock instead. He aimed the blow at the Apache's face, but the man twisted and the butt caught him on the shoulder.

That was enough to knock the Apache to the side. Sparkman kicked him in the belly. The cowboy knew he was fighting for his life, and that desperation gave him strength and speed he didn't know he had.

Unfortunately he was battling a man for whom fighting and killing were as natural as breathing. The Apache writhed out of the way when Sparkman tried again to hit him with the rifle. His left hand shot out, gripped Sparkman by the throat, and drove the back of the cowboy's head against the tank.

The blow stunned Sparkman, caused his vision to go blurry for a second, and made the world spin crazily around him. By the time he recovered his wits, the Apache had wrenched the knife loose and held the blade at Sparkman's throat.

Sparkman expected to die right then and there. The keen edge sliced into his skin and he felt the warm trickle of blood down his neck.

But the Apache held off and didn't put enough pressure on the blade to slice into

Sparkman's throat.

Instead he leaned close over the cowboy, his face only inches away from Sparkman's, and asked, "How many are in the house?"

It was hard to talk with a knife at his throat that way, but Sparkman managed to gasp, "You can . . . go to hell!"

The Indian pressed a little harder on the knife and went on, "Santiago Rubriz. Is he here at the ranch?"

Sparkman didn't see how it would hurt anything to answer that one. He said, "No. He went with . . . Texas John . . . after those damn . . . rustlers." Sparkman breathed raggedly through his clenched teeth for a second, then added, "You fellas better . . . light a shuck . . . before Slaughter gets back. You'll be mighty sorry . . . if he catches you."

The Apache smiled. If anything, it made him look uglier and more evil.

"What about Don Eduardo?"

"I don't know . . . a damn thing. And I wouldn't tell you . . . if I did."

"Then there is no reason to keep you alive."

Sparkman's heart jumped again. He wanted to cuss the Apache again, but there was no time for that. He felt the knife bite deep into his throat, burning hot and icy cold at the same time, and his body bucked up from the pain. He saw his own blood spout up like a fountain as his panic-stricken heart pumped it out through the gaping wound.

He knew he would never see Texas again. In fact, the last thing he saw was his killer standing up, knife in hand, blood dripping crimson from the blade . . .

The only thing that gave Joe Sparkman any comfort as he crossed the divide was the knowledge that his death would be avenged.

John Slaughter would see to that.

CHAPTER 18

Becker saw Bodaway walking through the cottonwood grove and frowned. He realized he hadn't seen his old friend for a while.

"Where have you been?" Becker asked.

"Getting rid of a problem," Bodaway replied.

"What problem?"

"The rifleman hidden on top of the water tank."

Bodaway pointed to the tank, the top of which was visible in the distance, rising higher than the roof of the ranch house.

"Wait a minute," Becker said with a frown. "One of Slaughter's men was up there?"

Bodaway grunted and said, "I would not have had to kill him if he wasn't."

"How did you know?"

"I saw the barrel of his rifle when he pointed it at you."

"At me?" Becker asked, surprised.

"While you were at the fence talking to

the woman."

Becker felt a little shiver go through him. He wasn't surprised that he'd been covered while he was parleying with Mrs. Slaughter, but the idea that a sharpshooter had targeted him from the top of the water tank was unexpected. Putting a man up there was actually a pretty smart move.

But evidently it hadn't paid off, because Bodaway had disposed of the *hombre.*

"So you killed him?"

Bodaway shrugged.

"What did you do with him?"

"Left him up there. What else would I do with him?"

There were still a couple hours of sunlight left. The body would start to stink by nightfall, lying out in the sun that way.

Maybe the people in the house would smell it, Becker thought. The idea made him smile a little. Nothing like the stench of death to make somebody's spirits fall. Maybe some of the defenders would start to think about giving up.

Not that it would really matter in the long run if they did. They were all going to die anyway.

Herb Woodbury came up to Becker and Bodaway and said, "The boys are startin' to wonder what we're gonna do, boss. Are we waitin' until the sun goes down to make our move?"

"That's right," Becker said. "Once it's dark I want a couple of men to get up close enough to the house to throw torches through some of the windows. If we set the place on fire inside, they won't have any choice but to come out."

"And we shoot 'em down when they do," Woodbury guessed.

"Have you forgotten why we're here?" Becker asked with a frown. "I want Don Eduardo and his wife alive."

Bodaway said, "The boy is not here."

Becker looked quickly at him and asked, "You mean Santiago?"

"I asked the man on the water tank about him. He said the boy went with Slaughter after the cattle."

Becker rubbed his jaw and said, "Well, that's pretty much what I figured. That makes it even more important for us to capture the don and doña and Mrs. Slaughter. The others will be coming back sooner or later, and we'll need hostages to make them surrender, too."

"Gonna make a clean sweep of it, eh?" Woodbury said.

"Whatever it takes to make sure Rubriz dies knowing that I've taken everything from him. That means his wife and son have to die first."

Bodaway said, "And the white men claim that Apaches are cruel."

For a second that comment annoyed Becker. Then he looked closer at Bodaway and realized that despite the solemn expression on his old friend's face, the Apache had just made a joke. Becker threw back his head and laughed.

Then he grew more serious, too, and said, "Nothing is too cruel for the man who murdered my father."

"Let me go out there," Don Eduardo said as he struggled to stand up. "That is the only chance any of you have to survive this madman's scheme."

"Eduardo, don't be insane," Belinda said. She put a hand on her husband's shoulder. "You know it wouldn't do any good. You heard what Mrs. Slaughter said."

Viola held out the note to Don Eduardo and said, "You can read it for yourself. He wants both of you. And don't think for a second that if he got you, he would spare the rest of us. Becker's a natural-born killer."

"No!" the don responded with unexpected vehemence. "She made him that way, that

215

woman. That evil woman!"

He was breathing hard. Dr. Fredericks came up on his other side and said, "You'd better take it easy, Don Eduardo. You've been through a rough time of it, and you're in no shape to work yourself into such a state."

With an angry frown, Rubriz leaned back on the sofa. Belinda perched on the edge beside him and took his hand. He lifted her hand in both of his and gently pressed his lips to the back of it.

"I am so sorry that you are in danger, my dear," he said. "This is my fault. I should never have trusted either of them."

"Either of them?" she repeated with a puzzled frown.

"Thaddeus Becker . . . and his wife." Don Eduardo sighed. "Although, to be fair, Thaddeus was a good man at one time. We fought side by side for freedom against the oppressors of my country. True, at first Thaddeus joined with us because he believed our side would emerge triumphant in the end, and he might become rich if he was one of us. But by the time that came about, he believed in our cause, I know it."

Viola thought the don might be wrong about that. A man who fought for money, or even for the hope of profit, seldom changed his stripes.

But she hadn't been there, she reminded herself. She had no way of knowing what had really been in Thaddeus Becker's heart and mind.

"It was Lusita," Don Eduardo went on. "She was the one who changed him. He saw her in Mexico City, at a ball to celebrate our victory, and lost all reason. It was the same ball where I met my own beloved Pilar." He looked over at Belinda. "I am sorry, I should not mention her —"

"Of course you can mention her," Belinda said. "I know you loved her. Of course you did. From everything you've told me, she was a wonderful woman. And she was Santiago's mother, so of course you still have feelings for her."

"They do not diminish my love for you."

Belinda leaned over and kissed him on the cheek. She murmured, "I know that."

Viola frowned slightly. She had spent the past eighteen hours intensely disliking Doña Belinda Rubriz, and now the woman had to go and act like a decent human being. Her affection for her husband seemed genuine.

But if it was, how could she be unfaithful to him with her own stepson?

"Lusita was quite taken with the dashing *gringo* adventurer, I suppose," Don Eduardo

217

went on. "But I should not bore you with this story."

"No, go on," Belinda urged him. "Anything that helps me get to know you better is all right with me, Eduardo."

And talking kept the don sitting there relatively quietly and resting, thought Viola. She glanced at Fredericks, and the doctor gave her a slight nod. He approved of Don Eduardo telling them about his past, too.

"You understand, these are things that have weighed on my heart and soul for many years. We were happy at first, there at the ranch: Thaddeus and Lusita, Pilar and me. But Lusita always had, how do you say it, a wandering eye. She claimed to love Thaddeus, but she thrived on the attention of men. It seemed to be like air and water to her, a necessity of life."

"I've known women like that," Belinda said.

She had probably been a woman like that in the past, Viola thought, then chided herself for being so judgmental.

"Thaddeus loved her so much, he could not see what she was really like," Don Eduardo said. "Or if he did, he persuaded himself to ignore it. But he gave no sign that he knew, even when she . . . even when she decided that she wanted to seduce me,

218

his own partner and comrade-in-arms."

"You resisted her, of course."

"Of course," Rubriz said. "Then when she became with child and presented Thaddeus with a fine son, I hoped that motherhood would force Lusita to put everything else behind her. That she would devote herself to her husband and the little boy. And for a time it seemed that would be so."

Viola said, "That little boy was Ned Becker, the man who's out there laying siege to this house now?"

With a solemn nod, Don Eduardo said, "Yes, it must be so. That is the name I remember him by. I have not seen him in many, many years. In truth, I thought that he was probably dead. I knew from friends in Mexico City that Lusita never returned to her family after she took the boy and left the ranch, after Thaddeus Becker's death."

Viola's head was spinning a little from trying to keep up with everything in Don Eduardo's story. It was a good example of how messy and complicated life could get for some people. She was glad that she had met the love of her life at a relatively early age and spent so many years happily married to John Slaughter.

"I wanted to believe that Lusita was just impulsive and misguided," the don continued. "But that hope was colored by memories of earlier, happier days. When she lied to her husband and made him believe that I had attacked her, she forced Thaddeus to take action that ultimately resulted in his death. I have no doubt that wherever they went after that, she filled her son's head with lies about the things I had done. She must have blamed me for what happened to Thaddeus, when I was only defending myself. And now Ned has come to reap the evil his mother sowed."

"Maybe you could talk to him," Belinda suggested. "Maybe if you explained the truth about everything, he'd see that he's wrong to hate you."

Don Eduardo looked at Viola and said, "You talked with him, señora. Did he seem to you like the sort of man who would listen to reason?"

"Not at all," Viola answered without hesitation. "He's been nursing his hate for too long. I don't think he could put it aside now. It's all he has left."

Don Eduardo spread his hands and said to his wife, "You see? There is nothing to be done. We must wait."

"Wait and hope that John gets back here in time," Viola said. "That . . . and be ready to fight for our lives if we don't get any help."

The sun was nearly down when Stonewall and Hermosa came in sight of the ranch. John thought there might be some sort of trouble here, so Stonewall was more nervous than he would have liked to admit. He had been watching for smoke in the sky that would indicate burning buildings and listening for the sound of gunfire, although it was beyond him why any of the rustlers would have doubled back to attack the ranch.

Instead, the place looked quiet and peaceful in the fading light. From a distance, Stonewall could make out the trees, the roof of the house, the water tank standing to one side a little higher than anything else.

He and Hermosa reined in, and Stonewall heaved a sigh of relief.

"Looks like John was wrong for once," he said. "That sure doesn't happen very often. I reckon we can ride on in —"

Hermosa reached over and gripped his arm.

"Wait," the *vaquero* said.

"What is it?" Stonewall asked with a frown. "Everything looks fine to me."

"Look there." Hermosa pointed. "Above the water tank."

Stonewall squinted, and as he did, he made out several dark shapes wheeling through the air. They were little more than dots at this distance, but he had seen such things often enough in the past to recognize them.

"Those are buzzards," he said.

As he watched, one of the carrion birds dipped down toward the water tank and disappeared. It must have landed on top of the tank, Stonewall realized. The other buzzards continued to circle.

"Something is dead up there," Hermosa said, his voice flat.

"Maybe a . . . a rat?" Stonewall suggested as a ball of sick fear began to form in his belly.

Hermosa shook his head and said, "Not a rat. One of the *zopilotes* would have picked it up and carried it off by now. What's up there is too big for them to lift."

"Well, an animal of some other sort, then," Stonewall said, but even he could hear how hollow his voice had become.

"An animal, yes," Hermosa repeated with a grave nod. "A man."

"We can't be sure about that. Anyway, what in blazes would a man be doing on top of the water tank?"

"A man might be up there to work on it.

222

But a dead man?"

Hermosa's shoulders rose and fell in an expressive shrug.

Stonewall took off his hat and scrubbed a hand over his face. It seemed like a week since he'd had any sleep, and he'd been in the saddle for so long that every muscle in his body ached. But for a second there he had felt a lot better when he thought everything was fine on the ranch after all.

Hermosa had kicked that right out from under him. Everything the *vaquero* said was correct. There had to be a dead man on top of the water tank.

That might well mean the trouble here was already over.

Viola might already be —

Stonewall swallowed hard and clapped his hat back on his head. He wasn't going to believe that anything had happened to his big sister until he had undeniable proof of it. Viola had always been extremely capable of taking care of herself, so Stonewall was going to assume she was fine.

Thanks to Hermosa's keen eyes, though, he knew they couldn't afford to go riding in openly, as if nothing were wrong.

Hermosa seemed to be thinking the same thing. He asked, "Which approach has the most cover?"

Stonewall scratched his jaw in thought for a moment, then said, "It'll take longer, but we need to circle all the way around to the south, across the border. There are more trees and buildings if we come in that way. If we can make it to the barn and the corrals, we'll have a good view of the front of the house from there, and maybe we can tell what's going on."

Hermosa nodded in agreement with the plan, then glanced at the sky and said, "It will be dark in an hour or so. Trouble often comes with the twilight."

"If it does," Stonewall said, "we'll be ready for it."

CHAPTER 19

Night fell quickly in Arizona Territory once the sun dipped below the horizon. Normally that wasn't a problem, but Viola hated to see it happen tonight.

The darkness meant they couldn't see the enemy coming.

And come they would, she thought as she knelt at one of the front windows and watched the dusky shadows gathering.

It was getting even darker inside the house. When the maids started to light the lamps, as they normally did at this time of day, Viola had told them to stop and added that they should blow out the ones they'd already lit. She didn't want any of the defenders silhouetted against the glow so they would be even better targets.

A footstep beside her made Viola look around. Dr. Fredericks stood there, crouching a little so he could look out the window.

"Better move back, doctor," she said.

"There's no telling when they might start throwing lead through these windows."

Fredericks retreated quickly. He said, "I'm afraid you have more experience at this sort of thing than I do, Mrs. Slaughter. I deal with the aftermath of trouble. I rarely find myself squarely in the middle of it like this."

"I know, and I wish you weren't here now. Not that I don't appreciate any help you can give us —"

"I know what you mean," Fredericks said. "I could have driven away and not been trapped here." His voice took on a determined tone as he continued, "But I have patients here, so I'm glad I stayed. I have every confidence that we're all going to be all right."

"So do I," Viola said.

That was stretching the truth, she thought, but she knew better than to give up hope. She had come through some dangerous situations before, and John hadn't always been at her side during those times, either.

"I don't know much about this sort of thing," Fredericks went on. "What do you think they'll do?"

Viola had been pondering that quite a bit herself. She said, "Unless their numbers are overwhelming, I don't believe they'll launch a full-scale attack on the house. If they had that many men, they would have already done it. So it's more likely they'll try to drive us out into the open. The best way to do that is with fire."

"Fire," Fredericks repeated. Viola heard the worry in his voice. "You mean they'll try to set the house on fire."

"That's right."

"Flaming arrows on the roof, perhaps, to borrow a trick from the savages?"

Viola shook her head and said, "The roof is slate. It won't burn easily. They might try to shoot flaming arrows through the windows or get close enough to throw torches through them. It'll be up to us to keep them from succeeding."

"The other people who are wounded could probably get out of the house if they had to, but Don Eduardo shouldn't be moved too much," the doctor said. "It could be very dangerous for him." Fredericks paused. "But not more dangerous than staying in here while the place burns down around him, of course."

"Maybe it won't come to that. We'll do our best to see that it doesn't."

"You know," Fredericks mused, "if this man Becker wants Don Eduardo and Mrs. Rubriz alive, he can't just massacre everyone wholesale. He'll have to take prisoners."

"Only until he has the ones he wants," Viola pointed out.

"And then everyone else . . ."

"Will be a problem to be disposed of," she said.

A large rock cairn jutted up from the flat ground covered with scrub grass. Stonewall and Hermosa crouched behind it, each man peering past the cairn toward the barn and corrals about two hundred yards away.

The cairn marked the border between the United States and Mexico, and right now it provided some cover for Stonewall and Hermosa, too. Stonewall hoped that in the fading light their shapes would blend in with that of the marker in case anyone happened to look in this direction.

"I see no one moving around," Hermosa said quietly. "Perhaps the ranch is deserted."

"Maybe. That might not be a good thing, though."

Stonewall hadn't seen any signs of life as they approached, either. They had left their horses a quarter of a mile behind them and proceeded on foot for about half that distance before dropping to hands and knees and crawling the rest of the way to the border marker.

Stonewall listened intently. He didn't hear anything. A cloak of silence seemed to have been dropped over the ranch. That was unusual in itself. There were evening chores to do, and a lot of times there was horseplay going on around the bunkhouse. The quiet was ominous.

"We need to get closer," Stonewall said. They had brought their rifles with them, so he picked up his and went on, "You stay here and cover me. When I get to those trees" — he pointed to the cottonwoods that grew near the barn — "I'll stop there and you can come on across."

"The ground between here and there is wide open," Hermosa pointed out. "Anyone who looks in this direction will see you."

"Yeah, I know, but we're not doin' any good out here. I reckon we'll just hope that anybody around the place who ain't friendly will have their eyes on the house instead of back here."

The *vaquero* didn't argue with that. He simply picked up his Winchester and gave Stonewall a grim nod.

Stonewall tugged his hat down tighter on his head, then burst out from behind the border marker and ran toward the trees. He zigzagged a little, just in case anybody was trying to draw a bead on him.

Running in boots wasn't easy. Like most *hombres* who had practically grown up in the saddle, Stonewall figured that any job a man couldn't do from horseback usually wasn't worth doing.

This evening, though, he had no choice. He summoned up all the speed he could as he ran with the rifle held at a slant across his chest.

His heart hammered wildly in his chest, and not just from the exertion. His muscles were braced for the shock of a bullet at any second.

That shock never came. He reached the cottonwoods and slid to a stop among them, pressing his back to one of the tree trunks.

After standing there a moment with his chest heaving as he tried to catch his breath, he took off his hat and waved at Hermosa. From here, Stonewall couldn't see the *vaquero* behind the border marker even though he knew Hermosa was there.

Hermosa emerged from the cairn's shelter and loped toward the trees. Now that Stonewall had crossed the stretch of open ground without drawing any fire, Hermosa obviously didn't feel quite as much urgency. Despite that, his long legs covered the ground quickly, and he joined Stonewall in the trees.

Stonewall gestured toward the barn and said in a half-whisper, "We can get in there now and take a look at the house. I'll go first."

"Be careful," Hermosa advised. "If there are bad men around, some are likely to be in there."

"Yeah, I know. But there's only one way to find out."

Bending low, Stonewall ran through the gloom, past the corral, and up to the back of the barn. There was a door here. He had it open and slipped through in a matter of heartbeats.

The hinges squealed a little more than he liked, though.

He stopped just inside the barn. The shadows were thicker in here. The double doors at the front were almost completely closed, but not quite. When he looked along the center aisle he saw a thin line of grayish light, indicating the gap between the doors.

Stonewall listened again but didn't hear anything out of the ordinary. Several milk cows were kept in stalls in here, and he heard them moving around a little. They seemed restless, and one of them mooed plaintively. A couple of others joined in.

Those simple sounds told him something.

The cows hadn't been milked this evening, and they weren't happy about it.

That was the last bit of evidence he needed to tell him something was very wrong here. A chore like milking the cows never would have been neglected otherwise.

He sniffed the air. Manure, straw, animal flesh . . . those were the only things he smelled. Tobacco smoke would have told him that someone was in here.

Of course, just because nobody was smoking a quirly in the barn didn't mean he was the only human occupant, he reminded himself. Maybe somebody was just being careful not to give away their presence.

Stonewall started toward the double doors.

His booted feet made no sound on the hard-packed dirt of the center aisle. The walk through the barn wasn't long, but his nerves were stretched so tight it seemed to take him an hour.

Finally he was at the doors. He leaned forward and peered through the gap. From here he could look across the two roads and the large open area where the party had been held the previous night and see the house behind the picket fence.

In this poor light, he couldn't tell if any smoke rose from either of the two chimneys.

The house sat there dark and quiet, flanked by a couple of outbuildings and the water tank, some tall cottonwoods looming behind it, several shorter trees and shrubs in front of it.

Stonewall regarded this place as his home, but it sure didn't feel very welcoming at the moment.

He was about to return to the back door and hiss at Hermosa, indicating that the *vaquero* should join him, but before he could turn away from the door he heard a faint noise close behind him. It was only a tiny scrape of boot leather against dirt, but that was enough.

Stonewall dived down and to the side as something swished over his head. He heard a grunt and then somebody stumbled into him.

Whoever this man was, he might be a friend, attacking Stonewall because he didn't know who he was. Stonewall didn't want to hurt him until he found out what was going on here.

Then the man let out a harsh, vile curse and Stonewall didn't recognize his gravelly voice. Stonewall lowered his head and lunged forward. His shoulder rammed into the man's legs. Stonewall hooked an arm around his knees and heaved. The man let out a yell as he went over backward and crashed to the ground.

Stonewall scrambled onto his knees and swung the Winchester one-handed, hoping the barrel would strike his attacker in the head and knock him out. The blow missed, however, and Stonewall had to put his other hand down to catch himself as he lost his balance.

That left his chin hanging out in the open for the kick that the man swept around at him. The blow knocked Stonewall across the aisle. He lost his hat and the rifle as he rolled over a couple of times and came up hard against the gate across the front of one of the stalls.

He started to pull himself up but froze as he heard the unmistakable sound of a revolver being cocked.

"Who the hell are you, mister?" the gravelly voice demanded. "Speak up or I'll start shootin'."

Stonewall didn't say anything. He figured the stranger didn't really care who he was. He just wanted Stonewall to say something so he could shoot at the sound of his voice.

Now that the man had committed himself and given away his own position, though, he couldn't afford to wait very long. Sure enough, only a couple of seconds went by before the man's nerve broke and he squeezed the trigger. Stonewall saw Colt flame bloom in the darkness as the sound of the shot assaulted his ears. The bullet thudded into a board somewhere as Stonewall threw himself onto his belly and palmed out his own Colt.

The gun roared and bucked in his hand as he triggered twice, bracketing the spot where he had seen the muzzle flash. He figured the man had ducked one way or the other after firing.

His ears were ringing from the shots, but he heard a choked scream. The man fired again, but the shots were wild, spasmodic, as if his finger was jerking the trigger with no conscious thought. He emptied the gun, and then Stonewall heard something hit the ground with a soggy thud.

He pushed himself up but had to grab the stall gate with his free hand to keep from falling again. That kick to the jaw had shaken him up more than he realized at first. As he stood there he heard rapid footsteps slap against the dirt and lifted his gun to shoot again if he needed to.

"Stonewall!"

That was Hermosa's voice. Stonewall sagged a little as he recognized it.

"Here," he called. "But be careful, I don't

know how many of them are in here."

No more shots sounded. A moment later the *vaquero* gripped Stonewall's arm and asked, "You are all right, *amigo*?"

"Feel like a mule kicked me, but other than that I'm fine," Stonewall told him. "I think there must've only been one fella in here, and I'm pretty sure I got him."

"One more thing you can be sure of," Hermosa said grimly. "If there are more of them, they know now that we're here."

The shots made Becker stiffen and turn his head. He had been looking toward the house, but now he gazed toward the southwest.

"Did those shots come from the barn?" he snapped.

"Sounded like it," Herb Woodbury replied.

"Who's over there?"

"Walt Bryce, I think. Maybe he thought he saw somethin' and got spooked."

"No," Becker said, "I counted seven shots." He turned to the Apache. "Bodaway —"

"I will find out what happened," Bodaway said before Becker could finish. The Apache faded away into the shadows.

Once Bodaway was gone, Becker said to his *segundo,* "We're not going to wait any longer. The men have the torches ready?"

"Yeah, but those folks in the house are gonna be on edge now," Woodbury said. "It'll be harder to sneak up on 'em."

"Do it anyway," Becker ordered. "It's time to put an end to this."

Woodbury hesitated, then said, "Boss, you've already waited a long time for your revenge. Maybe it wouldn't hurt anything to wait until the redskin gets back and we find out what's goin' on."

"No," Becker said, his voice as hard and cold as ice. "Have the men set the place on fire now. It's judgment day for Don Eduardo Rubriz."

Inside the house, Viola's heart seemed to jump into her throat when she heard the shots. She could tell they came from the barn.

"Jess," she said to the foreman, who knelt at one of the other windows, "did we leave anybody out there?"

"Just Joe Sparkman on top of the water tank, ma'am," Fisher replied. "Everybody on the place except for him and the men who went with your husband is in this house."

"It couldn't have been Joe, so who were they shooting at?"

"Beats me. Shadows, maybe."

Viola didn't think so. She couldn't be sure, but she thought she'd heard two different weapons going off. She had been around enough gunfights to know one when she heard it.

Did that mean help had arrived? Was John back?

She didn't know, but for the first time in a while she actually felt hopeful again — but also more frightened because for all she knew, her husband might be in danger or even hurt.

"Keep a close eye out," she told Fisher. "That might have been a signal, and even if it wasn't, it might prod them into starting something."

"Yes, ma'am."

Time stretched out maddeningly as several minutes ticked by. The echoes of the shots had died away, leaving the ranch cloaked once more in that sinister silence.

Then Fisher exclaimed, "There!" and straightened up. The rifle in his hands cracked as he thrust the barrel through the open window.

Viola kept her attention focused on the area outside the window she was covering. She saw a sudden flare as someone snapped a match to life.

"Watch out!" Fisher called. "They've got torches!"

Viola squeezed off a shot and felt the rifle buck against her shoulder. As she worked the Winchester's lever she saw a small explosion of flame in the darkness. It spun toward her and she had to throw herself backward to keep from being hit by the torch as it sailed through the window.

The blazing brand landed on the floor, bounced a couple of times, and came to a stop. Viola smelled kerosene from the torch as the rug began to burn.

CHAPTER 20

"We need to get back outside where we can move around," Hermosa told Stonewall. "We do not want to get trapped inside this barn."

That sounded like good advice to Stonewall. Without wasting time checking on the man he had shot, he and Hermosa turned and hurried out the barn's rear door as soon as Stonewall found the rifle he'd dropped.

They headed for the trees. More shots split the gathering night, these coming from the direction of the house.

Alarm made Stonewall's heart slug heavily in his chest. He knew Viola was probably in the house, trying to defend it from whoever the intruders were. He wanted to reach her, to make sure his sister was all right.

But if he charged blindly into the middle of the fracas it was more likely he would just get himself killed, and that wouldn't be any help to Viola at all.

Stonewall spotted a garish orange glare through the trees that made his already taut nerves constrict even more. He pointed it out to Hermosa and whispered urgently, "They're tryin' to set the house on fire!"

"It seems they are trying to make those inside flee."

"How can we stop 'em?"

"It may be too late for that."

The *vaquero*'s voice was grim, and Stonewall saw why. The flames were growing brighter. From here it looked like the house might already be on fire.

Rifle reports came from the northeast. Stonewall looked in that direction and spotted the flicker of muzzle flashes several hundred yards away. He pointed them out to Hermosa and said, "That's where the schoolhouse is. The kids of the married hands have classes there whenever John's got somebody around who can teach 'em."

"It appears to be where the invaders have taken cover," Hermosa said. "Is there a way to get behind it without crossing open ground where we would be seen?"

The question made an idea leap into Stonewall's head. He said, "There's a ditch that runs parallel with the road. If we stay pretty low, we can follow it most of the way and they shouldn't be able to spot us."

Hermosa nodded and said, "Let us go."

Stonewall dashed through the darkness. Full night had fallen now and the moon hadn't risen yet, so they had that on their side, anyway. But the silvery light of millions of stars was scattered down over the landscape. They could have used a few clouds to block that starlight, but the sky was dazzlingly clear, as it often was in this part of the country.

Stonewall reached the ditch, which was about five feet deep and six wide, and dropped into it. It had been dug to bring water to the trees near the barn when one of the infrequent rains fell. That hadn't occurred in a good while, though, so the sandy bottom was dry as a bone.

Stonewall crouched low and moved along at a fast trot with Hermosa following close behind him. The ditch ran for approximately five hundred yards, ending at the little lane beside the ranch cemetery.

The two men had covered about half that distance when a dark shape suddenly loomed up in front of Stonewall.

He barely had time to realize somebody was there before the man lunged forward and crashed into him, driving him back into Hermosa. The surprise attack knocked both of them into the bottom of the ditch.

Stonewall had the presence of mind to thrust his Winchester straight up and ram the barrel into the attacker's belly. Foul breath spewed into his face.

Hermosa writhed free of Stonewall's weight and surged up to tackle the man who had jumped them. As the two of them locked in hand-to-hand struggle, Hermosa gasped to Stonewall, "Go on! Help your sister!"

Stonewall didn't want to leave Hermosa, but he figured if anybody could take care of himself, it was the *vaquero*. Besides, Viola's safety had to come first. Stonewall scrambled to his feet, leaped past the two men, and ran along the ditch.

The shooting continued from the direction of the house as he reached the end of the ditch and climbed out to race past the cemetery. He was farther east now than the place where the schoolhouse sat, so the men using the adobe brick building for cover wouldn't be likely to see him as he circled in behind them.

He spared a thought for Hermosa and hoped the *vaquero* was all right. Then he turned his attention to the task before him. He was only one man and knew he would be outnumbered, but that might not matter if he could take his enemies by surprise and get the drop on them.

As he slipped into the trees behind the schoolhouse, he heard horses nearby, blowing and stamping. It made sense that whoever was attacking the ranch would leave their horses back here where they were more out of harm's way.

Stonewall catfooted among the cottonwoods and made his way carefully toward the animals. When he was close enough he could see them, a large, dark, restless mass. He thought one of the gunmen might be watching the horses, but apparently they were just tied back here.

Unsure whether to be disappointed or relieved — Stonewall had thought he might jump the horse guard and knock the man out of the fight, but that also would have meant the risk of getting caught himself — he moved closer and murmured to the horses so he wouldn't spook them even more. He took hold of a pair of taut reins, followed them to the sapling where they were fastened, and untied them. The horse pulled away.

One by one, Stonewall untied the other mounts. He didn't try to stampede the horses because that would have drawn attention to him. Instead he just let them drift away. Whoever the invaders were and whatever they wanted, they wouldn't be able to make a quick getaway now.

With that done, he moved closer to the schoolhouse. He had counted fourteen horses. The man he had shot in the barn and the *hombre* he and Hermosa had run into in the ditch accounted for two of their owners.

That left an even dozen men to carry out the assault on the house. Some of them had crept close enough to throw torches at the house and try to set it on fire.

Thankfully, they didn't seem to have succeeded. The orange glow that had blazed up briefly had died back down. The defenders must have put out the fire.

That didn't mean this bunch of killers would give up, however. They would try something else, unless Stonewall managed somehow to stop them.

He didn't get the chance to try. He heard something behind him, started to turn in the hope that Hermosa had disposed of his opponent and caught up to him, but instead he caught a glimpse in the starlight of a cruel, savage face framed by black hair bound back by a bandanna.

Apache!

That was Stonewall's last thought before

something exploded against his head and sent him tumbling down into an all-consuming blackness.

Viola reacted instantly when the rug blazed up from the kerosene-soaked torch. She grabbed one edge of the rug, lifted it, and threw it over the flames.

Then she lunged on top of it, snuffing out the fire with the rug and her own weight.

This wasn't the only place the attackers had succeeded in getting a torch inside the house, though. She heard shouting in some of the other rooms that told her the defenders there were battling other blazes.

With the stink of kerosene and burned rug in her nose, she grabbed the rifle she had dropped and leaped back to the window. She saw a man drawing back his arm to throw another of the burning brands and snapped a shot at him.

Instinct guided the bullet. The man cried out, spun around, and dropped the torch at his feet as he collapsed. The grass along the fence was fairly dry at this time of year. It caught fire and sent flames dancing along the man's body.

The fact that he didn't move told Viola she had killed him. That might bother her later, but at the moment it left her unmoved.

The man had attacked her home. As far as she was concerned he deserved whatever happened to him.

"Mrs. Slaughter, are you all right?"

The urgent question came from Dr. Fredericks behind her. Without looking around she said, "I'm fine, doctor. What about everyone else?"

"No one is hurt except for a few minor burns."

"The other fires?"

"They're out — for now. We were lucky they didn't spread too much. Your house sustained some damage, though."

"Damage can be repaired," Viola said. "A house can be rebuilt, if it comes to that. As long as we don't lose any more people, that's all I really care about."

She watched over the windowsill as the grass along the road continued to burn. The fire was bright for a few minutes, but then it began to die down as the fuel was exhausted. The smell of smoke lingered in the air.

From the window where he was posted, Jess Fisher said, "I don't see anybody else moving around out there. Looks like they've all pulled back except for that fella you drilled, Mrs. Slaughter."

As the smoke drifted over the house, Viola

caught a whiff of a sickly sweet smell that made her stomach turn over unpleasantly. She knew it came from the body of the man she had killed, which had been charred by the flames around it. She gagged a little at the thought.

"Mrs. Slaughter?" Fredericks asked.

"I'll be fine," she managed to say. "Don't worry, doctor."

"It's the smell, isn't it? It always got to me, too, during the war. I was a surgeon in the Union army, you know. It wasn't the things I saw in the field hospitals that bothered me the most, although Lord knows they were bad enough. It was always the smells."

Viola took a handful of .44-40 cartridges and concentrated on thumbing them through the Winchester's loading gate. Once she took her mind off what had happened, she found that her stomach calmed down quickly.

She had a job to do — defending this ranch — and she couldn't allow anything to interfere with that.

No matter how many men she had to kill.

Becker paced back and forth angrily behind the schoolhouse as Woodbury tried to explain how the defenders must have been

248

able to put out all the fires before they spread too much.

"I can see that," Becker interrupted. "I can see that the damned house isn't on fire like it's supposed to be. Did that failure cost us any men?"

"Pony Chamberlain didn't make it back," Woodbury said as he shook his head ruefully. "One of the boys told me Pony got hit just as he was about to throw his torch. He dropped it and it set fire to the grass around him instead. He must've been dead, 'cause he didn't move while it burned him."

"Serves him right for letting himself get shot," Becker muttered. Then he saw the surprised, upset look on his *segundo*'s face and knew he had gone too far. He added, "We'll make the bastards pay for killing him."

That seemed to mollify Woodbury. He nodded and said, "We damn sure will." He paused, then asked, "What are we gonna do now, boss?"

That was a frustrating question. Nothing they had tried so far had worked.

Before Becker could answer, Bodaway emerged from the trees carrying something draped over his shoulders. As the Apache came closer, Becker's eyes widened in surprise. Bodaway's burden was the body of a man, either unconscious or dead.

Bodaway came up to Becker and Wood-bury and dumped the body in front of them. In the starlight, Becker could tell that the man was young, with fair hair and a dark smear of blood across his face from a cut on his forehead.

"Who's this?" Becker demanded. "I thought all of Slaughter's people were holed up in the house."

"I found this one and another man trying to get behind you," Bodaway explained. "This one had reached the trees and turned your horses loose before I caught up to him."

A curse exploded from Becker's mouth. He turned to Woodbury and ordered, "Go get those horses rounded up."

Woodbury hurried to obey as Becker turned back to his old friend.

"Is he dead?" he asked as he nodded at the young man lying on the ground.

"Not this one. I left the other in a ditch over there."

Bodaway waved vaguely toward the barn.

"What about those shots earlier?"

"Your man in the barn is dead, as you thought."

"So we've lost two men," Becker said. "That's got to stop. Why didn't you go ahead and kill this son of a bitch?"

"I thought you might be able to make use of him. He is Señora Slaughter's brother."

That came as a surprise to Becker, too. He said, "How in the world do you know that?"

"Last night, before my men and I raided the party, I overheard some of the people talking while I was still hiding in the dark. I learned then that Viola Slaughter is his sister."

A smile tugged at Becker's thin lips as he looked down at the unconscious young man.

"Well, now," he said, "that was good thinking on your part, Bodaway, bringing him here alive instead of killing him. This little bastard might just come in handy."

CHAPTER 21

Stonewall wasn't out cold for long. He was a little surprised when he regained consciousness to find that he was still alive.

When the last thing you saw before you passed out was the cruel face of a bloodthirsty Apache warrior, you didn't really expect to wake up again.

It was obvious he wasn't dead, though. Not with the way his head hurt from being walloped like that. Unless that pounding racket was Satan's own imps playing a drum inside his skull instead of his own pulse.

No, he heard human voices somewhere nearby. He was definitely alive.

But that didn't mean he was all right. He could still be in a mighty bad spot. The next step was to open his eyes and find out exactly what was going on.

Easier said than done. Each eyelid seemed to weigh at least a thousand pounds, and he lacked the strength to lift them.

Finally he pried them up, and when he did he saw that he was lying on the ground with trees around him. Figures moved vaguely nearby. Those were the men he'd heard talking a moment earlier, he thought.

They didn't seem to be paying much attention to him. Maybe he could get up and slip away into the night. It was worth trying.

Or it would have been if he could move, he realized. As he tested his muscles, he discovered that he was tied hand and foot. Someone had pulled his arms behind his back and lashed his wrists together. Likewise a length of rope was bound around his ankles.

They hadn't gagged him, though. He could yell all he wanted to — for all the good that would do. He didn't figure there was anybody close by who would want to help him.

Actually, it might be better if they didn't even know he had come to, he decided. That way he stood a better chance of eavesdropping on his captors and figuring out his best course of action.

Sooner or later he would get a chance to make a bold, unexpected move, he told himself, and when the proper moment came, he needed to be ready.

At first he thought his eyes were adjusting to the starlight, but over the next few minutes as everything became brighter and took on a more silvery hue, Stonewall realized the moon was coming up. He could make out his surroundings a little better. The dark mass about fifty yards away became the double-cabin schoolhouse where the kids on the ranch were taught their lessons.

He even saw the Apache who had captured him, talking to a tall, lean man who held himself like he was the boss around here.

That *hombre* would soon find out how wrong he was, Stonewall told himself. When John Slaughter got back, everything would be different. He was the only boss on this ranch.

Except for Viola, of course.

The two men stopped talking and turned to walk toward him. Stonewall slitted his eyes as he watched them approach. He didn't move a muscle or give any other sign that he was conscious.

Turned out that was wasted effort on his part, because the first thing the tall white man did when he walked up was to draw back his foot and kick Stonewall in the side. The brutal blow made Stonewall gasp and jerk.

"Wake up, if you're not already," the man said. He hunkered on his heels next to Stonewall. "You hear me, boy?"

"I . . . hear you," Stonewall grated through the pain in his side. Felt like the son of a buck might've cracked one of his ribs.

"I know you're Stonewall Howell, John Slaughter's brother-in-law, so don't even think about lying to me. Where's Slaughter?"

"I don't know."

The man stood up and kicked him again, this time in the left shoulder. Pain shot down that arm for an agonizing few seconds before it went numb.

"I told you not to lie to me. You went with Slaughter when he chased after those rustled cattle. Why are you back here so soon?"

"My horse . . . went lame."

"That's a lie, too. Slaughter would have taken extra horses. And even if it were true, why would that other *hombre* come back with you?"

So they knew about Hermosa. Stonewall wondered if the Apache was the man they had run into in the ditch. If he was, the Indian's presence here didn't bode well for Hermosa.

"Did Slaughter send you back?" the man went on. "Did he know there was going to

255

be trouble here at the ranch?"

"Mister . . . John Slaughter's my boss . . . not just my brother-in-law. I don't ask him . . . to explain himself . . . I just do . . . what he tells me."

"So he told you to come back. Well, I thought as much. I don't suppose it really matters what tipped him off. I've heard that Slaughter is a pretty smart man. Now here's the important question."

The man placed his foot on Stonewall's shoulder, the one he had kicked a few minutes earlier, and bore down on it. Stonewall groaned as he felt his bones grinding together under the pressure.

"How far behind you is Slaughter? When will he get here?"

Stonewall couldn't answer because the pain in his shoulder made him throw his head back as a grimace stretched his mouth. After a moment his captor let up, and as the weight went away, the pain eased.

"I don't . . . know," Stonewall panted in a whisper. "I really . . . don't."

The man hunkered beside him again and said, "You think what I've been doing to you is bad? This man beside me, he's called *El Infierno*. The Fires of Hell. The name suits him, too. If you don't tell me what I want to know, I'm going to turn you over to him and let him ask the questions for a while. You think you'll like that any better?"

Anger welled up inside Stonewall. This *hombre* thought he could just waltz in here, kill people and raise all sorts of havoc, and then demand answers. Stonewall said, "Why don't you . . . go to hell?"

The Apache moved a step closer.

The white man raised a hand to stop him and said, "No, that's all right. I know you'd enjoy working on him, Bodaway, but we don't have time to waste. There's too good a chance Slaughter is headed back and will get here before morning."

He straightened and prodded Stonewall in the side with a boot toe. It wasn't really a kick this time, but it hurt anyway.

"Get him on his feet," the man ordered. "We can make use of him whether he talks or not."

Stonewall didn't like the sound of that.

Viola didn't know what Becker would try next, but with the rising of the moon she doubted if the invaders would attempt to sneak up on the house again. The moon was three-quarters full and cast a lot of light over the area around the ranch house.

She had started wondering about Joe Sparkman up on the water tank. She hadn't heard any shots from there during the earlier skirmish, and she was afraid Becker's men might have spotted him and killed him.

If that turned out to be true, it was one more score against Ned Becker that would need settling. Viola hadn't even known Sparkman's name before today, but if he was dead, he had died fighting for the Slaughter Ranch and he would be avenged.

Dr. Fredericks came up to the window where Viola had posted herself and said, "Don Eduardo wants to talk to you."

"I'm a little busy," Viola said without taking her eyes off the stretch of ground in front of the window.

Fredericks chuckled and held out his hand. He said, "Give me the rifle. I'll spell you long enough for you to go talk to the don. I told you before, I know how to use a gun."

Viola had to admit to herself that it would feel good to get up and move around a little. She had been kneeling here for quite a while. She made up her mind and handed the Winchester to Fredericks, then grasped the side of the window to brace herself as she stood up. She made sure to stay out of a direct line of fire.

"I'm not as young as I used to be," she commented as stiff muscles protested the movement.

"My dear lady, you're a child compared to most of us."

"I don't know about that. I'd say that Doña Belinda is a little younger than me. Is she still with her husband?"

"She's asleep in one of the chairs." Fredericks paused. "That may be why the don asked to speak with you. I think he was waiting for her to doze off."

Viola wasn't sure what that meant, but there was one way to find out. She nodded to Fredericks and went into the parlor. She didn't need a lamp to find her way around. She knew every square inch of this house, and even if she didn't, enough moonlight came in through the windows to reveal the shapes of the furniture.

Don Eduardo was sitting up on the sofa with pillows propped behind him. Fredericks must have thought that was all right since he'd just been in here. Viola went over to the sofa, perched on the arm, and said, "The doctor told me you wanted to talk to me, Don Eduardo."

He nodded and slowly lifted an arm to point at a wing chair set against the wall. Viola could make out Belinda's huddled form as she slept, claimed again by exhaustion.

"I thought while my wife was asleep I should take the opportunity to speak with you again, Señora Slaughter."

"Something you don't want Doña Belinda to hear?" Viola smiled. "If you're planning on flirting with me, Don Eduardo, you should realize by now that I'm a happily married woman."

The don laughed quietly and said, "I do realize that, señora. I only wish my Belinda was as happily married."

Viola tried not to wince. She hoped that he wasn't about to confide in her. She didn't want to hear his suspicions that his wife was cheating on him. In these desperate circumstances, if he did that she wasn't sure she could keep what she knew to herself.

"Her husband is a very stubborn man, though," Rubriz went on.

"Are you saying that my husband isn't stubborn? Because if you are, you don't know John Slaughter very well."

"No, I was talking only about my determination to do what must be done. I have to turn myself over to Ned Becker. If you will help me, señora, we can accomplish that while Belinda sleeps, so she will not try to stop me."

Viola didn't try to hide her irritation as she said, "We've already talked about this.

We're not going to give Becker what he wants. Anyway, it wouldn't do any good, since he's said that we have to surrender Doña Belinda to him as well as you."

"I am the one he really wants," Don Eduardo insisted. "I am the one he blames for his father's death. It was many, many years after that tragic occurrence before I even met Belinda. She had nothing to do with it. Surely once he has me in his power, he will see that and be satisfied."

"Satisfied to kill you, you mean."

Carefully, probably because of the bullet hole in his side, Don Eduardo shrugged.

"If such is to be my fate, I will regret it, of course. But I have enjoyed my life for the most part and if it is destined to end now, I can accept that."

"If my husband was here, he would tell you that we make our own destinies, Don Eduardo. John has always lived by that code."

The don let out a weary sigh and said, "People have died, Señora Slaughter. How many, I don't know, but more than should have because of me. It is my wish that no one else should die because of Ned Becker's hatred for me."

"That argument might work if I really believed he would let the rest of us go. But

261

that's never going to happen, and we both know it. He's a madman. If he gets his way, he'll kill us all, to cover his trail if for no other reason."

The moonlight was bright enough for Viola to see the tired but determined expression on the don's face. She wished he would stop wasting his energy arguing with her. She tried another tactic to get him to understand.

"Anyway, what would you do if your home was attacked and a lunatic wanted to kill one of your guests?" she asked. "Would you step back and let that happen?"

He glared at her for a few seconds, then abruptly laughed.

"You are an intelligent woman, Señora Slaughter. You appeal to my sense of honor, knowing that it means more to me than almost anything else in the world. Only two things mean more: my wife and my son."

Who are cuckolding you, thought Viola. That became less urgent, though, in a life-or-death situation such as the one in which they found themselves.

She stood up and said, "I'm sorry, Don Eduardo, we're not going to allow you to surrender —"

"Mrs. Slaughter," Dr. Fredericks said from the parlor doorway with a note of urgency in his voice. "Mr. Fisher says you need to come back in here right now."

That set Viola's heart to tripping faster. Something was happening, and under the circumstances she doubted if it could be anything good.

As she hurried past Fredericks, she told him, "Keep an eye on Don Eduardo. Don't let him do anything foolish."

"You can depend on me," Fredericks assured her as he handed over the rifle.

Viola took the Winchester and went over to the window where Jess Fisher was crouched.

"What is it?" she asked the foreman.

He nodded toward the road in front of the house and said, "They showed up out there a minute ago. I passed the word for everybody to hold their fire."

She looked through the window and gasped as she saw three figures standing in the road. The moonlight was bright enough for her to recognize Ned Becker as one of them. One of the other men appeared to be an Apache warrior.

And the third man, standing between Becker and the Indian with his hands tied behind his back, Becker's gun to his head, and the Apache's knife to his throat, was her brother Stonewall.

CHAPTER 22

Stonewall bit back a groan of despair as he stood there in the road between Becker and Bodaway. He hated the fact that he was being used as a weapon against his own sister.

Surely Viola was smart enough not to give these bastards what they wanted, no matter how much they threatened him. Even if she cooperated, they would double-cross her and kill everybody. He was sure of it.

"Mrs. Slaughter!" Becker called. "You hear me in there?"

"I hear you."

That was Viola's voice, all right, and the faint tremble in it told Stonewall that she was mad. Not scared, as somebody else might think if they heard it, but deep down, nail-chewing, blood-spitting mad. Stonewall knew that because he had been on the receiving end of such anger from her before. Not often, but enough to never forget it.

"You better listen to me," Becker went on.

"You can see I've got your brother. My thumb on the hammer of this gun is all that's keeping me from blowing his brains out, so don't get any ideas about trying some fancy trick shot. Anyway, even if you managed to kill me without this gun going off, my friend here would cut the little bastard's throat wide open before I even hit the ground."

"We're holding our fire," Viola said. "What do you want?"

Becker laughed.

"Why, you know that as well as I do. I want Don Eduardo and his wife, and I want you to surrender, as well. I plan to make a clean sweep of this when Rubriz's son gets back, and I don't want your husband interfering with that."

"You've gone to all this trouble and killed all those people for nothing, Becker," Viola responded. "Don Eduardo wasn't responsible for your father's death. Whatever your mother told you about what happened years ago was a lie."

Becker stiffened. Stonewall felt the muzzle of the man's gun press harder against his head. For a second he thought that Viola's words might have just gotten him killed.

Becker controlled himself enough not to shoot. He yelled, "You're a lying bitch! Rubriz is a murderer, and he has to pay for what he did. I'll see to it that he loses everything he holds dear before he dies! He'll be begging me to kill him and put him out of his misery!"

So that was what was going on, Stonewall thought. Some sort of loco vengeance quest. It made sense now, or at least as much sense as a scheme hatched by a lunatic could make.

Viola said, "If you let my brother go and ride away, you can make it into Mexico before anyone can stop you. The authorities down there probably won't come after you. This senseless killing can stop here and now."

"It's not senseless," Becker insisted. "It's justice. Rubriz deserves to die for his crimes, and anybody who gets in the way of that, well, it's just too bad about what happens to them."

Talking wasn't easy with the Apache's knife against his throat, but Stonewall croaked, "Mister, you're wastin' your time. I've known my sister all my life, and she's the stubbornest woman on the face of the earth. She'll never give you what you want."

"Not even to save your life?" Becker asked as his lips twisted in a snarl.

"Not even for that," Stonewall said. He

knew it was true, too. Viola would never back down in the face of evil.

"Well, that's her mistake. She'll see that I'm not bluffing." Becker's voice shook with the depth of his anger. "Bodaway —"

Stonewall figured Becker was about to order the Apache to cut his throat. He tensed, readying himself to make a desperate, last-ditch move that probably wouldn't accomplish a damned thing.

Before Becker could finish what he was about to say, Viola called, "Wait!"

An arrogant grin spread across Becker's face in the moonlight as he said, "So, you're ready to listen to reason, are you, Mrs. Slaughter?"

"You're the one who needs to listen," Viola said. "You've overplayed your hand again, Mr. Becker. If you kill my brother, we won't have any reason to hold our fire. You and your Apache friend will be riddled with lead before you can take two steps." She paused. "I'd say what we have here is a standoff . . . and the only way for you to break it is to release my brother, back away, and get off this ranch."

Becker's breath hissed angrily between his teeth. He said, "You're a fool. Do you think I'll give up my revenge that easily?"

"You can't get your revenge if you're

dead," Viola pointed out.

She was right, of course. Becker had believed he could waltz in here and terrorize his way into getting what he wanted.

It hadn't occurred to him that he would run up against a woman with a backbone of tempered steel. No matter how this turned out, Stonewall was proud of his sister.

The tension in the air would have continued to stretch out until it snapped, and there was no telling what sort of explosion might have resulted from that.

But before that could happen, an unsteady figure stumbled out of the shadows next to the house, extended shaking hands toward the men in the road, and called, "Ned! Ned, please don't do this! Don't hurt these people when the one you really want is me!"

"Rubriz!" Becker exclaimed.

The gun barrel came away from Stonewall's head as Becker's instincts made him jerk the weapon toward the don.

In the same instant, the front door of the ranch house slammed open as Doña Belinda charged outside screaming, "Eduardo!"

The Apache's knife moved away from Stonewall's neck just slightly, and he knew this would be his only chance. He lowered his head and rammed his shoulder into the man beside him.

Don Eduardo's sudden appearance outside took Viola by such surprise that for a moment all she could do was stare at him as he stumbled erratically toward the road.

Then Belinda rushed through the front room, threw the door open, and ran outside as well before anyone could stop her.

"Everyone hold your fire!" Viola shouted as she lunged to her feet and headed for the door, too.

Maybe she could grab Belinda and wrestle the blonde back inside before something happened to her.

As she emerged from the house, she caught a glimpse of Stonewall fighting with the Apache. She wasn't sure her brother was a match for the savage warrior, but she didn't have time right now to try to help him. She went after Belinda instead, who had just about reached Don Eduardo.

Unfortunately, so had Ned Becker. Becker could have gunned down Don Eduardo easily by now, but obviously just killing him wasn't enough to satisfy the crazed need for revenge that Becker felt.

Don Eduardo leaped between Becker and his wife and cried, "Belinda, get back!" She ignored him and grabbed his arm instead as he almost fell.

Becker was close enough to lash out with the gun in his hand. The barrel slammed against Don Eduardo's head and battered him to his knees as Belinda screamed. Viola lifted her rifle but couldn't get a shot at Becker because as Don Eduardo collapsed, Belinda threw herself at Becker and clawed at his face with her fingernails. She was directly in Viola's line of fire.

Viola had no idea what else was going on around the ranch house. All hell could have been breaking loose for all she knew. She ran closer, hoping to get a clear shot at Becker even though she knew that if she killed him, the rest of his men would probably open fire on her.

Becker swung his left arm in a backhanded blow that cracked across Belinda's face and sent her spinning off her feet. Then he lunged at Viola. She fired the Winchester, but Becker twisted aside at the last second and the bullet screamed harmlessly past him. He grabbed the rifle barrel and wrenched it aside.

The next instant a blow exploded against the side of Viola's head. The Winchester slid from her suddenly nerveless fingers. She felt herself hit the ground, then knew nothing after that.

Stonewall panted as he struggled against the Apache called Bodaway. His left hand was locked around Bodaway's right wrist, holding the knife away from his body. Stonewall's right hand had hold of Bodaway's throat. He dug in his thumb and fingers as hard as he could.

But Bodaway's left hand gripped Stonewall's throat, cutting off his air, and Stonewall knew it was a race to see who passed out first. The Apache was lithe and incredibly strong, a man whose business in life, basically, was killing.

Stonewall was young and strong, too, though. He just didn't know how long he could hold out. Already crimson rockets were exploding behind his eyes.

The sound of a shot nearby made Stonewall flinch. From the corner of his eye, he had seen Viola run out of the house a few seconds earlier, and he was afraid she might have been hit.

That distraction was enough to allow Bodaway to switch tactics. He let go of Stonewall's throat and hammered a fist into his temple instead. That blow was enough to stun Stonewall, already on the verge of passing out from being choked. His grip slipped off Bodaway's wrist, and he expected to feel eight inches of cold, deadly steel penetrating his throat or chest.

Instead Bodaway slammed the knife's handle against Stonewall's head. That finished the job of knocking him unconscious for the second time tonight.

If he had been awake, Stonewall wouldn't have given good odds on the chances of him waking up this time, either.

As soon as Mrs. Slaughter fell unconscious at Becker's feet, out of the line of fire, a rifle blasted from the house and a bullet whistled past his head. He crouched and looked around. Bodaway had just knocked Stonewall Howell to the ground.

"Leave the kid!" Becker called to his old friend. "Grab Mrs. Slaughter instead."

Becker then bent down, took hold of Belinda Rubriz's arm, and jerked her to her feet.

"You're coming with us, Don Eduardo," he ordered, then shouted, "Herb, give us some cover!"

Instantly, a barrage of rifle fire ripped out from the schoolhouse. Bullets slammed into the ranch house and forced the defenders to duck. Becker ran toward the school, forcing a stumbling Don Eduardo in front of him at gunpoint while he dragged the half-senseless Belinda.

Behind them trotted Bodaway with Viola Slaughter's unconscious form draped over his shoulders as Stonewall had been earlier. Even without the covering fire provided by Herb Woodbury and the other outlaws, the people in the house wouldn't have been able to shoot for fear of hitting Viola.

Things hadn't gone exactly according to plan, Becker thought, but they never did. The key to his genius lay in his ability to adapt his plan to the circumstances, whatever they might be.

A few moments later, he and Bodaway reached the schoolhouse with their prisoners. Stonewall Howell had been left behind, but that was all right. Becker had traded Stonewall for his sister, and that was a swap he would make any time.

John Slaughter would have been concerned about his brother-in-law's safety, of course, but he would be even more worried about his wife.

"Boss, are you all right?" Woodbury asked as the firing slacked off now that Becker and Bodaway were safe.

"I'm fine," Becker replied. "We've got what we need. We can get out of here now."

Woodbury frowned in confusion and said, "I thought we were gonna burn the place to the ground and kill any witnesses."

"That's not necessary. I've decided that we're going to finish this somewhere else."

Bodaway said, "Barranca Sangre."

Becker nodded.

"That's right. Slaughter's going to bring Santiago Rubriz there — alone — if he ever wants to see his wife alive again." He gave the whimpering Belinda a shove toward Woodbury and continued, "Hang on to her and see that she doesn't get away. You won't like what happens if she does, Herb."

Woodbury holstered his gun and took hold of Belinda with both hands. She shuddered and tried to pull away from him, but his grip was too strong.

Don Eduardo said, "You don't have to do this, Ned. Take me and let Belinda and Señora Slaughter stay here. They have nothing to do with your grudge against me."

"Forget it," Becker snapped. "You're all going. This isn't going to be over, Rubriz, until you've lost everything just like I did."

"You cannot mean that."

"The hell I don't." Becker looked at the Apache and went on, "Keep an eye on things while I write a note to leave for Slaughter. I want to be sure he knows exactly what to do to keep his wife from dying." Becker smiled. "At least . . . to keep her from dying too soon."

CHAPTER 23

Slaughter, Santiago, and the other men caught up to the hands driving the herd back to the ranch late in the afternoon.

Slaughter paused long enough to ask one of the cowboys, "Were you able to round up all the cattle after they scattered to hell and gone like that?"

The man tipped his hat back and nodded. "Yeah, I think so, boss. Pert-near all of 'em, anyway. What happened up yonder in the mountains? Did you catch up to those rustlers?"

"We did," Slaughter said grimly. "A couple of the scoundrels got away, but they were running so hard I doubt if we'll ever see them in this part of the country again."

"I reckon that means the others didn't get away."

"That's right. And we found out what this is all about, too." He didn't offer any further explanation, just asked, "How many men will it take to drive this herd back to the ranch?"

"Well . . . it'd be a lot of work, but four men could probably handle 'em, I reckon," the cowboy replied.

"All right. You'll be one of those four, Hal. Pick three more. The rest are coming with me back to the ranch as fast as we can get there."

"There really is trouble back there?" the cowboy asked with a worried look on his weatherbeaten face.

"I'll be surprised if there's not," Slaughter said.

A short time later, with a larger force behind him now, Slaughter was on the move again. When he looked at the sun hanging low in the sky, he knew it would be long after dark before they could reach the ranch. He hoped that whatever Ned Becker had planned, Viola and the men left behind at the ranch could handle it until reinforcements arrived.

As Santiago rode beside him, the young man said, "I'm sorry my family's history has brought danger to your family, Señor Slaughter. All this had nothing to do with you."

Slaughter grunted and said, "Wrong place at the wrong time, as the old saying goes, I suppose. Becker must have known that he couldn't make a move against your father on his own ranch. Don Eduardo was too well-defended there. He waited until the don was away from home and thought that would be easier."

"But that was foolish on his part, waiting until my father was visiting the famous Texas John Slaughter."

With a bleak, icy smile, Slaughter said, "The jury's still out on that. So far I haven't managed to do a hell of a lot to disrupt Becker's plans, whatever they may be."

"How could you know what to do when we didn't find out he was involved with this until a short time ago?"

Santiago had a point there, but it didn't make Slaughter feel any better.

Nothing was going to accomplish that until he got home and saw for himself that his wife was safe.

Slaughter pushed men and horses as hard as he could, but it was still hours after sundown by the time they approached the ranch. Stonewall and Hermosa should have gotten there quite a while earlier, though, so he hoped they had been able to give Viola a hand in case of trouble.

Stonewall was young but not green. He

had considerable experience as one of Slaughter's deputies, as well as being a top hand on the ranch. And Hermosa was a fighting man through and through, in Slaughter's judgment.

Slaughter had been watching the sky to the south. He knew the sort of orange glow that appeared whenever something big was on fire . . . like a ranch house. He hadn't seen anything of the sort, so that gave him hope.

He called a halt when he judged that he and his companions were about half a mile from their destination. As he leaned forward in the saddle he listened intently.

Santiago must have been doing the same thing, because after a moment the young man said, "I don't hear any gunfire."

"Neither do I," Slaughter said.

"That is a good sign, surely."

Slaughter shook his head and said, "Not necessarily. It may just mean that the fighting is over."

And that everyone there is dead, he added to himself, but he couldn't put that dire thought into words.

Slaughter heeled his horse into motion again. He rode at a more deliberate pace now. It was possible that some sort of ambush was waiting for them at the ranch, and he didn't want to charge blindly into it.

As they came closer he saw lights. Lots of lights, in fact, as if every lamp in the house was ablaze. That was cause for alarm in itself. Under normal circumstances, by this time of the evening everyone on the ranch would be settling down for a good night's sleep.

Slaughter's nerves wouldn't take it anymore. He kicked his horse into a gallop that didn't end until he hauled back on the reins and swung down from the saddle at the gate in the fence in front of the ranch house. Santiago and the rest of the men weren't far behind him.

The people in the house must have heard the hoofbeats. Slaughter hoped to see Viola step out of the front door and come onto the porch.

Instead it was the burly figure of the doctor from Douglas, Neal Fredericks, that appeared. Fredericks stood on the porch and wiped his hands on a rag.

In the light that spilled through the doorway and the windows, Slaughter saw the crimson splotches on the rag and knew they were bloodstains.

He threw the gate open and hurried into the yard.

"Doctor," he called. "What's happened

here? Where's Viola?"

"I have bad news, John," Fredericks said as Slaughter bounded up the steps to the porch.

Slaughter's hand closed tightly around the doctor's arm. Fredericks winced a little but didn't pull away.

"By God, don't tell me she's dead," Slaughter said. "Don't you tell me that."

"I don't know. She was alive when she left here, that's all I can be sure of."

"When she . . . left here?" Slaughter repeated, confused now. "Where in blazes did she go?"

"A man named Becker took her, along with Don Eduardo and Doña Belinda."

"No!" That shocked cry came from Santiago, who leaped down from his horse and charged up to the porch. "That cannot be!"

"I'm sorry, son, but that's what happened," Fredericks said. "Who are you?"

Slaughter said, "This is Santiago Rubriz, Don Eduardo's son." He struggled to control his raging emotions and went on, "You'd better start at the beginning and tell us what happened, doctor."

For the next few minutes, Fredericks did exactly that. Slaughter had to bite back both curses and groans as he heard about how Viola had been captured by the raiders, along with Don Eduardo and Doña Belinda.

Santiago interrupted to ask, "My stepmother, was she hurt?"

"Knocked around a little, but that's all, as far as I know." Fredericks frowned a little. "Your father was in much worse shape."

"You got the bullet out of him, though," Slaughter said.

Fredericks nodded and said, "Yes, but he lost a lot of blood. He was very weak and couldn't afford to lose any more. If that wound of his opened up again . . ."

The doctor's voice trailed off and he shook his head. His meaning was all too clear.

Something else occurred to Slaughter. He said, "My brother-in-law Stonewall and one of Don Eduardo's *vaqueros* were on their way here ahead of the rest of us. Have you seen any sign of them?"

Fredericks pointed over his shoulder with a thumb that still had bloodstains on it.

"In the parlor with the rest of the wounded," he said.

Slaughter stepped past the doctor and went inside. As he came into the parlor he spotted Stonewall sitting on a straight-backed chair as one of the maids wrapped a bandage around his head. The young man exclaimed, "John!" and would have stood up if Slaughter hadn't motioned for him to keep his seat.

Stonewall didn't appear to be in too bad of a shape. The same couldn't be said of Hermosa, who lay on the same sofa where Don Eduardo had been recuperating the last time Slaughter saw him. Thick bandages swathed the *vaquero*'s midsection. His eyes were closed. He looked dead, except for the fact that his chest was rising and falling lightly.

Slaughter and Santiago went over to Stonewall. He gestured toward the bandage on his head as the maid stepped back.

"Don't worry about this," Stonewall said. "I got knocked out a couple of times, but that's all. My head's too hard for that to have done any real damage."

"Tell us what happened," Slaughter snapped.

Stonewall provided his version of events, then added, "I figured that blasted Apache had killed Hermosa, but he was still alive when Doc Fredericks and Jess Fisher found him out yonder not far from the schoolhouse. Hermosa must've crawled out of the ditch after he tangled with the Apache, and that Apache left him for dead."

Fredericks said, "Any normal man would

have been dead. He'd been stabbed at least five times. To be honest, I'm shocked he's still alive. His insides must be made of rawhide, just like his outsides."

Slaughter stepped over to the sofa and looked down at the wounded *vaquero*. He told Fredericks, "Do everything you can for him, doctor."

"I will, don't worry about that."

"Was anyone else killed?"

"We found a man on top of the water tank," Fredericks said. "His throat had been cut."

"That was Joe Sparkman," Jess Fisher said gloomily. The ranch foreman had come into the room while Slaughter was talking to Stonewall. "Miz Slaughter put him up there to do some sharpshooting, but I reckon that damned Apache found him before he ever got a chance to take a hand."

Slaughter shook his head and asked, "Who is this Apache all of you keep talking about?"

"His name's Bodaway or something like that," Stonewall said. "From the way he and Becker act, they're old friends. I hear tell that Becker's got a bad grudge against Don Eduardo, and that's what caused all this ruckus."

"Ned Becker is a madman," Santiago said. "That is the only way to describe him."

"He may be a madman," Fredericks said, "but he's got a plan." He held out a folded piece of paper. "We found this message over by the schoolhouse, held down with a piece of broken brick. They used a bandanna and a sharp stick to make a flag they planted right beside it, so we couldn't miss it."

Slaughter took the paper and unfolded it. A fairly long message was written on it in a compact, precise hand. Ned Becker might be an outlaw, a murderer, and a lunatic, but apparently he was also an educated man, because it was his signature at the bottom of the missive.

Since the maid had finished bandaging Stonewall's head, the young man stood up and came over to join Slaughter, Santiago, and Fredericks beside the sofa where the unconscious Hermosa lay. The others watched Slaughter tensely as he read the message.

After a moment, Slaughter looked up from the paper.

"Becker is very clear about what he wants," Slaughter said. "I'm to bring Santiago with me, and the two of us — alone — are supposed to cross the border at dawn tomorrow and ride south until someone meets us. From there we'll be taken to the place where Becker is holding Viola, Don

Eduardo, and Doña Belinda. If I turn Santiago over to him, he says he'll let Viola and me leave and return here unharmed."

"I don't believe that for a second, John," Stonewall said. "That fella's loco, and the Apache's worse. We killed all of his war party when they raided the ranch last night. He'll want vengeance for them."

"You're not telling me anything I don't already know," Slaughter said. "And I sure wouldn't trust Becker's word after everything he's done." He looked at Santiago. "You're the last one he wants. What do you say about this?"

"I would gladly turn myself over to him if I thought it would save the lives of my father and . . . and stepmother. But I think Becker intends to kill all of us."

Fredericks said, "Judging by some of the things I heard him say to Mrs. Slaughter, I think you're right, young man."

"But what else can we do?" Santiago went on. "We don't know where Becker has taken the prisoners. If we're going to have any chance to rescue them, we have to play along with him."

Slaughter scratched his bearded chin and said, "Two of us against Becker, the Apache, and the rest of the gang? We won't have much of a chance."

Stonewall said, "I can bring some men and follow you, John. We'll be close by, close enough to help when the time comes."

Slaughter shook his head and held up the paper. "Becker's smart enough that he'll have somebody watching us. He'll know if there's a party following Santiago and me, and he's liable to kill Viola if we try to trick him."

"Well, dadgum it!" Stonewall burst out. "What else can we do? There's no other way to find out where they're holed up."

Slaughter didn't have an answer for that, but it was in the silence following Stonewall's angry words that a faint voice spoke up.

At first Slaughter couldn't tell where the voice came from. Then he looked down at the sofa and realized Hermosa was awake and trying to say something. He motioned for the others to remain quiet and dropped to one knee beside the sofa so he could lean closer to the *vaquero.*

"Are you trying to tell us something, Hermosa?" he asked.

The *vaquero*'s eyes were mere slits of pain as his lips moved. Slaughter heard him breathe two words of Spanish.

"Barranca . . . Sangre."

"Barranca Sangre," Slaughter repeated.

287

He looked up at the others and translated loosely, "Blood Canyon."

"I don't know where that is," Stonewall said. "I never heard of it."

"Nor have I," Santiago put in.

Hermosa whispered, "T-Tequila . . ."

"Will it hurt him, doctor?" Slaughter asked.

"It'll be painful, but it won't do any more damage than has already been done," Fredericks said.

Slaughter turned his head and told one of the maids, "Bring a glass of tequila."

The young woman hurried to obey. When she brought back the tequila a minute later, Slaughter took it and carefully held the glass to Hermosa's mouth. He trickled a little of the fiery liquor between the *vaquero*'s lips.

Hermosa sighed in apparent satisfaction. The tequila seemed to have an almost instant bracing effect. His voice was stronger as he said, "I know . . . Barranca Sangre. I heard the man say to the Apache . . . that was where they were going."

"How did you manage that?" Slaughter asked.

"The Apache thought . . . he killed me. But I . . . fooled him . . . I did not die . . . and when I could . . . I crawled out of the ditch . . . and went after him."

"Impossible," Fredericks said. "No man as badly wounded as this one could have been worried about going after his enemies."

"With all due respect, doctor, that's exactly what I'd expect from a man like Hermosa."

The *vaquero* chuckled dryly. He said, "Hate is . . . powerful medicine, doctor."

"So you got close enough to hear them talking about where they were going," Slaughter said.

"*Sí* . . . but that is all. My strength . . . she deserted me."

"That's all right," Slaughter assured him. "You've done more good by staying alive rather than getting yourself killed. Where do we find this Barranca Sangre?"

"I can . . . take you there."

"Out of the question," Fredericks said. "And I'm not just being overly cautious. Put this man on a horse or even in a wagon and he'll be dead before you go a mile. I guarantee it."

An idea occurred to Slaughter.

"What about a map?" he suggested. "Do you think you could draw a map so we can find the place, Hermosa?"

"Bring me . . . paper and a pencil," Hermosa said. "I can . . . draw a map."

Slaughter nodded to the same maid who

had brought the tequila, and once again she scurried off to fetch what Hermosa asked for.

"What good is this going to do?" Santiago wanted to know. "You already said that the men could not follow us, Señor Slaughter, because Becker would know about it."

"That's true," Slaughter said as he looked up at the men gathered around him. "But it might be a different story if Stonewall and the others were to get there first."

CHAPTER 24

Bodaway seemed to know where he was going, even in the dark. He led the group of riders as they penetrated deeper into the mountains across the border, in the upper reaches of the Sierra Madre Occidental.

Viola dozed off in the saddle from time to time. It seemed like forever since she'd actually stretched out on a bed and slept. It was unlikely that she'd get the chance to do so again any time soon, she thought — if in fact she ever did.

There was every chance in the world she was going to her death, and she knew it.

But she wasn't dead yet, so she still had hope. Becker was going to keep her alive as long as he had a use for her, and that meant until Santiago Rubriz was his prisoner as well.

John might catch up to them before that happened, Viola told herself. And if she got a chance to escape on her own without waiting for him, she would seize it.

Only if she could get the other two captives away, as well, though, and that seemed unlikely. Becker rode right beside Don Eduardo, leading the don's horse, and the man called Woodbury, who seemed to be Becker's second-in-command, had Belinda riding double with him, in front of his saddle.

The blonde wore a dull, defeated expression. She had been through too much. Her pampered existence hadn't prepared her for the danger and hardship she now faced. So she just shut her mind off to it, refused to think about what was going on. Viola could tell that by looking at her.

Don Eduardo, on the other hand, was still angry and defiant, but he was so weak it was a struggle for him to stay in the saddle. He wore a wool serape that one of Becker's men had given him, because when they left the ranch his only covering from the waist up were the bandages the doc had wrapped around him.

"I tell you again, Ned," the don said, "take me with you if you must, but I beg of you, allow my wife and Señora Slaughter to go back to the ranch."

"You begging me," Becker said mockingly. "I like that. The same way you begged my mother to be unfaithful to my father?"

"That never happened." Don Eduardo's voice was clear, although weak. "I never would have done such a thing to hurt my Pilar . . . or your father."

"You killed my father. You think that didn't hurt him?"

"I was defending myself. She had driven him mad . . ." Don Eduardo's words trailed off into a sigh. "No matter what I say, you will not believe it, will you, Ned?"

"Believe the word of a liar, an adulterer, and a murderer?" Becker let out a bark of cold laughter. "I don't think so."

"Then take your vengeance on me, but spare my wife and son."

Becker shook his head.

"They're part of this," he said. "We all are. We all have to play our roles."

"Mad . . ." Don Eduardo said under his breath.

Viola heard that, but if Becker did, he gave no sign of it. He kept riding, leading Don Eduardo's mount and following the Apache who rode about five yards in front of him.

The terrain was flat where they crossed the border, but within a few miles hills had begun to rear up from the arid, mesquite-dotted plains. Beyond the hills rose a range of low, rugged mountains. The riders were probably ten miles deep in those mountains by now, their path winding through canyons and climbing to passes. Viola looked to the east and saw a hint of rose in the sky.

The sun was on its way, rising as always, the universe going about its business no matter what the infinitely small creatures did who lived on this world.

Viola always felt insignificant when she was out in the middle of nowhere like this, and northern Mexico had plenty of nowhere.

How was John going to find her in this vast wilderness? She knew Becker planned to send a man back to meet John and Santiago and bring them to the gang's hideout, but John was too smart for that. He would know it was a trap and would come up with some other plan. Viola wouldn't allow herself to doubt, because doing so meant giving up hope, and she just wasn't the sort of person to do that.

So in the meantime she rode and wondered just how exhausted somebody had to be before they collapsed in a stupor. If she didn't get some real sleep soon, she might find out.

Becker called a halt every now and then so the horses could rest. During one of those breaks, Woodbury dismounted, then turned back to help Belinda down from the saddle.

Her dispirited demeanor suddenly vanished. Her head, which had been drooping far forward, snapped up, and her foot lashed out. The heel of her slipper struck Woodbury in the chest and knocked him back a step. He still had hold of the reins, but Belinda jerked them out of his hand, leaned forward, and kicked the horse in the sides as hard as she could. She shouted encouragement to the animal as it leaped into a gallop.

The escape attempt took Viola as much by surprise as it did everyone else. She recovered quickly, though. All eyes were on Belinda, so Viola made a move of her own.

No one had been leading her horse, because she was surrounded by the hardcases who worked for Becker. Now she jerked the reins to the side and sent her horse lunging into the mount of the man next to her left side. As the animals collided Viola reached out and plucked the outlaw's revolver from his holster.

She twisted in the saddle and triggered a couple of shots, aiming over the heads of the men around her. She didn't want to kill any of them, just spook them so they would get out of her way.

She wasn't going to leave Don Eduardo behind. That meant she had to get him away from Becker. She drove through the gap in the ring of startled guards and dashed toward the vengeance-seeking madman.

"Hold your fire!" Becker shouted as he hauled his horse around to see what was going on behind him. He must have spotted the fleeing Belinda. "Get the don's wife!"

He didn't see Viola coming in time. She lifted the Colt and fired. This time she was shooting to kill.

She knew, however, that being on the back of a galloping horse didn't lend itself to much accuracy. Her bullet must have missed. Becker didn't seem to be hit. He lost his grip on the reins of Don Eduardo's horse, though, when the don jerked the animal to the side.

Becker roared a curse and launched himself from the saddle as Viola tried to gallop past him. He crashed into her, and she couldn't stay mounted, either. Both of them toppled to the ground, landing so hard Viola was half-stunned. She tried to wriggle away from Becker, but her muscles responded sluggishly and he was able to fasten a hand around her arm.

"You bitch!" he yelled as he punched her in the belly with his other fist. Viola curled up around the pain of the brutal blow. She had dropped the gun when she hit the ground, so there was nothing else she could do.

Becker came up on his knees and shouted at his men to go after Don Eduardo. Viola didn't think either the don or Belinda would be able to get away. Becker had too many men, Belinda wasn't an experienced rider, and Don Eduardo was too weak from his injury.

She was right. By the time she recovered enough from the punch to sit up, some of Becker's men had caught the escapees and were bringing them back, leading the horses. Belinda sobbed in futility. Don Eduardo just sat there, hunched over a little in his saddle.

Becker stalked over and glared at them as he said, "That was foolish."

"Why?" Don Eduardo asked. "Are you not going to kill us anyway? Perhaps this way we would have died quicker and easier than what you have in mind for us."

"You can count on that. My father didn't die easy with your bullet in his back, Rubriz."

"He shot first," Don Eduardo said, his voice thin and reedy but filled with determination to get the words out. "He thought he had killed me. To be honest, I believed I was dying, too. I struck back at him the only way I could."

"Lies, all lies," Becker snapped. "Before he died, he told my mother what really happened, and she told me."

"Your mother told you what she wanted you to hear, not the truth. She wanted to make you hate me and blame me for what happened, when it was really all her doing."

Still sitting a few yards away on the ground, Viola thought Becker was going to pull his gun and shoot the don right then and there. That was how furious the outlaw looked. But with a visible effort, Becker suppressed that impulse. He turned away and walked back over to Viola.

As he extended a hand to help her to her feet, he said, "I'm sorry, Mrs. Slaughter. I shouldn't have lost my temper with you. This is nothing personal where you're concerned."

Viola gripped wrists with him and let him pull her up. She let go of him, slapped some of the dirt off her long skirt, and said, "You made it personal when you attacked my home, Mr. Becker. You'd do well to remember that."

"Maybe I will. Right now, though, my only interest in you is being able to persuade your husband to cooperate and deliver

Santiago Rubriz to me."

"John Slaughter will never cooperate with you," Viola said coldly.

"You'd better hope you're wrong," Becker said. "Because if you're not, there's a very good chance you're going to die sometime in the next twelve hours."

Their captors kept an even closer eye on them as they rode deeper into the mountains. After a while they turned east, went through a pass, and dropped down into a valley between the ranges that ran roughly north and south. To the east, on the far side of the valley, lay a canyon that cut through the mountains on that side.

The sun was almost up. As the group rode toward the canyon, the fiery orb peeked above the horizon. Viola caught her breath as she realized that the rising sun was framed by the notch formed by the canyon. The red sandstone cliffs and the garish crimson light made it look like the canyon was awash with blood.

"Barranca Sangre," Becker announced. "That's where we're going."

Viola felt a chill ripple through her at those words. The idea of going to a place called Blood Canyon would not be very inviting under the best of circumstances. As the prisoner of a madman, it was even worse.

Even though no one had asked Becker for an explanation, he seemed to like the sound of his own voice. He went on, "Bodaway's band lived here for a while, after they left the reservation in Arizona Territory. But the *Rurales* found the village and attacked it. They wiped out nearly everyone. Only Bodaway and a few warriors escaped. He spent the next year hunting down every man in that *Rurale* company and killing them all."

Viola could believe that. She had never seen any expression on the Apache's face other than cold, impassive hatred.

"One of the Mexicans lived for a little while after Bodaway was through with him," Becker continued. "He told the men who found him that looking into Bodaway's eyes was like looking into the flames of hell. That's how he got his name, *El Infierno.* It fits. His real name means Fire Maker."

"I'm not sure who you're talking to," Viola said. "None of us are interested in this."

Becker smiled at her.

"I just want you to know who you're dealing with. Bodaway always settles his scores. He lost fifteen good warriors when he raided your ranch."

"You were the one who told him to do it,"

Viola pointed out. "All to help you carry out this insane revenge scheme of yours."

"If you're trying to drive a wedge between us, Mrs. Slaughter, you're wasting your time. Bodaway and I are the only real friends either of us has left."

If the Apache heard that as he rode a few yards ahead of the others, he didn't show any sign. He continued leading the way into the canyon.

Viola could see all the way to the other end of Barranca Sangre. She estimated that it ran for a mile or more straight through the mountains. The group had covered about half that distance when a smaller canyon suddenly opened up to the left, running at right angles into the bigger one. The sandstone wall of the main canyon bulged out so that you couldn't see the smaller one until you reached its mouth.

The smaller canyon, fifty yards wide and maybe two hundred yards deep, ended at a blank wall of rock. A spring bubbled out of the sandstone at that point, creating a small pool and providing water for several cottonwoods and enough grass for the horses to graze. Half a dozen adobe *jacales* and a pole corral had been built near the pool.

"I've visited your home, Mrs. Slaughter," Becker said. "Now I have the pleasure of welcoming you to mine."

"This isn't a home," Viola said. "It's a hideout."

Becker shrugged and said, "Call it whatever you want. This is where we'll wait for your husband and young Rubriz."

They rode up to the huts and started to dismount. One of Becker's men riding beside Viola said, "You just stay right where you are until I tell you to get down, missy. Nobody else is tryin' any tricks today."

Viola didn't acknowledge the order, but she didn't swing down from the saddle until the outlaw told her to. Once her feet were on the ground, he took hold of her arm and marched her roughly toward one of the *jacales.*

Woodbury brought Belinda to the same hut. Both women were forced inside and the door closed after them. The door didn't have a bar or a lock on it, Viola noted, but she was sure at least one member of the gang would be standing guard outside all the time.

The *jacal* had no windows, but its roof was made of thatched limbs from the cottonwoods and there were enough cracks and gaps to let in some of the reddish light. Belinda looked rather sickly in that illumination, and Viola supposed that she did, too.

The single room was sparsely furnished with a rough-hewn table, a couple of equally crude chairs, and two bunks, one on each side wall. The bunks had no mattresses, only folded blankets on top of woven rope. Viola thought they looked pretty uncomfortable.

Despite that, Belinda sat on one of them, swung her legs up so she could lie down, and rolled over with her face to the adobe wall.

For some reason that irritated Viola. She said, "We need to talk about what we're going to do."

"We're going to die, that's what we're going to do," Belinda said without looking around. "That man Becker and his pet Indian are probably going to torture me to death while they make Eduardo watch. Maybe you'll be lucky and he'll just put a bullet through your brain."

"Not if we get away first," Viola insisted. "You tried to escape earlier. You must not want to give up."

Belinda began to sob quietly. Her back shook a little from the crying as she said, "I didn't make it even a hundred yards before they caught me. That proved to me how hopeless everything is. We're doomed and you know it."

Viola bit back the angry response that wanted to spring to her lips. No matter how bleak the situation looked, she wasn't going to give up. She couldn't. She wasn't made that way.

And John wouldn't want her to. She could almost sense his presence beside her, hear him whispering in her ear as he told her to stay strong and fight back against her captors if she got the chance.

Belinda needed something to jolt her out of her despair. Viola sensed that encouraging words wouldn't do a bit of good. But anger might, she decided, so she said, "How in the world did you wind up having a dirty little affair with your own stepson?"

Belinda jerked as if she'd been struck. She stiffened and rolled over on the bunk so she could look at Viola again. As she propped herself up on an elbow, she glared at Viola and snapped, "Don't talk about it like that. What's between Santiago and me isn't a dirty little affair. We love each other."

Viola folded her arms over her chest and said coldly, "Yet you married Don Eduardo."

"I love him, too."

"Of course you do," Viola said with obvious disbelief.

Belinda sat up and pushed herself to her

feet. Her chin jutted out defiantly as she said, "It's none of your business, but it happens to be true. Don Eduardo is like a father to me. When he asked me to marry him, he made it clear that I wouldn't have to . . . fulfill any wifely duties . . . with him. He said he wanted a beautiful young woman to be the mistress of his *hacienda* and to brighten his days for the time he had left. That's all."

What Belinda was saying took Viola by surprise. She couldn't comprehend a marriage where husband and wife didn't share everything there was to be shared. Her union with John Slaughter had never been that way, that was for sure.

Belinda looked and sounded as if she were being completely sincere, though.

"So the two of you have never . . ."

"That's right." Belinda's face was flushed. "And it's not proper to talk about such things."

"But you and Santiago . . ."

"Santiago and I love each other. Someday we'll be married. But I haven't been unfaithful to my husband. You can believe that or not. I don't really care."

Viola didn't know what to believe anymore. She had jumped to a conclusion, and maybe she'd been wrong. A part of her was a little ashamed that she had been so quick to rush to judgment. Yet logically she knew that most people would have thought the same thing if they had seen Belinda and Santiago together under that water tank.

"I'm sorry," she said. "What about Don Eduardo? Does he know?"

"About Santiago and me, you mean?" Belinda shrugged. "We haven't told him. I think he suspects, though. He's never given me any indication that he's upset about it. Maybe he's just glad that once he's gone, Santiago will have someone."

Viola supposed a person could look at it like that. The whole thing still seemed rather incomprehensible to her, but not everyone lived their lives the same way. She reminded herself that plenty of people had believed she was loco to marry someone so much older than herself.

The conversation between her and Belinda might have continued, but at that moment both women gasped and jumped a little as an unexpected sound cut through the morning air.

Somewhere nearby in Barranca Sangre, someone had just unleashed a bloodcurdling scream.

CHAPTER 25

All the horses Slaughter and his men had taken in pursuit of the rustlers were worn out, so they had to get fresh mounts from the remuda. While that was going on the servants put together bags of provisions in case the men were gone for several days.

Slaughter hoped that wouldn't be the case. According to the map Hermosa had drawn, along with the things the *vaquero* had to say, the canyon known as Barranca Sangre was less than a twelve-hour ride across the border into Mexico.

That meant if luck was on their side, they might have Viola home safely by nightfall the next day.

If it took longer than that, there was a chance they wouldn't be coming back at all.

Slaughter sat down with Stonewall in the dining room to go over the plan. He spread out the map on the table and said, "You're sure you can find the place?"

"I think so, John," the young man said.

"You can't just think so. Your sister's life may well be riding on this."

"I'll find it," Stonewall declared.

"If you have any doubts about your health or your mental condition, Jess can lead the rescue party. You've been knocked out twice in the past few hours."

Stonewall grinned and said, "I told you, this skull of mine is too thick for that to be a problem. It's not even dented."

Slaughter didn't doubt that, but it was the brain underneath the skull he was worried about. Stonewall appeared to be fine, but getting hit in the head was a tricky thing. Slaughter had known men to seem fine after an injury like that, only to drop dead a few days later. Other men had been knocked out, even once, and although they lived they were never the same afterward.

"All right," Slaughter said, "but if you feel like you can't handle it, you turn things over to Jess. Viola's safety is more important than anything else, at least as far as I'm concerned. Although I want to rescue Don Eduardo and his wife, too, of course."

Stonewall nodded and leaned forward.

"Let me take another look at that map," he said. "I know I'll have it with me, but I want to be sure where I'm going."

They had to hope, as well, that Hermosa had known what he was doing when he drew the map. The *vaquero* was gravely wounded, more dead than alive, according to Dr. Fredericks, and there was no way of knowing if his directions were accurate — or if his so-called knowledge of Barranca Sangre was just a product of a fevered imagination.

"There is a little box canyon just off Barranca Sangre with a spring in it," Hermosa had told them, fortifying himself with sips of tequila. "For several years a band of Apache lived there, until the *Rurales* almost wiped them out. After that some prospectors came to look for gold and silver in the mountains and built *jacales* there by the spring to use as their camp. When no one saw them again for almost a year, relatives bribed the *Rurales* to look for the men. They were all still there in Barranca Sangre — or their bones were, anyway. The rumors I heard said that terrible things had been done to them, probably while they were still alive. Since then no one has dared to go there."

"How do you know about it?" Slaughter had asked.

"As a young man I was restless. I explored across northern Sonora whenever I had the chance. And I always listened to the stories told in hushed tones in *cantinas.*"

"If it's true the place is, well, cursed," Stonewall had said, "how is it that Becker gets away with usin' it for his hideout?"

"There is no curse, not in the way you mean. There is only a survivor from that band of Apache, driven mad by hate and the need for revenge."

"The Apache who's workin' with Becker," Stonewall had exclaimed. "It's got to be him."

Hermosa had nodded, and even that much movement seemed to tire him greatly.

All of it made sense as far as Slaughter could tell. Anyway, he had no choice but to accept the *vaquero*'s story. Hermosa offered the only possible chance of turning the tables on the outlaws and rescuing the captives.

Slaughter's finger traced a path on the map as he and Stonewall bent over it.

"You'll need to take this way in," he said. "According to Hermosa it splits off from the regular trail, the route that Becker is most likely to use because he'll want to get back to his stronghold as quickly as he can. This little trail is rougher, and you'll have to be careful getting up to some of the passes along the way. But you can approach the canyon from the north instead of the west, the way the main trail does. That'll put you above the spring and those huts around it. That's bound to be where Becker will be keeping the prisoners."

Stonewall nodded and said, "We'll be able to ambush 'em. Maybe wipe out the whole bunch in one volley."

"I wouldn't count on that," Slaughter cautioned. "But you should be able to even the odds enough that Santiago and I will have a chance to get to the prisoners. If we can do that, we'll keep them safe."

"How are you gonna put up a fight? Becker won't let you carry any guns in there, I'll bet."

"No, I'm sure he won't," Slaughter said. "But he and his men will have guns, and I'm counting on the chance that Santiago and I can get our hands on some of them."

Stonewall nodded solemnly and said, "It's gonna be mighty dangerous, especially for the two of you. You'll be ridin' right into a hornet's nest."

"That's why we'll be counting on you and Jess and the other men to do some stinging of your own," Slaughter replied with a grim smile.

A short time later, everyone was ready to

leave. Stonewall and his group would ride out first, since the plan called for them to be in position above Barranca Sangre before Becker's emissary, whoever it was, brought Slaughter and Santiago to the hideout.

Once the men were mounted, Slaughter reached up, gripped his brother-in-law's hand, and said, "Good luck, son."

"You, too, John," Stonewall replied. He was riding the big roan Pacer, who'd had the day to rest after one of the hands rode him to Douglas to fetch Dr. Fredericks.

Santiago was there and shook hands with Stonewall as well. Then the riders, sixteen in all, left the ranch and headed south into Mexico.

"Will they be able to find the right trail in the dark?" Santiago asked as he and Slaughter watched the men ride away.

"It'll be close to sunup by the time they get to the place it branches off," Slaughter said. "We'll have to hope they can find it." He chuckled, but there wasn't much humor in the sound. "If they don't, you and I are going to be in a bad spot."

"I don't care. I'll dare anything to save my father and Belinda."

Slaughter thought it a little odd that the young man didn't refer to his father's wife as his stepmother or Doña Belinda, but at the moment that wasn't worth worrying about. They went back into the ranch house, where Slaughter conferred with Neal Fredericks.

"We're keeping you away from your practice in town, doctor," Slaughter said.

"I have patients here," Fredericks said. "There are a couple of midwives in Douglas who can take care of any birthing that needs to be done, and everything else will have to wait."

Santiago said, "I hope you can keep Hermosa alive, doctor. We owe him a great deal."

"I'm afraid that's almost out of my hands. Whatever has kept him alive this long is a higher power than any I can muster. But I'll do everything I can for him, I give you my word on that, young man."

As Slaughter was gathering up more ammunition, one of the maids approached him and said, "Señor Slaughter?"

"Yes, what is it?" he asked, then recognized her. "What can I do for you, Yolanda?"

"I know you go to rescue Señora Slaughter, and all my prayers for her safety go with you, señor. But is it a terrible thing if I pray that you deliver justice to the murderer of my Hector as well?"

Slaughter smiled, shook his head, and said

gently, "No, Yolanda, it's not a terrible thing. Hector was a fine young man, and his death should be avenged."

"But can I pray for a man to die, even a very bad man like the one who killed Hector?"

"Just pray that Señora Slaughter and the rest of us return home safely," Slaughter told her as he patted her shoulder. "That's the best thing you can do."

If they did that, there was a very good chance that the murder of Hector Alvarez — and all the other crimes committed by Ned Becker and his friends — would be avenged.

Santiago led the big black horse called *El Halcón* out of the corral. The stallion was saddled and ready to ride.

Slaughter nodded in approval, but he qualified it by saying, "I know that horse is fast and we're certainly liable to need that speed, but does he have the stamina?"

"He has the heart of a champion, Señor Slaughter. *El Halcón* will never falter."

"I hope you're right," Slaughter said. "Well, with any luck we won't need to make a run for it."

He had picked a big, rangy lineback dun for his mount. He had ridden the horse many times and knew that while the dun wasn't much for looks, it was strong and fast and would run all day if necessary.

Slaughter and Santiago swung up into their saddles and lifted hands in farewell to Dr. Fredericks, who stood on the porch watching them ride out, leading three saddled, riderless horses for the captives they hoped to rescue and bring back safely.

"Are you all right, Señor Slaughter?" Santiago asked as they left the ranch behind. "You have been going for a very long time without any rest."

"I'm a little tired," Slaughter admitted, "but that doesn't mean anything as long as my wife is in danger. I'll keep going for however long is necessary. I will say, though . . . when this is over a nice long nap will be most welcome."

"When our loved ones are threatened, our own comfort means nothing."

"We'll do everything we can to rescue your father, Santiago."

"And Belinda," the young man added.

There was that odd note in his voice again, Slaughter thought. He indulged his curiosity enough to comment, "No offense, but during the party the other night I got the impression you don't really care much for your stepmother."

"Certainly I care about her," Santiago said. "My father loves her. She is part of our family now."

"A lot of fellas don't like to see their mothers replaced."

Santiago laughed and said, "Believe me, Señor Slaughter, the very last thing Belinda has done is replace my mother."

Slaughter sensed that Santiago wanted to drop this line of conversation, so he didn't say anything else about Doña Belinda.

They had ridden past the border marker by now and continued south into Mexico. The moon and stars provided plenty of light for them to see where they were going, and Slaughter had no trouble letting those stars guide him in the right direction.

They talked only sporadically as they rode. Slaughter's mind was full of worry for Viola and, to a lesser extent, Don Eduardo and Doña Belinda. They had been guests in his house when they were kidnapped, and Slaughter considered the don a friend as well. Both of those things fueled the anger Slaughter felt at what Ned Becker had done.

Time had little meaning in a situation such as this. The eastern sky began to turn gray above the mountains that loomed in that direction. Slaughter knew that morning was only an hour or so away. He and Santiago had been riding most of the night.

"You're sure we are going the right way?" Santiago asked. "I thought perhaps Becker's man would have intercepted us by now."

"We're following the directions in Becker's note," Slaughter said. He patted his shirt pocket where he had put the folded paper. "There aren't many landmarks around here, but we've been going almost due south, the way he said." Slaughter eased back on the reins. "Let's stop and let the horses rest for a little while."

"I can keep riding," Santiago said.

"I know you can, but we don't want to wear out these animals." Slaughter patted the dun's shoulder. "They may wind up being more important than we are."

The two men dismounted. Slaughter had brought along several full canteens — nobody went anywhere in this arid country without carrying water — and used his hat to give the horses a drink. Then they let the animals graze a little on the sparse grass.

Santiago paced back and forth impatiently, ready to be on the move again. Slaughter just stood there breathing slowly, taking advantage of this opportunity to rest even though he couldn't sleep yet. After a while he poured a little water into the palm of his hand and used it to wash away the grit in his eyes.

The eastern sky had gone orange and gold. The sun would rise above the mountains soon. Santiago stopped his pacing, stared in that direction, and said, "Can we go now?"

"I reckon the horses have rested long enough," Slaughter said. He took hold of the horn and swung up into the saddle.

They had only gone another mile or so when Slaughter spotted a rider coming toward them from the mountains.

He pointed out the man to Santiago and said, "Looks like there's our escort."

"It's about time," the young man said. "I will try not to shoot him, but it will be difficult, knowing what he was a part of."

"Maybe," Slaughter said, "but we need him, so keep a tight rein on your temper."

As the gap between them closed, Slaughter studied their guide. The man was a stocky hardcase wearing a broad-brimmed brown hat with a round crown. A serape was draped over his ax-handle shoulders. A spade beard the color of rust jutted from his slab of a jaw.

Slaughter and Santiago reined in when about twenty feet separated them from the outlaw. The man brought his mount to a halt as well and gave them what almost seemed like a friendly nod.

"Mornin'," he greeted them. "You're the fellas I've been waitin' for."

He didn't phrase it like a question, but Slaughter said, "That's right. I'm John Slaughter, and this is Santiago Rubriz."

"You're alone, the way you're supposed to be?"

"You already know that," Slaughter said. "You've been watching us with a spyglass from up in those hills, haven't you?"

That brought a grin to the man's bearded face. "I've heard tell that you're pretty smart, Slaughter. I reckon that's right. Yeah, the boss said not to take any chances with you. He figured you'd do like you were told because you want to see that pretty little wife of yours again, but there was always a chance you'd try to pull some sort of trick."

"No tricks," Slaughter lied. "I'm just interested in getting my wife back safely."

"How about you, boy?" the outlaw addressed Santiago.

"Your boss gave me no choice," he snapped. "You have my father and stepmother. I will do everything I can to keep them alive."

"Well, that's between you and Becker. I'm just the errand boy." The man scratched his beard. "They call me Red, by the way.

Reckon you can see why."

"Owlhoots usually aren't very imaginative," Slaughter said dryly.

Red frowned and demanded, "Are you callin' me dumb?"

"You're not the one who came up with the name, are you?"

"Well, no, I ain't." Red shook his head. "Quit tryin' to mix me up. If you think I'll forget what I'm supposed to do, you're wrong. Now get down off those horses and shuck those guns. Where we're goin', you can't carry no weapons."

Slaughter glanced over at Santiago. He could tell that the youngster wanted to haul out his Colt and blast the red-bearded outlaw from the saddle.

But Santiago swallowed hard and then did what Red told him to do. Slaughter followed suit.

Within minutes, they were disarmed and Red had gathered up the rifles and pistols, stowing the handguns in a pack behind his saddle and lashing the Winchesters to one of the extra horses. Then he drew his own revolver and motioned for Slaughter and Santiago to ride in front of him.

"Straight toward them mountains," he said. "I'll tell you if you start goin' the wrong way. And rest easy, fellas. A couple of hours and we'll be where we're goin'. You'll get to see those folks you're so worried about."

"And they'll be all right?" Santiago asked. "We have your word on that?"

"Well . . . I reckon they'll still be alive," Red drawled. "That's about all I can promise you, though, especially where that old don's concerned."

CHAPTER 26

At the sound of the scream, Viola and Belinda both rushed to the door, which had a simple drawstring latch. Belinda reached it first, grabbed the string, and pulled. She jerked the door open.

Before they could take another step, two of the outlaws blocked their path. Each man held a rifle at a slant across his chest. The one closest to Belinda thrust the weapon at her in a hard shove that sent her staggering back against Viola. Belinda might have fallen if Viola hadn't caught and steadied her.

"You bitches ain't goin' nowhere," the other man snarled. "The boss said to keep you in there, and that's what we're gonna do."

"What's going on out there?" Belinda demanded in a hysterical voice. "What have you done to my husband?"

The two guards exchanged quick, ugly grins. The one who had shoved Belinda said, "The boss didn't say we couldn't let 'em take a look."

"No, I don't reckon he did," the other man agreed. He backed off a little and pointed his rifle at the two women. "You can step into the doorway, but that's as far as you go."

The door opening was barely wide enough for both Viola and Belinda to stand there and look out at the outlaw camp. As they did, Belinda gasped and then sobbed. She lifted her hands to her face and sagged against Viola, who put an arm around the blonde's shoulders and steadied her.

About twenty yards away, under one of the cottonwood trees, Becker and Bodaway had pulled Don Eduardo's arms up and lashed his wrists to a low-hanging branch. They had removed the serape first so his bandages were visible again, and Viola saw a crimson stain spreading slowly on the don's side.

The rough treatment had opened the bullet wound. It didn't appear to be bleeding very fast, but Don Eduardo couldn't really afford to lose any more of the life-giving fluid than he already had.

The don's toes barely touched the ground as he hung there. The pain of having that much weight dangling from his arms had to be excruciating, Viola knew, especially in his weakened condition. His head drooped forward and he looked like he had lost consciousness.

"You monsters!" Belinda screamed at Becker and the Apache.

Becker stepped back and turned toward the *jacal.*

"Monster?" he repeated. "Hardly. A monster sets out to steal another man's wife. A monster shoots an innocent man in the back. I'm not a monster. I'm just a man who wants to see justice done."

"Your own warped version of justice," Viola said coldly. "And you don't care how many truly innocent people you have to hurt to get it."

"Doesn't everyone have their own version of justice?" Becker shot back at her. "Who has the right to say that mine is any more warped than anyone else's?" He laughed. "And you should have figured out by now, Mrs. Slaughter, that there are no truly innocent people in this world. Not one."

Viola supposed she couldn't argue with his last statement. As for the rest of it, though, he was as loco as a hydrophobic skunk.

Becker evidently didn't want to argue. He gestured curtly at the women and went on,

"Put them back inside. The don's all right for now. This is just getting started."

Viola was afraid he was right about that. The guards forced her and Belinda back into the *jacal* and the door slammed closed once again.

Belinda collapsed on the bunk where she had been earlier and sobbed. Viola sat down in one of the crude chairs and let her cry. She would have offered words of hope, but she figured they wouldn't do any good right now.

She wasn't going to give up, though.

Somewhere, help was out there, and it was only a matter of staying alive until it got here.

Was he lost? Stonewall frowned at the map in his hand and asked himself that question, but he didn't know the answer.

"What do you think?" Jess Fisher said. "Is this where we're supposed to be?"

"Yeah," Stonewall said as he folded the map and replaced it in his shirt pocket. "This is the trail."

He lifted his eyes and looked at the narrow path that zigzagged up the almost sheer side of a mountain.

"You sure?" Fisher asked. "This looks

more like something a mountain goat would use."

"It's wide enough for a horse, and this is the way Hermosa drew it." Stonewall pointed to his left. "There's the sawtooth peak he put on the map, and over yonder is the flat-topped one. This trail leads up to a pass between 'em."

"All right. I trust you, Stonewall. This is the way we'll go."

Stonewall just wished he trusted himself. The possibility that he had gotten turned around somehow lurked in the back of his mind. Under other circumstances he might not have worried about it so much. He might have been content to wander around these hills and mountains until he found his way.

But his sister's life was on the line, along with the lives of Don Eduardo and Doña Belinda. He couldn't afford to make a mistake. He and the men with him had to beat John Slaughter and Santiago to Barranca Sangre so they could be ready when it was time to make their move. If they were late it could cost the others their lives.

Dithering around here wasn't going to do anybody any good, either, he told himself. He'd made his decision. It was time to stick to it.

"Let's go," he said as he lifted his reins and nudged his horse into motion. "I'll take the lead."

He walked Pacer onto the ledge. It was a natural formation, which meant its width varied and its surface was uneven in places. Pacer was a sure-footed mount, and he would need to be in order to make it up to the pass. Despite the urgency Stonewall felt, he knew he couldn't afford to rush the horse.

The sun was up already. Stonewall knew they ought to be farther along their route by now, but unfortunately there was nothing he could do about it other than keep pushing ahead and hope for the best.

The ground dropped away to Stonewall's right as he and Pacer continued to climb. He was widely regarded as fearless, but that wasn't exactly true. He didn't care much for heights. He was a flatlander at heart, and this land was anything but flat.

The ledge was a one-way trail, wide enough for only a single rider. Luckily it didn't seem to be heavily traveled, so he didn't think they were likely to meet anyone coming down.

As the path curved around a shoulder of rock, he took advantage of the opportunity to look behind him. Jess Fisher was second in line, about ten feet back, and then the other men strung out single file behind the *segundo*. Most of them looked tense and worried as the drop-off beside them increased, and Stonewall didn't blame them. If he never had to do anything like this again, it would be just fine with him.

After a few more minutes of following the torturous path, Stonewall felt relief flood through him when he spotted the pass up ahead. The ledge widened out into a broad, level trail that ran between two rocky upthrusts. Stonewall hoped that the descent on the far side of the pass wouldn't be as treacherous as the climb up here had been.

He turned his head to call to Jess Fisher and tell him that the end was in sight, and as he did a rifle cracked and a bullet whipped past his ear.

Stonewall heard a horse scream. He watched in horror as one of the animals farther back reared in pain. He knew the slug that had narrowly missed him had struck the animal. Whether or not the wound was fatal might not matter. The maddened horse's rear hooves skittered perilously close to the edge of the trail as the cowboy on its back struggled frantically to control his mount.

He wasn't going to be able to do it. The

others all knew that. Jess Fisher yelled, "Jump, Corey!"

The man kicked his feet free of the stirrups and flung himself out of the saddle just as the horse slipped over the brink. As the animal twisted screaming through the air, Corey landed at the edge and clawed at the trail to keep himself from falling. He would have to save himself. On this narrow path, none of the others could reach him in time to help him.

Fisher reacted with the skill of a top hand. He plucked up the coiled lasso that hung on his saddle, shook out a loop in the blink of an eye, and cast it with the unerring accuracy of a man who had made thousands of throws with a rope. Corey saw it coming and thrust his right arm up through the loop just as he started to slide into empty space. He caught hold of it and hung on for dear life.

Fisher had already dallied the lasso around his saddle horn. The rope would take the weight of a thousand-pound steer, so it had no trouble supporting one cowboy.

All that happened in less time than it would have taken to tell about it. There were other dangers to deal with. Another shot rang out and the slug whined off a rock. This time Stonewall spotted the spurt of powder-smoke from the pass. At least one bushwhacker lurked up there.

That made sense if this was really the back door to Barranca Sangre as Hermosa claimed. Ned Becker could have been cunning enough to post a guard or two here.

Stonewall knew that he and his men couldn't let that stop them. He hauled his Winchester from its saddle boot and returned the fire, spraying the pass with lead as fast as he could work the repeater's lever.

He didn't really have any targets at which to aim — the ambushers were well hidden somewhere in the pass — but if he threw enough bullets in there and they started to ricochet around . . .

That tactic was rewarded by the sight of a man stumbling out from behind a rock with a rifle in his hands, obviously wounded. He tried to lift the weapon for another shot, but Stonewall was too fast for him. Stonewall drilled the bushwhacker, and the .44-40 slug lifted the man in the air and dumped him on his back in the limp sprawl of death.

As the echoes of the shots faded away, Stonewall heard swift hoofbeats.

There had been a second guard, and he was getting away.

Stonewall knew what the man would do.

He would run back to Barranca Sangre as fast as he could and warn Becker that someone was approaching the canyon from the north. Those gunshots might have already done it, but the way the echoes bounced around off the slopes, there was a chance the sound wouldn't travel that far. They were still several miles away from the outlaw stronghold, Stonewall figured from his study of Hermosa's map.

As those thoughts flashed through Stonewall's mind, he was already acting. His boot heels jammed against Pacer's flanks and sent the big roan surging ahead. The trail was still narrow here, so Stonewall was taking a big risk by galloping his horse.

But letting Becker's man get away would be an even bigger risk. That would ruin the plan and likely result in Viola's death, along with Slaughter's.

Stonewall wasn't going to let that happen if he could prevent it.

He clutched the Winchester in his right hand and thrust it out to the side to help keep his balance as Pacer raced along the ledge. The trail began to widen, the drop-off became not as sheer, and suddenly Stonewall flashed into the pass. The rata-plan of Pacer's hoofbeats rebounded from the rocky walls that rose on both sides.

Stonewall was glad he wasn't in danger of plummeting to his death anymore, at least for the moment, but that didn't mean he was out of trouble. As he emerged from the pass he spotted his quarry ahead of him, riding down a fairly steep trail that ran through a field of boulders.

The man twisted around in his saddle and fired a pistol back at Stonewall. The odds against hitting anything from the back of a running horse at this range, especially with a handgun, were almost too high to think about. But bad luck happened, and sometimes a bullet was guided by a capricious fate.

Stonewall hauled back on Pacer's reins and brought the roan to a stop. He lifted his rifle to his shoulder and aimed carefully, drawing a bead on the rider in the distance. The outlaw was still in range of the Winchester. Stonewall let out his breath and stroked the trigger.

The rifle cracked and bucked against his shoulder, and as he peered over the sights he saw the rider suddenly swerve around a bend in the trail. A bright splash of silver appeared on a boulder where the bullet struck it. Stonewall's shot had missed.

And the varmint was out of sight now. Stonewall grated a curse and kicked Pacer into a run again.

The chase continued down the boulder-littered mountainside. Stonewall figured the rest of his bunch was following him by now, but that didn't really matter. This was a race between him and the man he was pursuing.

That thought made him remember the race he and Santiago Rubriz had planned to put on matching Pacer and *El Halcón*. That might never come about now, and Stonewall regretted missing the chance to compete against Santiago. There were a lot more important things to consider, of course, but it would have been nice to settle which of the horses was faster.

He caught a glimpse of the outlaw below him, where the trail had started to wind back and forth. An idea popped into Stonewall's head. A dangerous one, to be sure, but it might be his only chance to stop the man from warning Becker.

He veered off the trail and started cutting almost straight down the mountain.

Several times during that wild ride he thought Pacer was going to slip and go down, but the roan always caught his balance somehow as he lunged from rock to rock, over gullies, around outcroppings. The branches of a scrubby tree whipped at Stonewall's face, but he ducked his head and ignored them.

Taking this dangerous course allowed him to cut the outlaw's lead to almost nothing. He saw a big slab of rock thrusting out over the trail ahead of him. The man he was after hadn't come by here yet. Stonewall spotted him from the corner of his eye, galloping for all he was worth and swiveling his head around to check behind him.

The *hombre* didn't know the real danger was in front of him.

"Big jump ahead!" he called to Pacer. "But you can do it!"

Pacer's heart was gallant. Stonewall didn't ask him to slow down, so he didn't. He kept galloping full out and left the end of the rock slab in a soaring leap that carried both of them far out over the trail.

Stonewall had timed it perfectly. He left the saddle in a diving tackle that drove the outlaw off his horse.

The man hit the ground first with Stonewall on top of him. Even with the outlaw's body to cushion the impact, Stonewall felt like a mountain had risen up and swatted him. Dust swirled around them as Stonewall rolled over, but he couldn't cough. He didn't have any breath left in his body to do so.

He gasped a few times, swallowed some of

the dust and choked on it a little, then pushed himself up and looked to the side. The outlaw lay on his back a few feet away, his head twisted and set at a funny angle on his neck. Dust started to settle on his widely staring eyeballs, but he didn't blink.

The man was dead, his neck broken in the fall.

Stonewall groaned and let himself slump back down. His heart still pounded wildly and he had to fight to get his breath, but gradually he felt himself beginning to recover.

The sound of more hoofbeats made him look up. Pacer had landed safely and returned to him. The roan reached his head down and bumped Stonewall's shoulder with his nose.

"Yeah," Stonewall said in a weak voice. "I'm all right."

He heard more horses, and as he pulled himself upright by grasping Pacer's reins, he saw Jess Fisher and the other men riding toward him. Fisher called, "Stonewall, are you all right?"

"Yeah. Danged if I know how I didn't bust every bone in my body, but I don't think I'm hurt." He looked at the rest of the men and spotted the cowboy whose horse had fallen off the ledge riding double with another man. "Glad to see you made it, Corey."

"What do we do now?" Fisher asked.

"The same thing we set out to do," Stonewall replied with a note of grim determination in his voice. "We've got a rendezvous to keep at Barranca Sangre."

CHAPTER 27

After the outlaw called Red met Slaughter and Santiago, it still took them two more hours of riding to reach Barranca Sangre. That time seemed even longer than it really was to Slaughter as they followed a winding path through the mountains. These peaks might not tower like the Rockies, but they were still rugged enough to make for slow going.

Red was talkative, but it was just aimless chatter and didn't really help to pass the time. He wouldn't say anything about the captives except that they were fine when he left the camp. Slaughter had a hunch that Becker had ordered the man not to reveal too much.

Finally they descended into a valley and Red pointed out a canyon in the next range of mountains about two miles away.

"That's where we're goin'," he told them. "That's Barranca Sangre."

"How did it get the name Blood Canyon?" Slaughter asked. "It looks like a normal canyon to me."

"Right now it does, now that the sun's higher," Red agreed. "But earlier in the mornin', right after the sun's come up and it's shinin' through there on those sandstone walls, the place looks like it's filled with blood. It's a lot redder than this beard o' mine."

"I'll take your word for it," Slaughter said. "After today I'd just as soon never see this place again."

That brought a laugh from Red. The outlaw didn't explain what he thought was funny, but Slaughter had a pretty good idea.

Red didn't think Slaughter and Santiago would ever be leaving Barranca Sangre.

The three of them rode on toward the mouth of the canyon. The high walls rose imposingly around them as they entered. Slaughter knew from talking to Hermosa that there was a much smaller canyon running into this one at right angles where the actual camp was likely to be.

That speculation appeared to be correct because Slaughter could see the entire length of the main canyon and it was empty except for rocks, tufts of hardy grass, and a few stunted bushes growing along the base

338

of the walls.

Slaughter didn't spot the side canyon until they were practically on top of it. The natural formations of Barranca Sangre disguised it as cunningly as if someone had fashioned it that way. It was easy to see why the Apaches who had stumbled upon this place had decided to make their camp here. The isolation and the fact that it would be easy to defend made for a perfect hideout.

As soon as they rounded the shoulder of rock that partially concealed the entrance to the side canyon, Slaughter saw the *jacales* and the corral at the far end, around a pool where a spring bubbled out of the cliff face.

He also saw the motionless figure of Don Eduardo Rubriz hanging like a dead man by his wrists from a branch of one of the cottonwood trees.

Santiago saw that, too, and couldn't control himself. He let out an inarticulate cry of rage and kicked *El Halcón* into a gallop. Red yelled, "Hey!" but he was too slow to stop Santiago.

The hoofbeats rang out loudly inside the confines of the canyon and gave Becker's men ample warning that someone was coming in a hurry. The men who were already outside grabbed their guns, and several others burst out of the *jacales* ready for trouble.

When a tall, dark-haired man ran out of one of the huts and shouted, "Hold your fire!" Slaughter figured that had to be Ned Becker. He hadn't laid eyes on the man until now.

Red half-turned in his saddle and leveled his revolver at Slaughter.

"Don't you go gettin' any ideas, mister," he warned.

"I'm just sitting here," Slaughter said coolly. "I want to save my wife, not get both of us killed."

Red grunted and motioned with the gun for Slaughter to keep going toward the end of the side canyon.

By now Santiago had reached his father. He yanked the horse to a stop and flung himself out of the saddle before *El Halcón* stopped moving. The outlaws closed in around him, though, and one of them slammed the butt of his rifle between Santiago's shoulder blades and drove him to the ground before he could reach Don Eduardo.

"That's enough," Becker said as he made his way through the ring of men and pushed them back. As they spread out, Slaughter caught sight of Santiago again. The young man lay face down on the ground, writhing in pain from the blow that had knocked him

340

off his feet.

"Get him up," Becker snapped. A couple of the men took hold of Santiago's arms and hauled him to his feet.

Becker stepped closer, and as his men held Santiago, he cracked a brutal backhanded blow across the young man's face.

Slaughter saw that from the corner of his eye, but most of his attention was focused on looking around the camp, hoping to catch sight of Viola. He didn't see her or Belinda, but he noticed two men standing outside one of the *jacales* with its door shut. They had to be guarding the hut, he thought, and that meant the two women were probably in there.

When Red motioned for him to rein in, Slaughter did so. He sat there and carefully kept his face impassive. For Viola's sake, he couldn't afford to give in to the raging emotions he felt. Instead he kept them buried as deeply as he could inside him. He watched as Becker confronted Santiago.

With a sneer on his face, Becker demanded, "Do you remember me, kid?" He laughed and went on before Santiago had a chance to answer, "No, of course you don't. You were just a baby the last time I saw you. Hell, I barely remember it myself."

Santiago stood there silently, his chest

341

heaving. A trickle of blood ran from the corner of his mouth where Becker had struck him.

Becker leaned closer and thrust his face up next to Santiago's. Through clenched teeth, he said, "You're going to wish you never saw me again."

"I already . . . wish that," Santiago said.

Slaughter frowned as he looked at the two men staring at each other with such hatred. They were only a few years apart in age. Something struck him then about them, and his frown deepened. He couldn't quite figure out what it was.

Becker turned and jerked an arm toward the don.

"It looks like the old man's still passed out," he said. "Somebody wake him up. I reckon a bucket of water ought to do it."

While one of the outlaws went to fetch water from the pool, Becker sauntered over to Slaughter and Red. He grinned up at Slaughter and said, "So you're the famous Texas John."

"I'm John Slaughter. Where's my wife?"

"She's fine. You'll be seeing her soon. You've got a nice ranch, Slaughter, to go with that mighty pretty wife of yours."

"You don't need to hurt her," Slaughter said. "I've cooperated with you. I did exactly what you told me to do."

"That's right, you did. You brought me Santiago Rubriz." Becker glanced over at Slaughter's escort. "Did they come alone, Red?"

"As far as I could tell," Red said. "I checked their back trail for a long ways, and there was no sign of anybody followin' 'em."

Becker nodded and said, "That's good. I was hoping you'd be smart enough to do the right thing, Slaughter."

There was an unspoken threat in Slaughter's voice as he replied, "Like I said, I don't want anything to happen to Mrs. Slaughter."

"She's unharmed, I give you my word on that."

"Too bad the same thing can't be said for everyone else on my ranch."

Becker shrugged and said, "The course of justice often claims a few innocent victims along the way. It's regrettable, but it can't be helped."

The man who had gone to the pool came back carrying a bucket of water. Becker turned his attention back to Don Eduardo, but as he did he added to Slaughter, "You might as well get down from that horse. You're going to be here for a while."

"You could go ahead and give me my wife

and let us get out of here," Slaughter suggested.

"Not yet. I want you to see these people get what's coming to them."

That confirmed Slaughter's suspicion that Becker intended to kill him and Viola no matter what they did. The man wasn't going to murder three innocent people in front of them and then let them go. That was what Slaughter expected, of course, so he wasn't surprised.

Becker swaggered back over to where Don Eduardo hung from the cottonwood branch. His men still held Santiago nearby. Becker nodded to the man with the bucket, who threw the water in Don Eduardo's face.

Rubriz gasped and sputtered and came awake from the shock. He flinched involuntarily, as if to get away from any more water thrown in his direction. The rude awakening had already been accomplished, though.

Even worse for the don, Slaughter thought, was the sight of his son in the hands of his enemies. Don Eduardo stared at the young man and whispered, "Santiago."

"That's right," Becker said in smug self-satisfaction. "Now I have all three of you. Your happy little family. I must admit, I'm surprised you and your wife didn't have more children, Rubriz. Were you too busy trying to force your way into the beds of other men's wives?"

Don Eduardo swallowed. Water still dripped from his face, but somehow he managed to summon up some dignity as he said, "My Pilar was unable to have more children. It was one of the great regrets of her life. She would have enjoyed having a large family."

"Well, some things are beyond our control, I guess. Like what's about to happen to you and your wife and son." Becker looked around at his men. "Bring the women."

At last Slaughter was glad to hear something Becker had to say. He wanted to see Viola with his own eyes and know that she was all right.

A couple of the outlaws went over to the men guarding the *jacal* with the closed door and spoke to them. Then three of them leveled their guns at the door while the fourth man opened it, said something, and stepped back quickly. If it was anybody except Viola in there, Slaughter would have thought they were being overly cautious.

Where his wife was concerned, though, it paid to be careful if you were her enemy. She could be tricky when she wanted to.

Not with the odds stacked this high

against her, however. Viola came out of the *jacal* with Belinda, who seemed so shaken up by everything that had happened she could barely stay on her feet. Viola had her arm around the blonde's waist to support her as they emerged from the hut.

Then she saw Slaughter, and her eyes widened as their gazes met. He could tell she was excited to see him, but then she looked oddly disappointed.

Maybe that was because she'd expected him to come in here with all guns blazing and a salty crew of tough cowboys behind him. And to tell the truth, Slaughter had given that option some thought. He had decided that he stood a better chance of getting Viola out of here alive by taking a different tack.

As for him, he was so relieved to see she was all right that for a second he felt uncharacteristically weak in the knees. Viola was the most important person in his life. He wasn't sure how he would have ever gotten along without her. He hoped he never had to find out.

"Come over here, Mrs. Slaughter," Becker ordered. "Bring the doña with you."

"Come on, Belinda," Viola urged. She glared at Becker. "We have to cooperate . . . for now."

With the four outlaws close behind them, the women walked slowly toward the pool. Belinda kept her head down as if she didn't want to look at her husband until Don Eduardo said in a choked voice, "My love."

She finally lifted her eyes, and when she did, she must have seen her stepson because she exclaimed, "Santiago!"

"Yes," Don Eduardo said, sounding miserable. "I have doomed us all."

"You did nothing wrong, Father," Santiago said. "If anyone has doomed us, it is this madman with his twisted dreams of revenge."

"What we're doing here is justice, like I've said before," Becker insisted. He lifted a hand and pointed. "Strip the boy and stake him out right there, where the don and doña will have a good view. We're going to let Bodaway work on him for a while."

"No!" Belinda screamed. She tried to pull away from Viola, who tightened her grip.

"If you fight them, you're just playing into Becker's hands," she said. Belinda started sobbing and buried her face against Viola's shoulder.

Slaughter hadn't seen the Apache here in camp, but obviously Bodaway was still around if Becker was going to let him torture Santiago. Slaughter had seen what renegade Apaches could do to their captives. Santiago was in for a hellish ordeal, and it would be almost as bad for Don Eduardo and Belinda if they were forced to watch.

Slaughter glanced up at the rimrock and took his hat off. Red tensed and lifted his gun, which he was still holding.

"Take it easy," Slaughter said as he used his sleeve to wipe sweat from his face. "The sun's high enough that it's getting hot down here now."

"You'd better not have a gun or nothin' hidden in that hat," Red warned. The outlaw darted a nervous glance toward Becker. Clearly, he didn't want his boss to know that he hadn't thought to check Slaughter's hat for weapons.

Becker wasn't paying attention, though. He was watching in rapt attention as his men started ripping the clothes off a futilely struggling Santiago.

Slaughter put his hat back on. He had no way of knowing if Stonewall and the other men were up on the rim, but wiping his face with his sleeve was the signal they had agreed on. When Stonewall saw that, he knew it was up to him to open fire on the outlaws whenever he was ready.

It wasn't going to be easy, though, the way

Becker's men were grouped around the captives. Any shots aimed at them could endanger Slaughter and the others, too. Unfortunately, Slaughter knew he couldn't afford to wait any longer to give the signal.

Don Eduardo said, "Please, Ned, I beg of you, do not do this terrible thing. Go ahead and kill me. I'm an old man. I don't mind dying. Just let my wife and son and the Slaughters ride out of here unharmed."

"Nobody leaves until it's over," Becker snapped. "And the three of you will never leave. I'm going to destroy your family just like you destroyed mine, starting with your son."

Belinda was still crying as Viola held her. Slaughter waited for the crash of gunfire to drown out her sobs, but it didn't happen. No shots came from the rim.

Was Stonewall not up there? Had he and the rest of the men gotten lost and not even found the place? Slaughter was ready to make his move — he was going to dive at Viola and Belinda and tackle them to the ground, hopefully out of the line of fire — but he couldn't do anything until Stonewall opened the ball.

Becker's men had most of Santiago's clothes off now. Only a few tattered rags still clung to him. They started wrestling him toward the spot Becker had indicated, where one of the outlaws was using a mallet to drive picket stakes into the hard ground. Another man had some strips of rawhide they would use to lash Santiago's wrists and ankles to the stakes.

Clearly, Becker had done plenty of planning and preparing to put his crazed scheme into action.

Slaughter made an effort to keep what he was thinking and feeling from showing on his face. He didn't want to give anything away. But his nerves were stretching tighter and tighter as he waited for Stonewall.

Right from the start, he had known his plan was a gamble. There had been plenty of times in the past when he had wagered a great deal on the turn of a card or the roll of the dice.

He wasn't sure he had ever made a wager this big before.

One of the outlaws kicked Santiago's knees from behind so that the young man fell. His captors wrestled him onto his back. It took two men on each arm and leg to force him into position so that other men could begin tying him.

Belinda's sobs grew louder and more shrill. She was on the verge of hysterics, no matter how hard Viola tried to comfort her.

Bodaway emerged from behind one of the *jacales*. This was the first time Slaughter had seen him, too, although he might have caught a glimpse of the Apache during the fighting at the ranch two nights earlier. As Bodaway walked slowly toward Santiago, the men who had finished lashing the young man to the stakes stood up and backed away.

"Please, Ned, you cannot do this thing," Don Eduardo said to Becker. "You do not know what a terrible thing this is you are about to do."

Becker folded his arms over his chest and smirked as he said, "I know exactly what I'm doing, old man. I'm going to stand back and enjoy watching while Bodaway peels every inch of skin off your son's body. It'll take hours to kill him that way. He might not even die until nightfall."

"Noooo," Don Eduardo wailed. "You cannot!"

"Why not?" Becker demanded. "Give me one good reason."

Don Eduardo stared wild-eyed at him and howled, "Because he is your brother!"

CHAPTER 28

If Don Eduardo had suddenly sprouted wings and a tail, a more shocked silence could not have fallen over the canyon.

Slaughter wasn't surprised as completely as the others, however, because he realized now that was what he had noticed when Becker and Santiago were standing close together with their faces only inches apart. The resemblance between them had been plain to see.

Becker wasn't going to accept it, though. He shouted at Don Eduardo, "That's a damned lie!"

Don Eduardo shook his head wearily and said, "No, it is the truth. You are my son, Ned. Your mother, she was a very compelling woman. I . . . I fear I was not as strong as I should have been, the first time she approached me."

Becker just stood there, staring, shaking his head in angry disbelief.

After a moment Don Eduardo went on, "Thaddeus believed you to be his son, even after your mother insisted on naming you Edward. She . . . she said it was to honor your father's partner. I hoped that things would be different then. I thought that with you to care for, your mother would change." He sighed. "For a time it appeared that might be true, but in the end, she was still the same, determined to get what she wanted no matter what the cost. And this time it led to the bad trouble between your father and me that took his life."

"It's a pack of filthy lies," Becker insisted. His voice shook with rage. "She never would have done such a thing, no matter what she was forced into later by your treachery, Rubriz. I don't believe it, and it doesn't change anything."

Slaughter glanced around. He could tell from their faces, everyone else in the canyon accepted Don Eduardo's story, even if Becker refused to. They all had eyes. Now that the relationship between Becker and Santiago had been pointed out, the others could see the resemblance, too.

But Becker was right about it not changing anything. He was still in charge here. He jerked a hand toward his half brother's prone form and snapped, "Make him scream, Bodaway."

As expressionless as always, the Apache drew his knife from the sash around his waist and stepped toward Santiago.

The whipcrack of a rifle split the air.

Bodaway spun around and dropped the knife as the impact of slug striking flesh sounded like an ax splitting wood.

That shot had barely rung out when more followed it, filling the canyon with their racket.

Slaughter was on the move before Bodaway even hit the ground. He lunged toward Viola and Belinda and spread his arms wide to encompass both of them. He grabbed them and pulled them down with him as he dived to the ground. Bullets buzzing like angry hornets filled the air.

"Stay down!" Slaughter told the women. "Viola, don't let her up!"

He would have preferred a more peaceful reunion with his wife, but there was no time to keep her in his arms. He scrambled onto his hands and knees and went after the knife that Bodaway had dropped when he was shot.

His hand had just closed around the knife's handle when strong fingers clamped on to his wrist. Slaughter jerked his head around and saw Bodaway lunging at him.

There was blood on the Apache's torso from the bullet wound, but he was far from dead.

Bodaway tried to grab Slaughter by the throat with his other hand, but Slaughter blocked it with his forearm. The two men rolled over as they struggled. Slaughter drove a knee toward Bodaway's groin, but the Apache twisted away from the blow.

Slaughter was vaguely aware of shouted curses punctuating the continued gunfire. He knew a battle royal was going on around him. He wanted to know whether Becker was still alive or whether the shots from the canyon rim had cut him down.

But he couldn't afford to take his attention off Bodaway for even a split second, because he knew the Apache would kill him.

Somebody else would have to deal with Ned Becker.

Belinda screamed and shook as the shooting continued, but Viola was pretty sure the blonde hadn't been hit. John had gotten them out of the way very quickly when this particular hell broke loose.

She lifted her head and looked around. When the shooting started, Becker's men had scattered to hunt cover and now they were firing up at the rimrock with rifles and pistols. More lead slashed down from up there and a couple of the outlaws who hadn't concealed themselves well enough behind rocks and trees cried out and fell as slugs ripped through their bodies.

Viola had no way of knowing exactly who was up there, but she was certain John had planned things this way. Somehow, he had gotten men into position to attempt a rescue. She wouldn't be surprised if her brother Stonewall was among them. The young firebrand never wanted to miss out on any action.

Viola's breath caught in her throat as she spotted Ned Becker stumbling toward Don Eduardo with a gun in his hand. Becker shouted hoarsely, "I won't be cheated of my revenge! Whatever else happens, you're going to die, old man!"

John had told her to stay down, but Becker was about to shoot Don Eduardo and Viola knew she was the only one close enough to stop him. John was wrestling with the Apache, who was wounded but not dead.

"Stay here," she told Belinda, then surged to her feet, hoping she wasn't standing up in the path of a stray bullet.

Becker had his thumb looped over the hammer of his revolver and was raising it to shoot Don Eduardo when Viola lowered her shoulder and rammed into him from behind.

She was a petite woman, but her life as a cowgirl had given her a considerable amount of wiry strength. The impact of her collision with Becker caused the outlaw to fly forward. He landed almost at Don Eduardo's feet. Somehow Becker managed to hang on to his gun. He twisted around, came up on his knees, and pointed the revolver at Viola, who lay a few yards away.

"You bitch!" Becker yelled.

Before he could pull the trigger, Don Eduardo lifted his legs and scissored them around Becker's neck, jerking him backward. That put even more weight on the don's wrists, but he hung on with grim determination.

"Señora Slaughter!" he gasped. "Take my wife and get out of here!"

That might be the best thing for them to do, Viola decided. She rolled over and leaped up.

But as she did, the still-struggling John and Bodaway rolled against her legs and knocked them right out from under her, dumping her on top of them.

Slaughter was shocked when Viola landed

on him with a startled cry. He had told her and Belinda to stay down, but obviously that hadn't happened. And now she was in the middle of what amounted to a battle between two desperate wildcats.

That distraction allowed Bodaway to writhe out of Slaughter's grip. The Apache still had the knife. He slashed the blade at Viola's throat. Slaughter caught hold of the back of her dress and jerked her out of the way just in time. The razor-sharp edge missed her throat by no more than an inch or two.

Her hand shot out with fingers hooked like talons. They dug into Bodaway's eyes. For the first time the Apache showed a real reaction. He yelled in pain.

Slaughter's gaze fell on a chunk of sandstone about as big as two fists put together. He snatched it up and swung it over his head as he shouldered Viola out of the way.

Slaughter used the momentum of the roundhouse swing to drive the rock down as hard as he could into Bodaway's face. He heard the crunch of bone shattering. Bodaway spasmed, his back arching off the ground. His arms and legs twitched violently.

Then he sagged back limply. His eyes stared up sightlessly from his ruined face, which had been battered out of shape by the terrible blow.

Shots still rang out, but now there were fewer of them. Slaughter hoped that meant Stonewall and the men with him were winning the fight against Becker's outlaws.

He dropped the rock and grabbed the knife Bodaway had dropped in his death throes. Slaughter lunged over to Santiago and started sawing on the rawhide thongs binding the young man to the pickets. The knife's keen edge made it short work.

"John!" Viola cried.

Slaughter jerked around and saw Don Eduardo with his legs locked around Becker's neck, trying to choke him. Becker's face was dark red with trapped blood. But he still had his gun, and he managed to lift it above his head and fire a shot that ripped into Don Eduardo's belly.

Freed now, Santiago plucked the knife from Slaughter's hand and drove himself at Becker with a roar of fury. Don Eduardo's legs fell away from Becker's neck, releasing him. Becker saw Santiago charging him and came up to meet him, gun spouting flame as he did so.

Santiago shuddered as the bullet struck him, but momentum carried him forward into Becker, who went over backward. The muscles in Santiago's arms and shoulders bunched as he drove the knife into his half brother's chest again and again, striking as deeply with the steel as he could.

Finally Santiago's injury caught up to him and he slumped atop Becker's body. The knife was buried in Becker's chest. The vengeance Becker had sought claimed him instead.

Slaughter scrambled up and lifted Viola to her feet. An eerie silence fell over Barranca Sangre as echoes of the shots rolled away and died.

"See to Belinda," Slaughter told Viola, then he hurried over to Santiago and Becker.

The outlaw was dead, no doubt about that. Slaughter grasped Santiago's shoulder and rolled the young man onto his back. There was a bloody bullet hole high on Santiago's left shoulder, but he didn't appear to be hurt too badly.

The same couldn't be said of his gutshot father.

Slaughter pulled the knife out of Becker's chest and went to Don Eduardo. The don's head lolled far forward as he hung from the cottonwood branch. Slaughter thought he was dead already, but Don Eduardo lifted his head and forced a smile onto his lips.

"My wife?" he whispered. "My son?"

Slaughter looked around. Viola and Belinda were helping Santiago to his feet.

"They're all right," Slaughter told the don. "They're going to be fine."

"Thanks to . . . *El Señor Dios* . . . and you, Don Juan. Thank you . . ."

The others reached them as Slaughter cut the ropes holding Don Eduardo up and lowered him gently to the ground. Santiago and Belinda dropped to their knees beside him, clutching him desperately.

"Do not . . . mourn me," he rasped. "I lived my life . . . good and bad . . . and the evil that came to me . . . was of my own doing."

"No," Santiago said. "It was not your fault
—"

As if he hadn't heard, Don Eduardo went on, "The two of you . . . have given me much happiness . . . Now you must . . . comfort each other . . . be happy together . . . yes, I know . . . it is a good thing . . . those I love . . . should be together . . . as I am now . . . with your mother . . ."

His eyes closed, and he sighed a long, last breath.

Ned Becker's crazed hatred had claimed its final victim.

As Santiago and Belinda cried over Don Eduardo's body, Slaughter drew Viola into his arms and held her tightly against him. Her arms went around his waist with equal fervor. In the midst of this tragedy, they were together again, and that was something to be celebrated.

The sound of hoofbeats made Slaughter look around. He saw Stonewall and several of the other men from the ranch riding into the side canyon.

"Viola! John!" Stonewall cried as he hurried his horse toward them. He reined in, swung down from the saddle, and clapped hands on their shoulders. "I was afraid we weren't going to get here in time. You're all right, both of you?"

Viola nodded and said, "Of course we are. We're together, aren't we?"

Stonewall threw his arms around both of them in an enthusiastic hug.

After a moment, Slaughter said, "This, uh, isn't very dignified, Deputy."

"No, sir, it's not," Stonewall agreed. "But we're a long way from Tombstone, aren't we, Sheriff?"

Slaughter couldn't argue with that.

All of Becker's men were dead, picked off one by one by the riflemen on the canyon rim. They were left for the scavengers, and if anyone other than the coyotes and the buzzards ever saw the scattered bones, the sinister reputation of Barranca Sangre would grow that much more.

The only one buried in that lonely canyon was Ned Becker. Santiago insisted on it.

"He was mad, and he killed our father, but he was still my brother," the young man said.

That was a more generous attitude than Slaughter would have taken, but it was Santiago's decision to make.

Santiago, Belinda, and the don's men who had accompanied the rescue party took Don Eduardo's body back to his ranch, where he was laid to rest beside his beloved Pilar.

Two weeks later, Hermosa returned to the ranch as well, but he was alive, still recuperating from the wounds he had suffered at Bodaway's hands but growing stronger with each passing day. Dr. Fredericks insisted that the *vaquero* was a medical miracle. Hermosa just shrugged and said that he was too tough for some Apache to kill him.

And eight months later, John Slaughter, Viola, and Stonewall traveled to the ranch as well to attend the wedding of Santiago and Belinda. There was a great *fiesta,* and after they had eaten, the crowd adjourned to the race course Santiago had laid out.

Stonewall led Pacer to the starting line to join Santiago and *El Halcón*. With a big smile, Santiago said, "So, we will settle this at last, eh, *amigo*?"

"Sure, if that's what you want," Stonewall said. "I figure if I'd just got married, though, I could come up with somethin' better to do than have some ol' horse race."

"Yes, of course, but this is important, too. A matter of honor for us both."

"Maybe, but my honor's gonna be just fine no matter how this comes out."

Viola held a parasol to shade her from the sun as she and Slaughter stood with the spectators waiting for the race to begin. Belinda was with them, looking stronger and happier than she had in all the time they had known her.

"I may have misjudged her . . . a little," Viola had admitted to Slaughter. "She wasn't really doing anything Don Eduardo didn't want her to do, and she tried to be as honorable as she could about it. I still think she has some growing up to do, though."

"They can grow up together," Slaughter had said. "Santiago's a good man. They'll be all right."

Pacer and *El Halcón* both seemed eager to get started on this race. Stonewall and

Santiago swung up into their saddles, and then Santiago looked around and called, "Señor Slaughter, will you start us off?"

Slaughter nodded and said, "It'd be my pleasure."

He walked out and stood next to the starting line, drawing his pearl-handled Colt as he did so.

"Get ready," he said as he lifted the gun. "All set?"

Grim, determined nods from the two young men.

"Go," John Slaughter said as he pulled the trigger and fired into the air. The two magnificent horses burst forward, galloping full out.

The race was on.

ABOUT THE AUTHORS

William W. Johnstone has written nearly three hundred novels of western adventure, military action, chilling suspense, and survival. His bestselling books include *The Family Jensen; The Mountain Man; Flintlock; MacCallister; Savage Texas; Luke Jensen, Bounty Hunter;* and the thrillers *Black Friday, The Doomsday Bunker,* and *Trigger Warning.*

J. A. Johnstone learned to write from the master himself, Uncle William W. Johnstone, with whom J. A. has co-written numerous bestselling series including The Mountain Man; Those Jensen Boys; and Preacher, The First Mountain Man.

The employees of Thorndike Press hope you have enjoyed this Large Print book. All our Thorndike, Wheeler, and Kennebec Large Print titles are designed for easy reading, and all our books are made to last. Other Thorndike Press Large Print books are available at your library, through selected bookstores, or directly from us.

For information about titles, please call:
(800) 223-1244

or visit our website at:
gale.com/thorndike

To share your comments, please write:
Publisher
Thorndike Press
10 Water St., Suite 310
Waterville, ME 04901